THE HIGHEST MOUNTAIN

The Whinburg Township Amish • Book Eight

ADINA SENFT

This is a work of fiction. Names, characters, places, and incidents are a product of the author's imagination. Locales and public names are sometimes used for atmospheric purposes. Any resemblance to actual people, living or dead, or to businesses, companies, events, institutions, or locales is completely coincidental.

Cover design by Seedlings Online. Images from Shutterstock and the author's collection, used by permission.

Edited by Leslie Peterson, Write Away Editorial.

The Highest Mountain / Adina Senft—1st ed.

ISBN 978-1-939087-73-7

❀ Created with Vellum

For Jeff

Denkes to the Amish of the San Luis and Wet Mountain Valleys, who shared their stories and their love of their mountain home with me.

Thanks also to the members of the Colorado Wildlife Department for helping me catch the poachers at the ranch.

And thanks once again to Leslie Peterson for her insight and guidance.

PRAISE FOR ADINA SENFT

“Senft has crafted an appealing tale of searching for one’s true identity. An interesting study of two mothers and how they have coped—one with her loss, the other with her guilt, and the role of faith in that process.”

— BOOKLIFE, ON *THE LONGEST ROAD*

"With a complex mix of both younger and older characters and a complex storyline, this book is truly a success."

— BRODART BOOKS & LIBRARY SERVICES,
ON *THE WOUNDED HEART*

"[A] genuine must read for those who love Amish fiction. Readers will not be able to put this book down until finished, it is just that great and filled with rich characterization.... a five star recommended book."

— AMISH READER ON *HERB OF GRACE*

IN THIS SERIES

THE WHINBURG TOWNSHIP AMISH

The Wounded Heart
The Hidden Life
The Tempted Soul
Herb of Grace
Keys of Heaven
Balm of Gilead
The Longest Road
The Highest Mountain
The Sweetest Song
"The Heart's Return" (novella)

In the mountain of the height of Israel will I plant it; and it shall bring forth boughs, and bear fruit, and be a goodly cedar: and under it shall dwell all fowl of every wing; in the shadow of the branches thereof shall they dwell.

—Ezekiel 17:23 (KJV)

"In the lowly place of prayer, God can lift you up to the highest mountain."

—Whinburg Township Amish proverb

THE HIGHEST MOUNTAIN

I
WHINBURG TOWNSHIP, PENNSYLVANIA

Early May

She had only one choice—dig the poor plant out of the ground and throw it on the compost pile. Because as even the smallest *Maedel* could tell you, everything on the farm had a job, and the borage wasn't doing its share.

With a a black sweater over her dress and kitchen apron, her blond hair wound into a modest bun at her nape and covered by a *Duchly*, or scarf, Amanda Yoder bent to see if there was any hope for the plant. Her sister-in-law Sarah Byler had given it to her the previous autumn. "Borage for courage, my *Grossmammi* always said," she'd told her with gentle cheer. Amanda had been looking forward to a healthy bush with beautiful, edible blue flowers like the one that grew over the hill at the Byler place. Sarah, the *Dokterfraa*, was a genius with plants. She'd assured Amanda that the borage would grow anywhere, but there was a good chance that *anywhere* didn't include this little corner of the garden.

Amanda hated digging things up. It was silly, of course. At

twenty-four, she had long ago learned to be practical about farm life, from gardening to poultry and livestock. But still she felt as though she was hurting the plant, hauling it out of the soil where maybe it had been comfortable, and plunking it down in a whole new place where the soil might be different, the light might be different, and the plants around it would be different.

Different was a little bit scary.

You big silly. That's the whole point. It's clear that the soil and light here aren't what borage needs. If you want a useful plant, go fetch the spade and get to work.

She never had trouble pulling out the sunflowers once they were finished, or the vegetables either—maybe because once the plant had yielded its fruit and seed, it quietly died so that the next generation could be fruitful. But borage wasn't like that. Herbs in general didn't seem to be like that. They just kept giving and giving.

With a spurt of determination, Amanda turned to get the spade out of the garden shed.

"Hi, Amanda!" called a feminine voice from somewhere down their long lane, shaded by maples that were just coming into bud. A moment later, two people came strolling around her mother's ornamental spruces. Hannah Riehl was wearing an Amish dress, but under it she wore a pair of pants because they were having a cold snap, and she'd forgotten her covering. She had once gone by the *Englisch* name of Megan Pearson until she had been restored by God's hand to her Amish family. It took an Amish girl years to learn the *Ordnung* and what was expected of her as a member of the *Gmee*, the church congregation, so it was no surprise that Hannah was having a hard time getting everything right.

The important thing was that she was back with people

who loved her, like a plant finally transplanted into the right soil.

Beside her was her ... friend? Special friend? Amanda was never sure what to call Ben Troyer. Other than *fence-jumper*, which was what some of the other *Youngie* called him. The bishop's son. His father's greatest joy—and greatest grief.

Ben was as unwelcome as a cell phone in his father's house. Daniel Troyer was a sensible, good-humored bishop in many ways, but with the eyes of the congregation on him, he had to toe the line. Particularly when his son stood on the other side of it. The price of Ben's coming home and rejoining the family was to join church first, and so far Ben hadn't been willing to do that.

He and Sam Riehl, Hannah's brother, lived in a mobile home in a little town far enough from Willow Creek to live an *Englisch* life, and close enough to be drawn back again and again. Since neither had ever been baptized into church, they weren't shunned, exactly, but Amanda figured it couldn't be easy for their parents to treat them as visitors rather than family.

So here they were, Ben half out and Hannah half in, trying to figure out where they ought to put down their roots.

A third person walked a little bit behind—Samuel. He'd spent thirteen years blaming himself for his sisters' being taken away by the Pearsons that day. Amanda wasn't altogether sure he'd stopped blaming himself, even after their miraculous return. Because of course they'd come back different. *Englisch*. The youngest, Ashley—still refusing to answer to her Amish name of Leah—had stuck to her plan and gone to college last fall. She wrote a letter to the family once in a while, but mostly she texted and posted things on Facebook so that Hannah could see them on the cell phone she was supposed to have given up when she'd come to stay.

Even Bishop Daniel had paused on that one. How could he expect a girl who hadn't been brought up Amish to follow the *Ordnung*? He knew, of course, that a number of the *Youngie* had cell phones, but nobody would be foolish enough to use one within earshot of the bishop.

"What are you up to?" Hannah asked as she crossed the lawn. "Isn't it kind of cold for gardening?"

Amanda smiled in greeting. As strange and troubled as Hannah was, she liked her. She kind of wished they could be real friends—both baptized, and therefore sisters in fellowship if not in blood. Maybe one day that would happen, but for now Amanda would be content in the place where God seemed to want her: that of unofficial teacher about being young and Amish.

"It is cold, but it won't last long." She waved at the borage. She could have sworn it shivered at the gesture. "Sarah gave this to me last year, but it's not thriving. I don't know what to do for it except dig it up and move it somewhere."

"What is it?" Hannah inspected the leggy, unhappy plant.

"It's called borage. She said it would grow anywhere, but it's not. What are you up to?" Her smile took in the boys, too.

"Day off." Ben was not a waster of words. Of his life, maybe, but not words. "We thought we'd go for a walk up the creek."

Lots of the *Youngie* did. It felt private down in the creek bed, and the rush of water hid confidences from anyone walking on the road above, or working in the fields on either side. It was pretty there, with all kinds of plants and trees that liked shelter. Things bloomed down there that hardly got a chance to sprout in the fields where the full force of a Pennsylvania winter could freeze them overnight.

"Come with us?" Hannah said. "I'll research what to do with your borage on my phone." ... *once we're out of sight.* Amanda heard the unspoken end to the sentence.

Most of her chores were done, and there was no harm in taking a walk. Besides, if she learned what to do with the plant, it couldn't be called wasting time. Not that Mamm would ever say such a thing, especially with these three. If the *gut Gott* had given her the opportunity to stroll along the creek and be an example to these lost lambs, then she must take it.

Plus, it sounded like fun. "I'll just wash my hands."

The borage looked a little relieved as it waved in the breeze.

The first thing Amanda saw when they skidded down to the bottom of the slick, muddy path was a wild lilac blooming on the western slope. She felt as though God had just given her a gift, and this sure sign that spring was really here lifted her spirits. They rose even more when Hannah waved her phone.

"Borage, right? With the blue flowers and fuzzy looking leaves?"

"*Ja*, that's the one."

Hannah rattled off a number of facts, but only one stuck in Amanda's mind. "*Well drained.* The poor thing. I put it in the bottom end of the garden where the rain always puddles. No wonder it won't grow. It's probably drowning."

Sam folded his hand over the phone in his sister's palm. "Put it away. Me and Ben have something to talk over with you girls."

"I knew it." Hannah gave him one of those squinty-eyed looks designed to tell him she was on to him . She slid the phone into her skirt pocket. "Spotting ulterior motives is my specialty."

You girls? And that included her, Amanda? Unless it involved gardening or quilting, she couldn't imagine a single thing that either Ben Troyer or Samuel Riehl would talk to her about in confidence. Ben's suggestion of a walk in the creek bed should have given her a clue that something unusual was up, but she was no expert in ulterior motives. She probably wouldn't recognize one if it landed on her nose.

"Remember last summer, when Joe Byler and Simon Yoder went to work on that ranch in Colorado?" Ben asked.

"I'm not likely to forget it," Amanda said. Here at least were facts she knew. "Simon hurt his foot and about made Sarah frantic until she could get a cure sent out in a box. Joe doctored him and did it well, too."

"What does your friend's foot have to do with us?"

Ben half smiled at Hannah. "His foot? Nothing. But the ranch where it happened? Maybe something."

"All right, Mr. Mysterious, spit it out."

With a clutch in her chest that was almost like a little spurt of envy, Amanda wondered how such give and take between a boy and a girl could look so easy and be so hard. Last year, she'd had a brief season of rebellion and had gone riding in Samuel's cousin Jesse Riehl's car, knowing full well it would anger Dat and grieve Mamm. In the Bible people were possessed of demons, and during that brief season, she had almost felt that way.

She had had hopes of a man who had hopes of another woman. Before Sarah had married Englisch Henry, Silas Lapp had come to Willow Creek to visit. What a mix-up that had been, with Sarah trying to make a match between Amanda and Silas, and his family trying to make on between him and Sarah.

For Amanda, every meeting of the families had made it both easy to see him and horribly painful to do so. Being overlooked in the end had simply been too much to stand. Young Jesse had been her answer. He might have been a fence-jumper, but at least he talked with her, though not of anything very substantial.

However, they'd been in a car wreck and that had ended that. She'd said good-bye to him and the next thing she knew, he was appearing on a worldly television reality show called *Shunning Amish*. He had been paid an astonishing sum of money and had emigrated to Australia. Even his parents had not heard from him since, and she didn't expect to either.

But now Samuel picked up the conversation. "They'll be looking for help out there in Colorado, and if we don't write soon, others will get the best jobs."

Samuel and Ben wanted to go to Colorado? Amanda felt a little breathless. Granted, they weren't church members like Simon, but still ... she had known them both nearly all her life. It had been difficult enough seeing Simon go last year—or rather, hearing that he'd gone, since he and Joe had snuck off and caught the train before Sarah or anybody could stop them.

"You want to go to Colorado?" she finally managed. "Are Simon and Joe going back, too?"

"I don't know. Simon might. I don't see much of Joe," Samuel confessed. "But I want to go. I'm sick to death of building RVs and never seeing the sun from one day to the next. I want to do something outdoors. Simon and Joe worked with the horses on pack trips. I bet I could do that. I'd muck out stalls if I had to, just to get away." He gazed west across the creek to the opposite bank, thirty feet in the direction he wanted to go. "Do something different. See something different."

Now was the moment when she ought to suggest that the lack lay not in his surroundings, but in his heart. That being transformed by the renewing of his mind, accepting God's will, and joining the Amish church would be the surest way to find contentment.

But she didn't.

Because now her breath was coming as fast as the rush of the creek beside them. Because the idea flooding her head was so new, so foreign that she could hardly catch it long enough to look it over for flaws.

"Have a nice time," Hannah said, waving a hand as though the boys were already leaving.

"Oh, it wouldn't be just us," Ben told her. "You girls could get jobs out there, too. Come with us. Have an adventure."

An adventure! That was the last word anyone would connect with her—plain, stay-at-home Amanda Yoder, with a figure honed by one too many pieces of bread at supper and an inability to say no to pie. Why would they ask her and not someone like Rosanne Kanagy, who was always in the middle of doings here?

"What would we do?" The same things she did every day? She'd never been to a ranch in her life, but it couldn't be all that different from a farm, could it? There would be cooking, and cleaning, and laundry—maybe even with an electric washing machine. The wild rush of possibility slowed, leaching away into common sense the way water leached into the ground and disappeared.

Except in the muddy part at the bottom of Mamm's garden.

"I don't know," Ben said. "House things, I guess. You'd be a *Maud*, maybe, and make up the guests' rooms. Or cook. Can you talk to Simon about it for us? Find out as much as you can?"

"Sure," she said, a little taken aback. "But can't you?"

The boys glanced at one another. "I don't know how plain Sarah and Englisch Henry are these days."

"How plain they are?" Hannah repeated, clearly not understanding. "Aren't all Amish plain if you're in church?"

"He means how strict they are," Amanda explained. "We say a family is plain or fancy depending on how they keep the *Ordnung*."

"Oh. Fifty shades of plain, huh?" Then she grinned, as though she'd made a joke.

Amanda had no idea what that meant, but she smiled anyway. "Maybe. But Sarah and Henry keep a godly house, and she wasn't happy about Simon going before. You'd be welcome, of course, but don't get your hopes up about Simon going again."

"It's worth a try," Samuel said, his aimless amble of a walk taking on purpose as he headed for the bridge that crossed the creek ahead. That was Red Bridge Road, which would take them past Englisch Henry's new pottery studio on the way back to the Yoder place. The studio faced the road and welcomed tourists by the dozen in the summer.

"No time like the present." Ben set off too, energy causing his boots to make deeper prints in the soft bank.

Hannah wasn't about to be left behind, and looked back at Amanda. "Come on."

"I don't know why." But in spite of herself, she was picking up her pace. The boys were already several yards ahead. "I'm not going to Colorado. They just want me there because Simon is my nephew and they think I can get what they want to know out of him."

"Your nephew?" Hannah let her catch up, and then they followed the boys, who were now halfway up the path to the road. "You're not old enough to have a nephew bigger than a baby."

"I'm twenty-four. I'm the youngest. Sarah's first husband was my oldest brother. He died of cancer."

"Oh." Hannah glanced back. "I'm sorry."

"He has gone to God," Amanda said simply. "There is nothing to be sorry about."

"I guess not, if you put it that way."

At the Byler place, where once her brother Michael had tilled the fields, they heard the rhythmic sound of the potter's wheel coming from inside the studio.

Amanda led the little parade away from the door. "Henry doesn't like to be interrupted when he's working the clay. He says it falls over and sulks if he takes his attention off it."

"It's Simon we want," Ben pointed out. "He's probably in the barn."

Simon was not that predictable, but Amanda didn't say so. Instead, she waved at Sarah, who had come out onto the front porch, a pestle in one hand.

"Guder mariye," her sister-in-law called. To Amanda, she was more like a sister; indeed, *Schweschder* was the word she used in her head instead of *Gschwei*, sister-in-law. They were only a handful of years apart in age, though Amanda supposed they were miles apart in experience of life.

"We're looking for Simon," she said. "Is he home today?"

"In the barn polishing tack," Sarah said. "At least, that's what he's supposed to be doing. But you know Simon."

She did. Mercurial, always moving, always coming up with ideas that as often as not sounded more wonderful in theory than they turned out to be useful in practice.

She waved in thanks, and Sarah went back in the house, where the immediate pounding of the pestle told Amanda she was compiling a cure for someone. They found Simon, not in the tack room, but draped over one of the horses, talking to her in a soothing tone.

He straightened in surprise when they clustered around the stall opening. "Hi, Amanda. And Ben and Samuel. And wow, Hannah too. I didn't know you all knew each other."

Hannah had that slightly dazzled look that girls got when confronted with Simon for the first time. Better acquaintance seemed to provide its own antidote, but it sometimes took a while.

Amanda supposed he was very good-looking, but she knew him well enough to see beyond the surface to the man he was becoming. Or would become, if God worked him a little harder. Which she hoped would happen someday, or some poor girl would be saddled with him for life and wonder what on earth had happened.

"Ben and Samuel are thinking they might like to go to Colorado, to work on the ranch where you and Joe went last year," she said. Clearly her job was to smooth the way, so she got on with it. "We were hoping you could tell them a little of how to go about it."

"What the people there are like," Samuel said.

"What kind of jobs there are. For us," Ben added.

Hannah elbowed him. "Us, too. You know ... just in case we wanted to think about it."

Simon's brows rose as he glanced at Amanda, as though he were thinking, *Us? I thought you weren't interested.*

"Well now, let me see," he said. "This is a pretty tall order." He kept them in suspense for a minute while he pretended to recall the previous summer. That was Simon. Enjoying the attention of four people to the full, with information only he could provide. It was a wonder he hadn't charged them admission first.

"The ranch where we were is north of Westcliffe, in the hills close to a little town called Amistad. It's called the Lost Creek Ranch because the creek that runs below the house is seasonal. It dries up late in the summer."

"That's good," Amanda said. "Otherwise you'd have to cross it every time you went outside, wouldn't you?"

"No, it's down in the meadow, far from the house." He grinned at her. He knew she didn't have any illusions about him and loved him anyway. "The family is called Gunderson. She's his third wife, and he's really rich. His kids live with his first wife, and the ranch is what he does now that he's retired."

"What did he do before?" Hannah asked. "Stock trading?"

"No, they have cattle still."

"I meant—"

"He was in computers. That's all I know. I only saw him a couple of times. Mostly the hands deal with the foremen, Jim Strever and Rob Lozano. We all slept in the bunkhouse, but we took our meals at the big house, in the staff dining room."

"How many houses are there?" Samuel wanted to know.

Simon ticked off his fingers, leaning on the patient mare, who was probably used to him. "Big house, bunkhouse, six or eight guest cabins, four staff cabins, barn, chicken house big enough to put up a whole family, and event center." Four blank faces. "That's where they hold dances and things. Weddings. You know."

Amanda tried to imagine what an event center on a ranch might look like, but all she could come up with was the big space on the second level of their barn, where Sarah's and Henry's wedding had been held. It probably wasn't like that.

"We were the horse wranglers for the pack trips, but there are other jobs. Cowboyin', for one, mending fences and moving the cattle from one place to another. Fishing guide. Mechanic. There are all kinds of jobs and they work you hard."

"But they're fair?" Samuel said. "What's the pay like?"

Simon told him, and Samuel's eyes went wide. "That's pretty fair." He and Ben exchanged a glance, and Amanda wondered what the wages were like at the RV factory. Maybe not as good as cowboyin' in Colorado. And what would happen when the summer was over and they came home? Even if they had a little saved, they had to get work. Would the factory take them back?

But that was none of her business, was it?

"What about women?" Hannah asked. "I could ride a horse and move cows, I bet. How hard can it be?"

"I don't know—cows are unpredictable. Give me horses any day." Simon patted the mare with affection. "But women work in the house. Housekeeping, cook, waitresses. Teresa—she's the cook—she says the dirt never stops coming in and going out. She says it's probably the same dirt, like it's an ocean and dirt is the tide."

There was enough dirt in the Amish life that Amanda didn't feel too inclined to race across to the other side of the country to see more of it.

"Do you have the address there? Do you think we can get jobs if we write now?" Ben asked, a little diffidently. He didn't know Simon all that well; she could tell the respect pleased her nephew.

"I bet you could. But don't bother writing. It's faster to phone."

"But it's long distance," Samuel said. "We don't have long distance at our trailer. Too expensive and no one to call."

"There's always the phone shanty out on the road. Daadi doesn't hold with telephones on his place, but ..." Simon glanced at Amanda. "There's always Henry's phone in the studio."

Amanda actually stepped back, bumping into Hannah. "I'm not phoning Colorado from Henry's phone. It would cost a fortune, and besides—"

"Besides what?" Hannah asked. "Ow. Get off my foot. It doesn't matter anyway. I have nationwide coverage. We'll just use my cell." She pulled it out of her pocket and peered at the screen. "Well, we would if I had a charge. Guess we'll have to go into town and have a coffee so I can plug in."

"Don't let your dad catch you," Simon mocked.

Hannah lifted her chin, as though he was being too forward even for a nineteen-year-old brought up *Englisch*. "You leave my dad to me," she said coolly. "Come on, Ben. Give us a ride to town?"

"I can take you," Simon offered, so smoothly that anyone might have missed that it was an apology. "I can hitch up Dulcie here quick as anything."

"That's okay." Hannah was already heading for the big square of light coming in the barn doors.

"Aren't you forgetting something?" He smiled, and Amanda realized what he meant a beat before Samuel said, "What?"

"You need the phone number, don't you?" Simon's eyes twinkled with the pleasure of having the last word.

But Hannah was a match for him. She rolled her own heavenward, as if he were hopelessly behind. "Dude. They're a commercial ranch. They have a website. The number will be on it. Thanks for your help."

Ben nodded to him and followed Samuel and his sister out the door.

"*Denki*, Simon," Amanda said softly. No one liked to be humiliated, Simon least of all. "It was kind of you to give them the information they wanted."

"*Ja*, especially when they could have looked it all up on a website," he said pleasantly.

He didn't fool her a bit. "No one even thought of that until now. But it doesn't matter. It's just a crazy idea. They'll be tired of it in a day or two. None of us has the money for a train ticket anyway."

"Did you think it was crazy when Joe and I went last summer?" He walked into the tack room and picked up part of a harness lying over a sawhorse, as if he really meant to do the job he was supposed to have been doing all along.

"*Ja*, I did. But it worked out, and you had a few adventures along the way."

"Maybe I'll go with them if they go through with it," he said casually. "They'd have an easier time with someone there to show them the ropes."

She wasn't so sure Hannah would agree. "I'm sure they would," was all she said, though. "I'd better go. See you."

He nodded over the harness, his clever hands already busy with saddle soap and warm water.

Amanda tried to beg off going into Willow Creek to the café, but the others were having none of it. "There's nothing to do in the garden until it dries out, and you can move that plant of yours later," Samuel said. "We're in this together."

No, they weren't. "But I have to start supper soon," she protested. "My parents will be back from Willow Creek at five."

"Then hurry up," Hannah said from the front seat of Ben's old red wreck of a car, which he'd parked out on the road earlier out of consideration for Dat's feelings. "I won't charge my phone all the way. Just enough to make the call, I promise. Half an hour, tops."

Hannah was as good as her word. No sooner had she plugged her little phone into the wall at the café and it showed signs of life than she pushed her coffee aside on the Formica tabletop and got down to business. Amanda had brief glimpses of tempting pictures of mountains and cattle on the tiny screen before Hannah found the phone number.

"Hello," she said pleasantly when someone picked up. "I'd like to speak to the person in charge of hiring summer staff, please."

Goodness. It was as though she'd stepped through a mirror and become another person. Not the girl in the black jeans and T-shirt and with purple highlights in her hair who had driven into Willow Creek last fall looking for her real family. Not the sort-of Amish girl who was trying to fit in without really understanding why the Amish did things they way they had always done. But another person.

The one who could get a job in the *Englisch* world.

Unlike Amanda, who wouldn't even know where to start.

She heard a couple of clicks, and then a different voice answered. Since she was sitting in the booth next to Hannah, Amanda could hear quite clearly.

"Hello, this is Silvia Gunderson. I understand you're looking for a temporary position this summer?"

"Yes." Hannah glanced at them. "Actually, I'm calling from Pennsylvania. My name is Me—um, Hannah Riehl, and I'm sitting here with the aunt of one of the Amish boys you hired last year—Simon Yoder?"

"Oh, yes. I remember Simon well. How is his foot?"

"All healed up, I'm happy to say. Anyway, he's told us all kinds of stories about how wonderful it is there, and we wondered if you might have positions for two young men and two young women. I'm nineteen and Amanda is twenty-four."

Amanda's stomach seemed to fall through the floor. Wait a minute! She wasn't going. Why was Hannah lying to this lady?

"And you're all Amish?"

Again that glance, one that seemed to ask for confirmation ... or forgiveness. "Yes."

Ben's brows rose, and Amanda put her cup down in sheer amazement that she would say such a thing. Anyone could see the moment they got off the train that three of the four weren't Amish.

Not yet. Or not any more.

"I have to say, Joe and Simon certainly did good work here last year. And with the influx of tourists to Custer County who come simply to see the Amish and visit their businesses, it seems we might be able to find a place for you and your friends. What experience do you have?"

Another glance. Really, Amanda should be the one on the phone. Then at least the woman would know what she'd really be getting.

"Well, Ben Troyer and Samuel Riehl have a lot of experience with construction. They've both been working in the RV factory here. But they're outdoorsy types, and really good with horses. You know. The way most Amish men are."

"As good as Simon?"

"Oh yes," Hannah assured her without even a blink. "He's even thinking of coming back."

There was a slight pause. "Is that right? And what about you and your friend?"

"I've been a barista, so I've got experience in waiting tables and in cleaning," Hannah said. "And Amanda is a really good cook and she can clean. Plus she designs and makes quilts, and can make jam and can fruit and that kind of thing."

"Excellent. We're fully staffed in the kitchen—Teresa Rodriguez is the head chef. The menus I have here are as close as you can get to *haute cuisine* outside of Denver, so we won't have much call for home canning. I hope your friend can join our housekeeping staff with you."

"We'd both be happy to do that." Hannah made an apologetic face to Amanda, who leaned her chin on her hand and resisted the urge to roll her eyes. How many times did she have to say she wasn't going?

"Tell you what," the woman said. "Have Simon give me a call. If he vouches for you, you can consider yourselves hired. If it works out, can you be here on the first of May?"

Amanda sat up. The first of May! That was only a couple of weeks off—and this was the most important part of the year at church. They couldn't go until after Communion. Did Hannah not know that?

"I'm pretty sure we could," Hannah said cautiously, clearly wondering why Amanda looked so alarmed. "The boys will have to give notice at the factory, of course."

"Of course. Give me a number where I can reach you, and we'll talk again soon."

Hannah gave it to her, and with a whoosh of breath, pressed the button that disconnected the call. "Wow. We might have jobs this summer. In Colorado. How about that?"

"*We* might not," Amanda said with asperity. "The people you made up out of thin air might, though."

"Oh, would you relax?" Hannah took a gulp of her fancy coffee. "It's called marketing."

"It's called lying."

"Not really." Samuel was trying not to smile, and failing. "Everything she said was true. Mostly. Or it was."

"Except that business about waiting tables," Ben put in. "When did you do that?"

"I used to work at a coffee bar," Hannah informed him, a little defensively. "Baristas had to bus the tables as well as make the drinks."

Amanda pushed back her chair. "Well, good luck trying to get a recommendation out of Simon, after you were so huffy to him. I'm going home." She held up a hand as Ben started to get up. "Don't worry—I'll get a ride. Mamm and Dat should be going by soon."

Which turned out to be the case. She waved down her parents, who were on their way out of Willow Creek, and climbed into the familiar buggy that smelled of horse and wool blankets and road dust. She thought of her poor borage plant at home.

She would dig it up when they got back—not to throw it out, but to put it where it could flourish. And put this nonsense about Colorado out of her head.

2

Instead of calling Hannah's cell like a normal person, Simon Yoder rattled down the gravel lane at Jonathan and Rebecca Riehl's place and pulled up next to the fence, where he jumped out of the buggy and tied up his horse. Hannah's younger sister Barbie goggled through the window in the kitchen door.

"Mamm, it's Simon Yoder. Did you ask for a cure from the *Dokterfraa*?"

Sometimes Simon delivered things for his mother, but most often it was his younger brother, Caleb, who did it. Hannah had already figured out why Simon had come—because why not deliver the bad news in person so you could give the girl who had been lippy to you what she deserved?

Mamm opened the door when Simon knocked, and the twins lifted their heads from the puzzle they were putting together at the kitchen table. The seven-year-old boys were so energetic it took all the girls in the family to keep up with them, but puzzles were the one thing guaranteed to keep them in one spot, sometimes for a whole hour. Since Simon wasn't from their church, and wasn't a member of their extended family, they lost interest and went back to work.

"Guder owed, Rebecca," he said, nodding to Hannah's mother.

"Guder owed, Simon." She stood aside to let him in. "I don't remember Sarah saying she'd send me a cure. Did I forget something?"

"Neh, I'm not here for Mamm. I wanted a word with Hannah, is all."

Oh, surely not. She hadn't said anything about the plan, mostly because she'd given up on it. Was he really going to blurt it all out right here in the kitchen, with Dat not ten feet away in the sitting room reading the paper?

Hannah adored Rebecca, the mother she and Ashley—Leah—had been taken away from nearly fourteen years ago. But it was taking a little longer for her to warm up to her father, Jonathan. Maybe because hanging on every word he said to her was the weight of expectation, of hope that she would stop going in circles and commit to one way of life or the other. Since Hannah wasn't capable of that at the moment, and didn't know when she would be, being around him was kind of ... fraught.

"In person," she said with just enough of a lilt that he might take it for disbelief that he didn't just call her, and Mamm might take it for gratitude. "Walk me out to the garden. I want to see if the peas are up yet."

"Of course they're up," Barbie said. "We were weeding them just today, remember?"

Sweet Barbie, who couldn't take her eyes off Simon. Clueless Barbie, who deserved a much nicer boy now that she was sixteen and old enough to take her half-*Englisch* sister to singing and sit next to her in church on the single women's benches instead of with Mamm and the little ones.

"Oh, that's right," Hannah said. "Come outside anyway, Simon. We don't need to disturb—"

"No one is disturbing us," came the bass voice from the sitting room, followed by the sounds of a paper being folded up.

Hannah closed her eyes briefly. So much for trying to do this in private. Simon was going to enjoy this even more.

Rebecca took a fresh rhubarb pie from the cold cupboard and began to slice it. "You'll have some pie with us, Simon?"

"Denki, that would be nice." He sat in Daadi Riehl's chair at the end, since Hannah's grandparents had retired to the *Daadi Haus* after supper. "So, Hannah, like I was saying, I heard back from Mrs. Gunderson a little while after you left."

"She said she was going to call you. To ask for your opinion." *Stay calm.* It didn't matter. Dat could hardly get mad for something she wasn't going to do, could he?

"Who is Mrs. Gunderson?" Rebecca asked. Jonathan came in and she put a fat slice of pie in front of him, then Simon, and indicated they should help themselves to the cream jug.

The little boys pushed aside their half-finished puzzle and sat up straight in anticipation, and Barbie made good and sure she delivered the cream to Simon personally after Jonathan had poured some on his pie.

Simon nodded to Barbie, who blushed scarlet and subsided in her own chair halfway down the table. "Mrs. Gunderson is the wife of the man who owns the ranch in Colorado where me and Joe Byler got work last summer."

After a beat of silence, Jonathan said, "And this woman has something to say to our Hannah?"

She had to take this conversation away from Simon before

her father's tone got any quieter. "I've been talking with Amanda Yoder about maybe going out there to work," she said, as if it didn't matter much. "So I spoke with Mrs. Gunderson this afternoon about it, and she said that if Simon vouched for us, we might consider ourselves hired." She hardly tasted the bite of rhubarb pie, though Rebecca was a fabulous cook. "I don't suppose that happened, though."

Simon grinned at her. Clearly he was having way too much fun forcing her to tell the whole story in front of her family. Both her parents had laid down their forks and were gaping at her in astonishment.

"Why wouldn't it?" Simon asked. "I had nothing but good things to say about my aunt ... and you, from what I know of you. Or Ben and Samuel. But anyway—"

"Ben!" Jonathan said. "Ben Troyer?"

"Samuel!" Rebecca repeated. "What is this? What is going on, Hannah?"

Don't panic. Treat it as though it's completely normal. Getting a summer job is *normal. It's Simon who's making the whole thing look underhanded, blast him.*

"Ben and Sam were there too," she said mildly. "Sam thought he'd be good as a hunting guide, or working with the horses like Simon did last year. Joe probably isn't going now that he's farming his own leases."

How Amish she sounded. As though she hadn't learned all this and committed it to memory, the way she might have studied for a trigonometry exam in her old life if she'd cared enough to do that. In fact, she took learning about the people here, their family connections, and their lives a lot more seriously than she ever had trig.

"To Colorado." Her father's voice sounded flat. "To work on an *Englisch* ranch."

She nodded. *"Denkes* for the recommendation, Simon." It galled her to owe him anything, but the words had to be said. "It was nice of you."

"Better this woman had written to your parents, Hannah," Jonathan said. "What do you mean by making all these plans without speaking to us first? Simon, what does your mother think of all this?"

"Well, after last year she'll probably take it a little easier," he said. "As long as I don't drop an anvil on my foot, she'll be happy I'm working."

"You're going too?" Barbie blurted, then blushed again and ducked her head.

"I might," he said easily. "Mrs. Gunderson offered me my job back, with a little raise to sweeten the pot. But of course I have to talk it over with Mamm and Henry. They might need me."

"Well, Hannah is certainly needed here." Jonathan pushed his empty plate away and stood. "And we have no money for train tickets and the like. She needs to ask for God's guidance and seek His will about the rest of her life, not go gadding around the continent with fence jumpers. I'm sure your grandparents will think the same. Corinne can't do without her girl at home, and that's the end of it."

In one way, it was good to have a place where you were needed—though Hannah suspected that Barbie and Katie were just as capable of helping Mamm now as they had been for the thirteen years of her absence. But in another way, having her choice taken away from her just like that ... it irked her. Even if she'd already resigned herself to not going, it still ought to be her decision.

And now it wasn't.

She was just taking a breath to argue when Rebecca laid a

gentle hand on her leg under the tablecloth. That pressure said, *Be quiet for now. Do this for me, and don't say the words I know you want to say.*

Hannah drew the angry breath deep into her lungs and let it out again. The hand slipped from her leg and her mother said, "Thank you for coming all this way to give Hannah the message, Simon."

"It was no trouble. It's only three miles and Dulcie needed the exercise. Guess I'd best be heading her home, though. It's almost dark. *Guder nacht*, all."

"Guder nacht," Hannah said in a fair approximation of politeness in front of the little kids. They chorused their good nights, all except for Barbie, who didn't dare show her preference any further in front of her dad.

Hannah could only hope Jonathan would put a stop to any preferences in Simon's direction in as big a hurry as he'd just squashed Hannah's own possibilities for the summer.

When the sound of buggy wheels crunched off down the lane and faded, Dat got up. "I'll see to the cows. Boys, come with me."

The cows had been milked ages ago, but he always went out last thing before bed to say good night to them. Hannah was half convinced the big scary animals watched for him every evening, too.

When they were gone and Barbie had taken Katie upstairs to brush teeth and hair, Hannah was left to clear the table and wash the pie plates and silverware.

She looked over her shoulder at her mother, who was wiping down the table. "I wasn't going to go, you know," she said. "I can't believe Simon told Mrs. Gunderson all that stuff. He doesn't even know me."

"He obviously thought you wanted to go." The circles of

shiny damp on the oilcloth grew smaller and finally stopped. "And Samuel? He would quit his steady work at the RV factory over a summer job? He would go so far away from us?"

"He's pretty far away now," Hannah pointed out gently. "He's confused. Seeing a new place is something to do with himself when he doesn't really have anything going on here. Something different."

"But Colorado." The pain in her mother's voice pricked Hannah's heart in sympathy.

"I don't think he'll go, Mamm. Not if we can't all go. And Dat made it pretty clear I can't, even if I could pay my own way. Which I can."

Rebecca looked up from folding the washcloth into smaller and smaller squares. "You can? How?"

"Sewing." Hannah smiled. "That Blooming Nine-Patch I made, remember? I still have two hundred dollars from the auction. I've never spent it."

"And you shouldn't, either. That's your money, and you need to put it in the bank."

She shouldn't say this. But something inside her pushed the words out. "Dat can't really tell me what to do, Mamm. I'm not really Amish. And I'll be twenty soon."

Rebecca looked down as she shook out the cloth, and crossed the kitchen to hang it over the faucet. "I know it. And he knows it." She looked up. "Corinne and Isaac will never consent to Amanda's going."

"But Samuel and Ben—"

"There is nothing stopping them. It's different for boys—and their families have no say in their lives now."

"It isn't different at all. People get summer jobs all the time."

"But *people* aren't Amish," her mother said. "An Amish girl stays home and learns housekeeping until the *gut Gott* chooses a man for her who will make her a wife and mother."

"I'm sure that happens in Colorado, too." How did anybody know if God was really behind meeting The One, or if it was just random chance and sheer luck? "I mean, the Amish folks out there must have boarded trains and moved house. They built a settlement, right? They couldn't have done that if they'd stayed home."

"God moved them, in their hearts." Rebecca crossed the worn linoleum and took Hannah's hands, damp from the dishes. "Don't be so quick to leave me, *Liewi*. I've only just got you back again."

There was no reply to that but a hug. And when Dat came in a moment later with the twins and saw them, his face relaxed just a little.

But it could have been because of the cows.

AMANDA WAS ENJOYING A CUP OF MEADOW TEA IN THE kitchen with Sarah and Englisch Henry when Simon came in from putting the horse away for the night.

"Hullo, Amanda," he said, pulling down a mug for himself and pouring a cup. He settled into his place at the table. "I was just over to Riehls' with a message for Hannah. You were my next stop."

"Aren't you the busy one." She smiled at him with affection unalloyed by knowing him so well. "What did you have to say to her?"

"Oh, I think you know. And Jonathan wasn't pleased, I can tell you."

"I imagine not," Sarah said quietly. "If you had been taken

from me for thirteen years, I'd be pretty hesitant about your taking yourself away to Colorado, too. Not that I wasn't last year, mind you. But it turned out all right."

Amanda buried her smile in her cup as Simon was unable to stop the jerk of his head in surprise that his mother knew what his veiled remarks referred to. He knew perfectly well Amanda often talked things over with Sarah as well as with his grandmother. The only secret she'd ever kept from Corinne was her brief friendship with Jesse, and look how that had turned out. Corinne had found out in the most painful way possible—with a call from the hospital.

The truth was that if you did the things God approved of, you had nothing to keep secrets about. Freedom of spirit was the result—and you could talk about anything with anyone without fear of being judged or causing offense.

Simon, it seemed, had yet to learn this valuable lesson. But he would. In time.

He shifted on the hard chair and took a sip of tea. "I vouched for the two of you with Mrs. Gunderson, and she's willing to offer you both a job in housekeeping starting May first. It will be June first, though. I told her that."

"No one from here could leave with Council Meeting coming up on Sunday, and Communion Sunday two weeks after that," Sarah said. "Goodness. Aside from what everyone in the *Gmee* would say, that would be no way to serve God—flitting off during the most important services of the year."

"I know, Mamm," Simon said. "She wants the others to call if they agree, and to tell her when they'll be arriving so she can have someone meet the bus."

"That's kind of her," Henry said. "Is the ranch some way out of town?"

"Nearly a hundred miles from where the train comes in,"

Simon told him. "That's why you have to take the bus for the last leg. Things are a lot farther apart there than they are here."

"I remember," he said quietly. "I used to live in Denver. Never got to the San Luis or the Wet Mountain Valleys though."

"I guess Hannah won't, either," Simon told them. "Jonathan forbade it."

"Mamm did too," Amanda admitted. "Well, not forbade, exactly. But she can't handle all the work alone, so that's that."

"It seems a shame," Sarah said. "I could give her a hand, and Caleb can help her in the garden."

Henry nodded in agreement—Amanda hadn't seen the two of them disagree yet. But they were practically newlyweds still. "He's a lot of help to me, but if he's more help to his grandmother, then he should divide his time between the studio and the farm. And Simon, you too. You can lend your grandfather a hand in the fields."

"I don't think I'll be here," Simon said slowly. "Mrs. Gunderson offered me my job back, with a raise. I might head out there again if Ben and Samuel go. Or even if they don't."

Quietly, Sarah Byler put down her cup, but she still gripped it with both hands. "To Colorado? On June first?"

"The pay is good, Mamm," he said quickly. "It's work I like, with people I like."

"*Englisch* people," she reminded him. "How often did you get to church last year? Maybe only two or three times, Joe said. You'd do better to get work here and do your share to support our family."

Simon's gaze flicked to Henry and back to his mother. Would he dare say something about Henry's ability to support the family? But he couldn't. Amanda wasn't privy to their finances, but from things her mother had let drop by accident, Sarah didn't have to scrimp and save anymore, or even sell her cures in the Amish Market in Willow Creek. She was a *Dokter-fraa* because she liked the path where God had directed her, not because every penny mattered, and God had blessed her for her joyful obedience.

"I'm nearly twenty-two, Mamm. Old enough to make my own decisions."

"Yes, you are," she agreed. "It's not my place to stop you, only to advise you."

"Last summer didn't satisfy your urge to travel?" Amanda asked, to give the situation a moment to cool down. "It seemed like a grand adventure to me."

Simon shrugged. "It was fun, but it's also a job. A good job, that pays better than anything I could get here. Even Ben said that the pay beat what he's making at the RV factory."

"I'm just afraid that you'll like it so much you won't come back." Sarah touched his hand. "I don't think I could bear that."

"If I didn't, it would be God's will." He turned his palm over to squeeze her fingers.

Simon's will, more like.

But that wasn't fair of her, Amanda chided herself. She had enough to do keeping her own spiritual garden in order. She'd best not be peeking over the fence and making remarks about his, or the heavenly husbandman might decide it was time to give her a good pruning.

"I'm for bed." Simon got up, kissed his mother, and laid a hand on Henry's shoulder.

Henry smiled as he climbed the stairs. "Caleb is reading—tell him to blow out the lantern."

"I'll walk you home, Amanda," Sarah said, standing to clear the cups.

"Nonsense. I've been walking that path for years."

"Let me have the pleasure of a stroll with you. I'll do the dishes when I get back."

At which point Amanda realized that there was nowhere better for a private word between sisters-in-law than the hill between this property and that of her parents, left to grow wild because of the herbs Sarah harvested there in the summer. So she said nothing until they had reached the top, knee deep in last year's grass and mallow and dock, and she could see the lights of home shining through the chilly spring darkness.

"If you want me to, I'll have a little talk with Corinne about your going," Sarah said at last.

Amanda's desire for something different struggled with her fear of change. Fear—or maybe the sheer weight of the familiar—won. "Don't," she said. "It's true. Mamm needs me."

"It's also true that we can work together to get done what we need to. Priscilla Mast and Rosanne Kanagy can both help, and I'll pay them a little."

"But why?" The moon was up, but covered in racing clouds. She could see Sarah's white organdy *Kapp*, and the pale oval of her pretty face, but not much more since her black jacket covered her to the hips. "I don't understand why you're encouraging me to go. You should be doing the opposite, like everyone else. Like me."

Sarah hesitated, her head turned away. Then her eyes glittered a little as she gazed into Amanda's face. They were of a height, though Sarah was more slender. "I think it would be good if Simon had someone there with him, if Joe Byler is going to stay home. One of his family. You're such a steady person. He could count on you."

Steady in her case meant *stuck* and finding reasons to be content with it. And count on her to do what? What was worrying Sarah that she would so unexpectedly lend her support to something Amanda's parents disapproved of? What did she think Simon would do out there in Colorado without someone to keep an eye on him?

"Are you afraid that Ben and Samuel might influence him?" she asked at last. It was the only reason she could see.

"Perhaps a little. I don't know what it is. I just feel an urging in my spirit for you to go." Sarah put her back to the wind and pulled her coat more closely around her. It didn't seem to have enough fabric in it for the job. "For him. For yourself."

Her jacket wouldn't quite fasten up. Sarah was still slender, but only from the back.

"Liewi, are you expecting?"

Sarah drew in a breath of surprise. "We were talking about you, in case you hadn't noticed. Yes, I am. I was going to tell everyone on Sunday after Council Meeting."

"Oh, I'm so happy for you and Henry!" Amanda threw her arms around her, and there it was, the little tummy making itself known where it hadn't before. "Simon and Caleb to have a little *bruder* or *schweschder*!"

There was nothing Amanda wouldn't do for Sarah. Even last year, when she'd been upset and jealous and behaving badly over the unsuccessful matchmaking episode, she had loved her sister-in-law, and that love had been returned with a whole heart. Sarah had never asked her for anything, but she had been there for Amanda many a time.

Now she was encouraging her to have an adventure. Wasn't

this the very thing that might cure her sorrow at never being someone's first choice? She was being chosen now, thanks to Simon and his winsome ways with people.

And she would be home in time for the baby's birth, to help Sarah during the first few months. The trip wouldn't last forever. Suddenly it had an ending date, and somehow that made it less frightening. More like something she could handle.

"All right," she said suddenly. "If you can convince Mamm and Dat that I should go, I will. I have my auction money, and the money I made at the Amish Market last fall. So a train ticket will be no burden to them. And I will be home in October, to help you once the *Boppli* is born."

"Gut." She could see the white shine of Sarah's smile. "I confess that I've been torn between encouraging you to go for your own good, and wanting you to stay, for mine. But perhaps when Jonathan and Rebecca Riehl hear that you are going, they will reconsider about Hannah, and you will have a friend to share your adventure with."

But that was too much to ask for. That would take the hand of God itself.

ꕥ 3 ꕥ

"I can't believe I'm actually here!" Hannah exclaimed. Standing on the westbound platform of the Lancaster train station, she bounced on her toes like a child.

"Neither can I," Amanda said in the kind of tone that made Hannah recall just what agony her own folks had put her through since the night Englisch Henry's Sarah had come over to have a visit with them. Amanda's folks hadn't been overjoyed about losing her for a whole summer, either, but she'd rather face Amanda's parents any day than her own father. What was it about Sarah Byler that got under your skin and made you think about things the way she saw them?

Of course, Jonathan had made it sound like he was only giving permission because God's will was at work and there was a larger task at hand than simply getting a summer job. Maybe it was God's will or maybe it wasn't. Maybe it was simply guts and good timing.

Whatever. The point was, she was off on an adventure with people she liked, and here came the train, huffing and roaring to a stop under the old-fashioned, shedlike roof of the station with its funny white gingerbread trim.

"I can believe it," Ben said with satisfaction. "I knew you girls would come along. Who would miss an adventure like this?"

"You'd better hope the boss at the factory takes us on again when we come back," Samuel pointed out as he hefted his bag to his shoulder and they prepared to board.

"Who says we're coming back?"

But Hannah just laughed. Ben was kidding, in his laconic, stingy-with-words way. Of course they'd come back. But who could think about the end of the adventure when it was just beginning?

They could have flown and been in Denver in, like, four hours. But the Amish didn't fly. Flying required a picture ID, and when you took the Bible seriously on the subject of graven images, you didn't get your picture taken, even for a driver's license. The Amish didn't drive cars, either, of course. They had ID cards to be out and about on the roads, and had to pass a test to drive a horse and buggy, but there weren't any pictures on those cards. Simon had to show his at the ticket counter, and so had Amanda.

The only train Hannah had ever been on was one trip into New York City when she was twelve, to see *The Lion King* on Broadway. The people she had called parents for most of her life had avoided trains and subways for the most part. They'd kidnapped her and Ashley from the hill behind the Riehl farm when they were little, and brought them up as their own. Hannah figured they'd done most of their traveling in the car so that other people would be less able to identify them.

But she still had her driver's license from the state of New York, and she had decided to dress *Englisch* for this trip instead of Amish. Which meant jeans that kind of squeezed her around the waist where they never had before, thanks to Mamm's good cooking. At the ranch, she'd be cleaning toilets and riding horses, and the jeans would be comfortable again in no time.

Nobody paid much attention to their little group in Lancaster, which was Amish Central where everyone was used to the sight of plain folks. Even in Pittsburgh there were a couple of groups in away bonnets and straw hats. Naturally Simon got talking to them, and before you knew it, they were being invited over to share the goodies packed in hampers and coolers.

But by the time they got to Chicago and made the transfer to the *Southwest Chief* heading for Trinidad, Colorado, Hannah was not only exhausted, she was irritated at the way people stared at the unfamiliar sight of Simon and Amanda.

"Don't glare at those people like that," Amanda said mildly, turning from the view of the mountains and catching her giving the hairy eyeball to a family down the aisle. "There's no reason to be angry. They're just curious."

"Staring is rude."

"Is that why you're dressed *Englisch*?" Amanda never missed a trick. "So people won't stare?"

"No." Hannah tried not to sound defensive, but she wasn't sure she pulled it off. "I just thought it would be easier. Three *Englisch*, two Amish, all traveling together as friends. How often do you see that?"

But Amanda only smiled and gazed out at the scenery, leaving Hannah, who had learned to be honest with herself, to the inescapable conclusion that she'd dressed *Englisch* because she was indeed afraid of just this kind of attention. The people she'd called her parents had avoided it—had warned them against attracting attention every time they set foot outside the door.

She hadn't realized that her old sense of caution would crop up again during the first real trip she'd taken since coming back to her real family. But it was more than that. She dressed Amish in Whinburg Township because she was with the Amish. She wanted to fit in. Now that she was back in the *Englisch* world, what was wrong with wanting to fit in here?

Hannah knew the answer. Of course no one was forcing her to adopt the clothes when she hadn't adopted the religion. Yet. But the fact was that she'd been born Amish. She could look as plain as Amanda—had brought more Amish clothes than *Englisch*, in fact. Three dresses, three aprons (two bib aprons for work, and a belt apron and cape for Sunday), and three *Kapps*. Just in case Mrs. Gunderson had been serious about wanting Amish girls. She could uphold as much of the *Ordnung* of her district as she could remember, just like Amanda. It wasn't like Mrs. Gunderson would know the difference.

On her days off she could be like Ben, who dressed in jeans and a plaid shirt, and no one paid any attention to him.

Except her. She always knew where he was, with some weird internal radar that pinged when his car went by on the county highway, for instance, or told her when he was coming down the aisle of this train car on his way back from the bathroom.

"Come on up into the observation car," he said as he stopped by her seat. "That's the way to see the mountains."

It wasn't until they were climbing the steps to the second level, several cars forward, that it occurred to her she should have invited Amanda along. But how many opportunities was she going to get to be alone with Ben?

She'd better take what she could get while she could.

The observation car with its glass top and sides was a lot warmer than she'd expected, despite the air conditioning doing its best. They slid into a two-seater table and Hannah took in the long view, with the late afternoon sun sinking behind yet another range of mountains that lay ahead.

"I wish we'd thought to come up here right after we left Denver," she said. "The Rockies were great, but we could have seen them better from here."

"I came up to get a table, but there weren't any left," Ben said. "But we can still enjoy this."

"I am." But no matter how beautiful the scenery, there were also views a girl had to take in when they were sitting right opposite her.

"You're supposed to be looking at the mountains, not me," Ben told her after a few minutes. "Do I have something on my face?"

"No." She smiled. "I like looking at your face. But don't get a swelled head over it or I'll change my mind and stare at Simon instead."

"Plenty of girls do," Ben acknowledged with a roll of his eyes. "But I hope he doesn't come up here. I need some time away from him. With you."

That was enough to make her melt inside just a little.

He was facing forward, gazing into the west. "Half of me wants to just stay on this train and keep going. To stay between places, and not arrive anywhere."

"Don't you want to get to the ranch, and start work? Do new things and meet new people?"

"*Ja,* some. But this way, we can just talk and be and not have to do, you know?"

"If you're my dad, life is all about the doing."

"Mine, too. But we're not our parents."

"That's part of the problem," came out of her mouth before she thought, as though she'd been hypnotized by the sound of the wheels on the track.

"Why is it a problem?"

She took his hand, sliding her fingers between his two clasped ones. To her relief, that hard grip relaxed and he turned his palm over to meet hers. "You know. If we were like our parents, we'd want their life. The Amish life."

"You sound like you haven't made up your mind."

"Of course not. Have you? All the way, for good, I mean?"

"Oh, ja."

"Says the guy who replies in *Deitsch*."

He looked surprised for a second. "I did, didn't I? I'll have to watch that. Say *yeah* instead." His gaze slid from hers to watch the landscape slip past. Slip into the past. "The farther away this train takes me, the more my mind makes itself up."

Well, she'd sort of known that, hadn't she? The problem was, she wasn't in the same place. What if he decided to keep on going in October and she wanted to return? To go home. What would happen to them, the couple who were holding hands right now?

The air conditioning seemed to blow a little cooler. But maybe that was because the sun was going down.

Her life had been like riding a train for months now. Just going along in a kind of moving between-place, enjoying the scenery but not committing to a destination and paying the price for the ticket. But that couldn't last forever. Sooner or later, life would demand that she choose a destination. Or God would. Or Dat would.

What would she choose?

As though it were giving her some kind of answer, the train

slowed and the other occupants of the viewing car got up and began to collect their belongings. A tinny voice announced the next station in five miles. Their station.

"Looks like the between is over and we're coming to the end of the line," Ben said, giving her hand a quick squeeze and pulling her to her feet. "Simon says we go over to the bus station for the last part. Not far now."

She didn't have the nerve to ask him all the questions tumbling around in her tired brain. But the next time she caught him looking like he wanted to ride off into the sunset, she'd better get up the nerve to talk about it. Right now she wasn't going to spoil the trip thinking about it. She needed every bit of energy to get where she was going.

They didn't have a whole lot of luggage to wrestle, not like the family whose three kids had been staring at Amanda over the backs of the seats. They had four giant suitcases, a baby stroller, and a cooler. Everything Hannah had brought fit in her backpack, and Amanda carried a suitcase so old it didn't even have wheels. The boys had black gym bags.

The bus was nearly empty, but that didn't make it go any faster. The closer they got to their destination, the longer the trip seemed to take. After what seemed like a lifetime on the bus—but according to Hannah's watch was only about an hour—they got off in Westcliffe.

Despite the fact that she'd been glued to the window the whole way, Amanda gazed upward in amazement. "The sky. Look at it. It's so big. And there is the evening star."

Big, and deep blue except for a glowing strip of green along the jagged tops of the mountains. Sure enough, there was the evening star, pricking out because it was so late in the day.

"I hope someone remembers to get us," Samuel said a little nervously. "Simon, you called from Denver, *ja*?"

"I said I would, and I did," Simon said, as tired as the rest of them, and just as irritated. "They'll be here. Stop worrying." But his gaze strained up the street, looking north.

Was that where their ride was coming from? Hannah barely knew north from west, but she knew cars. They had to be sending a van. You couldn't cram five people into a pickup unless you put them in the bed, and that was illegal, right?

In a moment a white van roared around the corner and passed them. Hannah had just enough time to read LOST CREEK RANCH painted on the side before Amanda said, "I don't think they saw us."

The van swung around in a U-turn right in the middle of an intersection and zoomed to a stop next to them, rocking on its wheels. The window dropped open and a kid no older than Simon leaned on one elbow, pushing his cowboy hat up with a finger. "You the Amish kids?" Then recognition crossed his face. "Simon Yoder? You back? You're a glutton for punishment, ain't you?"

"Hey, Reese. I'm back, and I brought reinforcements." Simon grinned, as though this was a joke.

"Hop in, or supper will be all gone before we get there."

Hannah had had enough of food out of vending machines; she wasted no time in scrambling into the van, with Amanda and Ben beside her. Samuel crawled into the very back, and Simon—because he was Simon—slid into the passenger seat in the front. He'd barely got the door closed when Reese took off, dust spiraling up behind them in their red taillights.

Hannah tried to take in some of what they passed, but once they left town, there was nothing but darkness, punctuated now and again by the lights of houses way off in the distance. She finally gave up and focused on Simon's conversation with Reese, but it was hardly more helpful. A lot of names she didn't know, including those of what must be horses. And a lot about an upcoming pack trip where it sounded like the boys would be needed.

She was so tired that she must have dozed, because the next thing she knew, they were bumping over something in the ground that made her teeth rattle and woke her up. "What was that?"

"Cattle guard," Reese said. "Here we are. Welcome to the Lost Creek Ranch."

After a long hill that felt and sounded like a gravel road, he pulled the van into a barn whose doors stood open as if it was expecting them. Hannah had a confused impression of buildings and yard lights and not much else, until they climbed a slope and the big house came into view.

The big house. They weren't kidding.

Hannah tried not to gape, but Amanda murmured, "Holy smokes!" as though she couldn't help herself. For her, this was the equivalent of an *Englisch* kid using a swear word.

The house jutted out from the slope like the prow of a ship, every tall, angled window alight. Around it, a wide deck with log railings and dotted with chaise lounges came to a point in the middle, enhancing the illusion. The house was built of stone halfway up, and then logs the rest of the way, warm red and gold in the skillfully placed lighting. From inside came the sound of cutlery and conversation, with what sounded like music in the background—a fiddle and a guitar.

Ben and Samuel headed toward the wide stone staircase up to the deck, but Reese waved them back. "Nope, not that way. Staff entrance is downstairs."

It turned out there was a whole other level down below the deck, behind a huge space devoted to a patio and the biggest swimming pool Hannah had ever seen. For the first time she understood what *Olympic sized* meant, lit in a rectangle of glimmering blue-green.

"It's all so big," Amanda breathed as Reese led them under the deck, and through a double door of intricately carved wood. "How do they expect us to clean it?"

Good question. Maybe they should sign up for something a little more manageable instead, like cooking for twenty on a pack trip.

They crossed a media room where comfortable chairs were grouped around a plasma TV on the wall, a pool table and a grand piano faced each other, and couches formed reading nooks or places where people could play board games on low tables. Then, through a swinging door, they entered a dining room full of what must be employees, all shoveling down their food. Cowboy hats hung on pegs on the walls, and there seemed to be two men for every woman.

Everyone looked up to take them in. Hannah felt Amanda shrink behind her.

"Staff eat here," Reese told them, and the noise of eating resumed. "Kitchen's through there." He nodded at a set of double swinging doors. From behind them, a clatter of cooking and plating food issued. "Teresa Rodriguez is the boss of all of us."

As though she'd heard her name, a woman backed through the door with two platters in her hands. She couldn't have been more than thirty, or taller than about five foot five, but it was clear that as far as the staff were concerned, she ruled the roost.

"I thought you said she was the cook," Amanda whispered to Simon. "Not the boss."

But he had no time to reply. "Simon Yoder," Teresa greeted him as she set the plates down and rested her hands on her hips. "I'm glad you've come back to us—and brought your friends, too. I hope you learned something on your last visit. How about some introductions?"

He did, and got a smile out of Teresa and several others when he introduced Amanda as his aunt.

"Great to meet you all," Teresa said with a smile that lit up her face. "You must be exhausted. Come on, drop your bags there by the door, sit and get something to eat, and then I'll show you girls where you'll be sleeping. Simon, you'll take the boys to the bunkhouse afterward and get them settled—you're in the same bunk you had last time."

"Thank you, ma'am."

Ma'am? Hannah made a mental note to ask Simon why he called her that as she pulled out a chair and settled into it. In their own districts, the Amish didn't use honorifics—she'd been told that *ma'am*, for instance, was short for *madame*, which meant *my lady*. *Sir* came from *mon sieur*, or *my lord*, which no Amish person would ever say. The only Lord they recognized was the One in heaven. Even *Mr.* and *Mrs.*—contractions of *Master* and *Mistress*—made them hesitate.

The person next to her passed her a bowl of potatoes and her stomach growled. But Hannah had barely got one on her plate when the double doors opened again.

The cowboys pushed back their chairs and stood, and the woman who had come in, blonde and slender and with cheekbones that could put her on the cover of a magazine, waved them into their seats.

"I heard Simon and his Amish friends were here," she said, her gaze raking the table until she found him. "How was your trip?"

"It was great, thank you, Mrs. Gunderson."

Mrs. Gunderson! So this was the owner's wife—the third

wife, the one who had hired them. Wasn't she beauti that sleek look that the spa and a strict fitness regime gave woman. Hannah found herself correcting her posture.

"Introduce me to your friends, Simon."

So he went through the whole rigmarole again. By the time he got to Hannah, though, Mrs. Gunderson's look of confusion had pulled itself into a frown. Simon fell silent ... and so did the whole room.

Every single person in it seemed to be staring at them and chewing like a bunch of cows, waiting for Mrs. Gunderson to explain what was the matter. Some—that dark-eyed girl across the table, for instance, in the white shirt and black pants that were probably her uniform—looked downright entertained.

"Are you all Amish?" Mrs. Gunderson said, looking them over. "I understood you were. But only two of you look it. Is that a regional difference?"

Ben and Samuel gulped hard enough to swallow their tongues. Simon elbowed her softly in the ribs.

Um. Hannah guessed the answer was up to her.

"Simon is Amish, ma'am. Amanda has been a church member for four years or so. I—I guess that leaves Ben and Samuel and me. We're, um, well, the boys left the church a couple of years ago, and I just found out I was born Amish and came back to my birth family."

"So you're not Amish?"

"Well, not yet, ma'am. Strictly speaking. You have to join church for that." Good grief, did she have to explain her life story in front of all these people? "It's kind of complicated."

Mrs. Gunderson crossed her arms over the kind of bosom Hannah had always wished she had. "You were the one I talked to on the phone, weren't you? You want to explain why you told me you all were Amish?"

from having to admit she'd used a little

...e from Amish families," he said easily. "Their ...urch doesn't make a difference, does it?"

... you want weekends off to go into Amistad to ch... e said shortly. "The five of you, I'd like to see you in my offic... after you finish eating. Simon will show you where it is."

She turned and left as suddenly as she'd come, and with a sound like the wind moving in dry grass, people visibly relaxed. Soon the scrape of forks on plates and the murmur of conversation rose again, though a lot softer and more guarded than it had been before. Hannah intercepted a bowl of beef stew and ladled it over her potato, along with some vegetables and pickles, but her stomach felt tight, as though the food would get squeezed back up. She'd faint if she didn't eat something, though, and whoever had made this stew was an artist. The meat was tender, the gravy savory and rich with herbs and just the right amount of fat.

"This is really good," she said, her mouth full.

"Thanks." Teresa had heard her, all the way down there at the end with a dozen people between them. "Don't let the boss lady scare you. She's like that. Blunt. Doesn't waste words."

Hannah smiled, though it took some effort. Amanda just ate her food methodically, her face pale, as though she thought she might be in trouble and eating would help someone be on her side.

Why did their employer care so much about their being Amish?

They found out soon enough. Hannah had just enough time to gulp down a slice of pecan pie—to die for, just like the stew—when Simon stood and waved them toward the door Mrs. Gunderson had used.

"At least if we're going to be fired because we haven't joined church, it'll be on a full stomach," Ben murmured to her as they climbed a set of log stairs, walked down a corridor toward the front of the house, and sidled into an office as big as a schoolroom.

Mrs. Gunderson looked up from a sleek silver laptop, closed it, and came around the desk. Behind her, the view over the hills to the snow-covered mountains beyond would be breathtaking in daylight. The tall windows should have dwarfed their boss, but Hannah had a feeling it would take a lot to do that. This must be the view from the main part of the house, too, where the guitar and fiddle had been playing. Imagine being able to sit in a comfortable chair and look at the mountains all day long.

"Have a seat."

Hannah sank into an armchair upholstered in a cheery English print that somehow complemented the plaid pattern of the thick rug lying on the hardwood floor. The desk was cherry and looked solid yet kind of feminine, and the walls were paneled in bookshelves stuffed full of books. A fire crackled in the fireplace, which had a big stone hearth you could sit on to warm your back.

Mrs. Gunderson sank onto the sofa, and Simon—being Simon—settled into it as well. The rest took chairs like Hannah's. "So I'm a little confused," she said. "I hired Amish staff, and yet three of you don't look it, and now I find out that technically you're not even Amish. You mind explaining to me what happened?"

Simon started to say something, but Samuel interrupted him. "Can I ask a question first, Mrs. Gunderson?"

"Sure."

"Are you going to fire us for not being Amish?"

To his credit, he didn't wilt under that direct blue gaze. "The state of Colorado has strong feelings about hiring and firing on the basis of color, gender, sexual orientation, or religion," she said.

"Does that mean yes or no?"

"It means no. But I need to get this straightened out. Let me explain why."

Even Simon seemed to lean in to pay attention.

"It's come to my attention that the Amish folks here in the Wet Mountain Valley, and over west in the San Luis Valley, have begun to do some pretty nice things for the local economy. They establish businesses, they get on well with their neighbors, they don't cause trouble ... and the tourists have begun to come here to visit them."

"They do that at home in Lancaster County, too," Amanda ventured shyly. "We try not to let it bother us, because their money is very welcome."

"Exactly. You've hit the nail on the head, Amanda."

Amanda looked pleased, and clearly a little puzzled at how she'd managed to make the boss lady nod her head so decidedly.

"It's become apparent to me that as the only dude ranch in these mountains with Amish staff, we can offer something the other ranches can't. We can put it on our website. Your work here becomes more than simply housekeeping or cooking or wrangling. You become a sought-after element of a holiday for folks who might come here instead of going to Lancaster County."

"You mean ... like a tourist attraction?" Ben said. His face had the same expression as it had a little while ago, when he'd tasted the pie and discovered how sweet it was. Not a fan of too much sugar, was her Ben.

"In a way. No one's going to be staring at you or having their picture taken with you, but there's nothing stopping you from being pleasant and helpful and ... Amish. And making them feel that because they spent their vacation at Lost Creek, they got a little bit extra. Something different, that they'd otherwise have to travel a lot farther to find. You see what I mean?"

Hannah did. She'd only ever had a part-time job at a coffee bar, but she'd sat in more than one staff meeting where the managers had fretted about marketing and outreach and trying to do special things that would bring customers in there instead of to the chain coffee bar at the mall.

"If it helps, ma'am, I brought Amish clothes with me," she said. "I don't know if Ben and Samuel did, too, but if they didn't, I bet they could ask one of the local ladies to stitch them up a couple of shirts and pairs of pants."

"Jeans are better for working with horses," Simon said. "That's what I wound up wearing last year. More protection on the trail, too."

"True," Mrs. Gunderson said. "But it's the shirt and suspenders, and the straw hat in place of a Stetson or a Resistol, that people are going to see first. Like what you have on, Simon."

He grinned at her.

"The Amish folks here have to get their hats and things from somewhere. I'm going into town tomorrow, so Simon, if you call the butcher in Amistad and inquire where you might get some, I can drop you wherever he says while I do my errands."

"Yes, ma'am. Sam and Ben will likely need a couple of shirts apiece. Will that come out of their wages?"

Hannah's brother had been squirming as though the chair were stuffed with nettles. Now he half rose out of his seat, then exchanged a glance with Ben and subsided.

"That's a fair question." She considered Samuel, and then her gaze moved to the others. "Half of me is feeling deceived, and the other half just wants to get on with it because I don't have time to deal with nonsense like this. I'll think on it."

Thank goodness she'd brought those Amish dresses! Relief at not being part of the *nonsense* washed through Hannah in a wave. When they started work tomorrow, there'd be no difference between her and Amanda—at least as far as clothes went. She'd washed most of the purple out of her hair months ago, but the twist and bob was another thing altogether. She'd master her hair if it was the last thing she did.

No one would be able to tell she wasn't Amish. Not even the Amish themselves.

And Ben and Sam would just have to get with the program. Because after all they'd done to get here, nobody was getting back on that train over a shirt and some suspenders.

No matter which way the train was going.

4

Amanda hadn't really known what to expect when she arrived in Colorado. Simon had tried to describe it, but *mountains* didn't really do justice to the Sangre de Cristo Range, leaping out of the plain like the shout of an archangel. *Big house* was completely inadequate for the mansion, which was half home, half hotel, and altogether intimidating and strange. And while *bunkhouse* sounded a little more like something a person could actually sleep in, *staff quarters* was ... well, she hadn't expected this.

The girl sitting across the table from her and Hannah—the one who seemed to find it funny that they were getting in trouble for not all looking Amish—had been instructed by Teresa to get them settled in.

"I'm Bonita James," she said, leading them outside and across the courtyard, where they climbed a shallow slope planted in junipers and flowering shrubs. "I'm housekeeping, like you. You'll be in cabin four with me and Jenny Ruiz. We already have the top bunks, so you'll have to make do with the bottom ones."

"We have a cabin?" Hannah asked. "I thought those would be for guests."

"Guests get a room with a view," Bonita said. "Staff quarters are here, behind the house. No view."

As long as they didn't have to sleep in the bunkhouse with all the cowboys, Amanda wasn't going to complain. And in the next moment, as Bonita led them into the last cabin on the left, at the end of the tidy gravel path, she decided she'd never complain again.

"This is staff quarters?" she blurted, gaping at the inside of it. "More like a palace."

The floors were honey-colored pine, with rugs in a geometric pattern in reds and grays scattered about. Two bunk beds were set against each log wall, and beyond them were a couple of armchairs, a TV set, and a cooktop where a person could make coffee or a simple dinner. A microwave oven and a toaster sat on the counter, a mini fridge below it, and the bathroom was at the back.

The tourists could sleep here and feel like kings. How could the cabins with views possibly be nicer than this? Then again, Satan had showed Jesus all the palaces of the world and offered them to Him. Such a beautiful cabin was the reward for accepting what Mrs. Gunderson wanted—an Amish staff who would attract the tourists. Amanda's stomach was still churning from the shock.

Her mind said, *The other staff wear uniforms. Be glad she is not asking you to wear black pants and a white shirt with buttons down the front. You knew what she wanted when you agreed to come.*

But her heart cried, *It's advertising. Your clothes are symbols of your faith, not something to go on the website!*

Amanda felt close to tears. She was exhausted—there were

too many people—she needed time to think and get used to a situation she'd never been in before.

"You won't think it's a palace when you have to dust log walls twice a week," Bonita said, breaking into the chaos of Amanda's thoughts. "I'll show you the ropes in the morning. Closet's there to hang your stuff. Jenny sort of took over the second. Just push her things out of the way."

"One closet for two people?" Hannah asked. "I guess that leaves you and me sharing, then."

"No, mine's full."

"No problem," Hannah said cheerfully. "This it?"

And before Amanda could pull herself together long enough to caution her about antagonizing Bonita, about showing the spirit of peace, about *Demut*—humility—Hannah had opened the closet, pushed the confusion of clothes aside, and made herself a space at one end.

"Hey!" Bonita cried. "What are you doing?"

Hannah shrugged. "What you just said. Pushing stuff out of the way."

"Jenny has much less stuff than I do," Bonita snapped. "Which is why I suggested you both use her closet."

"Two people each." Hannah wasn't backing down, and Amanda didn't know what to do, other than to try to make peace herself. She couldn't live with these angry voices. They just made her feel worse.

"It's all right, Hannah," she said. "I can just keep my things in my suitcase. It will be like a dresser drawer I can just close and slide under my bed. Then you can use Jenny's closet."

"It isn't Jenny's closet, or Bonita's closet. They're employee closets, two people each. If Bonita has a problem with that, she can take it up with Teresa."

"Teresa doesn't deal with that kind of thing." Bonita's gaze sparked venom. "She'll just tell you to work out your problems."

"Oh, I don't have a problem. But if you do, then you need to work it out with yourself."

The door behind them opened, and Amanda braced herself. The newcomer had to be Jenny, a girl about the same age as Hannah, with rippling black hair pulled into a ponytail and the same black pants and white blouse.

"Oh, hey, I wondered if you'd be our roommates," she said by way of greeting. "I hope you don't have a lot of stuff. Bonita is the worst closet hog you ever saw."

"No," Hannah said in a tone that implied she'd never think that. "My things fit just fine. Amanda, better unpack now. We'll probably be on the run tomorrow, trying to learn everything."

"Yes, scrubbing toilets is so complicated," Bonita pointed out with an edge to her voice. "Hey, don't touch that dress. It's one of my good ones."

"We're partnered up tomorrow," Jenny said, and glanced at Amanda. "Want to come with me?"

If she wasn't walking to town to catch the bus back to the train station. At least this *Englisch* girl seemed inclined to be friendly. But Bonita spoke before she could either shake her head or nod.

"Amanda's working with me tomorrow. I've had about enough of this one." She jerked her chin at Hannah, who just grinned and gave the loaded hangers another shove.

Amanda let out a despairing breath. Maybe she should take Hannah outside and speak with her. Bonita flounced into a chair and turned on the TV, blasting music into the room and a picture of a pair of glittery people doing some kind of gymnastics on a big stage.

"Come on, Bee, turn it down. *Celebrity Dance-Off* is almost over anyway."

When she got no answer, Jenny walked over and did something with a plastic thing with a bunch of buttons on it, and the noise fell to a level they could at least talk over.

Amanda lifted her suitcase on to the bed. She would unpack for tonight, and talk the situation over with the others as soon as she could. Simon would understand her dilemma—though the fact that he had got them all into this wasn't lost on her. Had the Amish-as-advertising plan been something he'd had to deal with last year? Probably not. From what she'd said, it sounded like a new development.

"Is it all right?" she asked Jenny, indicating the closet.

"Help yourself. Is that all you brought?"

Amanda nodded. She hung up her four dresses—her favorite green one that Sarah always said was becoming, a taupe and a purple for work, and black for Sunday. The underthings better stay in the suitcase, and since the room had no pegs for their *Kapps*, maybe her spare ones should stay where they would stay clean, too.

"What are those?" Jenny said.

"My coverings." She held up the heart-shaped *Kapp*, the light shining through the white organdy, and indicated the *Duchly* that lay under it. "I'll probably use these for heavy work, though, and keep the *Kapps* nice."

"Don't bet on it." Hannah turned from squeezing her own dresses into the foot of space in the closet on the other side. "I have a feeling the boss lady will want us in a *Kapp*. A *Duchly* doesn't look very Amish."

"But I only brought three," Amanda said. Never mind. She could just wash them more often. "Besides, how you look is only part of being Amish."

But Hannah didn't take the hint. She only shrugged and turned back to her task.

Jenny was still staring at her *Kapp*. "How does it stay on? How come you don't tie the ribbons?"

"We call them strings." Amanda smiled shyly. "And they stay on with straight pins. See?" She dipped her head to point. "Here on top, and one on either side."

Jenny's tanned brow bent into a frown. "Aren't you afraid you're going to stick yourself? Why not bobby pins?"

"Those are not permitted by the *Ordnung*—the standard where we live. They are worldly. And we learn how to pin on a *Kapp* when we're very small."

"Bobby pins are worldly?" Bonita inquired without turning around. "I've heard of weird, but that's extreme."

Which silenced Amanda. The girl was free to think what she liked and make whatever comments her human nature put on her tongue. Amanda's responsibility was to obey the *Ordnung* and through it, keep her human nature and its tendency to vanity in check. Bobby pins had become fashionable in the nineteen-twenties, when *Englisch* women had begun to cut their hair and pin it into marcel waves with the "bob pins." The Lancaster County elders at the time had universally agreed that Amish women wouldn't be using such pins, made to make short hair glamorous, and that was that.

She went into the bathroom to wash and brush her teeth, and to slip into her nightgown. When she came out, she took down her hair and brushed it. She felt a little shy doing something so intimate in front of two girls who weren't relatives. On the other hand, she didn't want to take too long in the bathroom in case someone needed to use it.

"Your hair is so long," Hannah said in admiration. "Mine's never going to grow that long. How often do you cut it?"

Amanda shrugged. "Once a year?"

"You need to deal with those split ends," Bonita said, turning around in the chair to watch her braid it up for the night. "And a heavy dose of conditioner wouldn't hurt, either."

"Leave her alone," Jenny told her. "What's got into you? You're just jealous you don't have blond hair to your waist."

"First, hair that long is a pain in the neck, and second, blond does nothing for my skin tone. It doesn't for hers either. You should color it something darker, Amanda. Maybe a honey caramel. You're so pale."

The hot flush of embarrassment flooded into her cheeks. Which only made the blemishes stand out more.

Hannah advanced toward the other girl, taking the attention away from Amanda, hopefully for enough time that the blush would subside. "Dude, first, she's Amish, so she doesn't color her hair or wear makeup or anything, and second, she doesn't have to do what you say."

Amanda wanted to put a cautioning hand on Hannah's arm, but if she did that, Hannah would probably get even more annoyed—and the attention would be back on her again.

"Dude?" Bonita looked like she'd scored a point. "That's so Amish. I bet you flunked *Ordlung* or whatever."

Hannah didn't bother to reply, thank goodness. She simply made a clicking sound of disgust with her tongue, and marched into the bathroom with her little travel bag. In a moment they heard the shower running.

Amanda climbed under the covers, and found the bed surprisingly comfortable. Luxurious, even. Certainly softer than her bed at home, which had once been her brother Michael's.

Oh, goodness. What was she thinking?

She pushed back the crisp sheets and patterned wool blanket, and slid out of bed to kneel beside it. Behind her, the TV changed from the racket of music and applause to something that sounded tense and scary. The girls had fallen silent. What a blessing. Amanda folded her hands and did her best to tune out the noise and settle her mind and heart with the Lord's Prayer.

She prayed it over twice, and had just got to *Lead us not into temptation* when the water shut off. *For Thine is the kingdom, the power and the glory—*

The bathroom door opened. "For Pete's sake, you barbarians, turn off the TV! Can't you see she's trying to pray? What is wrong with you?"

The racket shut off as abruptly as it had been turned on. It was all Amanda could do to keep her eyes closed and wrestle her mind back to the familiar words.

Forever and ever—

"Freedom of religion, girlie. I don't have to do a thing you say."

The TV came back on, but Amanda would prefer that to the angry voices rising over it.

"Are you always this nasty and inconsiderate?" Hannah demanded.

"Are you always this noisy when your friend is trying to pray?" came the silky reply.

Lord, help me to be strong and to please You. Help me not to be afraid. I'm always afraid, and now it's worse than ever, in this strange place with people who don't like me.

"Give me that!" The TV shut off, then turned on.

Be with Mamm and Dat, and Sarah and Henry and Caleb and the little Boppli coming, and all my family and friends at home. Please send the spirit of the peacemaker to Hannah, and help her learn how it is to be a servant.

"For Pete's sake—what are you guys, two years old?" Jenny finally said in exasperation.

Amanda pushed herself up off her knees. The plank floor was just as hard as it was at home. She'd pull one of the rugs over next time. Or maybe she'd say her prayers in the bathroom.

Better yet, in the shower, where no one would hear or see and be offended.

AMANDA SLEPT IN, NOT UNTIL FIVE IN HER OWN TIME ZONE, but this one, worn out from the previous day. No one was awake yet. She said her prayers in the cool gray dawn, then put on her purple dress in preparation for a day of toilets and dusting log walls. Something propelled her outside—maybe to get a little space between herself and the three sleeping girls in the cabin. Or maybe she simply needed some time alone with the One who had created the magnificence rising up all around her.

She hadn't been able to see much in the dark last night. But as she slipped out of the door, the first thing she saw was the sheer grandeur of the house. And this was the back of it! But dwarfing even the biggest house she'd ever seen were the mountains behind her, rearing up into a sky that was turning from cobalt to azure to sheer blue, even as she watched. The ranch was situated on the western slope of one range, and looked across the Wet Mountain Valley to the eastern slope of another. The rising sun left them in shadow for now while it lit the faraway slopes of the Sangre de Cristo, turning them gold and green and distant blue.

At her back, the scrubby trees that Simon had called *piñon* pines rose on the slopes, and in the hush before the day began, she could hear the rush of Lost Creek. She'd always found solace in the creek bed at home. Maybe in the whisper of water, she'd hear that still small voice again.

She left the staff cabins behind her, following a path that meandered over the face of the hill in the direction of the sound of water. Now and again the way was punctuated by a small staircase of rock built into the steep parts, or a log that held up the hillside where it was muddy. Lizards darted away from her feet, and birds twittered in the pines. A hundred feet up, a huge bird glided and tilted in the updraft, no doubt scanning the ground below for its breakfast.

How different this was from Lancaster County! At first glance it looked bare and bleak and forbidding. But when you stopped to take it in—when you just stopped—you could smell the spicy scent of those pines, draw the dry air into your lungs, and let the sound of the wind and the feel of the coolness spilling down the slope refresh your soul.

She found the waterfall a few blissful minutes later, chattering out of a deep rocky crevice, then widening into the long meadow down across the road in front of the house, where it flowed away to the south. Two tiny figures were walking out to its banks—fly fishermen. Guests, no doubt, up at the crack of dawn to see if they could pull some brook trout out of the water.

Amanda smiled. Dat loved to fish whenever he had a spare hour—though at this time of day he was usually in the milking parlor with the cows.

"There's a smile to brighten the day before the sun comes."

Amanda whirled to see a man coming up the road below—an Amish man. He had stopped his big Percheron pulling the market wagon in the middle of the one-lane road and because of the noise of the waterfall, she hadn't even heard them approach.

"I think you're too far away to see whether I smile or not." How good it felt good to speak *Deitsch*, the language of home and family! She'd been speaking English for Hannah's sake for days.

He seemed to be a big man, from what she could tell from fifty feet above, with broad shoulders under a burgundy shirt and brown canvas jacket. His brown broadfall pants were held up by black suspenders, and his face was clean shaven.

A single man. Not that it mattered to her. Men tended not to pay her any mind, and that was fine. The one God intended for her would pay attention, and until that time she simply needed to tend her spiritual garden and try not to feel it when she was the oldest young person in any group of *Youngie*.

Easier said than done, most of the time.

"My name is Joshua King, and these are my brothers Peter and Moses." Two boys in their early teens were sitting on the back of the wagon, which was full of something under a tarpaulin. Both boys waved, and Amanda waved back.

"I'm Amanda Yoder, from Willow Creek in Lancaster County," she called. "We just came yesterday, to work here."

"We? Did your family come, too?"

Did he always conduct conversations at a distance, hallooing across the wilderness as though he was alone and no one would hear him?

"My nephew, and three of our friends."

"Dei bruderskind? Yoder? Are you related to Simon Yoder? He was here last year, with a friend of his."

"Ja," she said. "He is my brother's child."

"You look far too young to be Simon's *Aendi*," Joshua King said firmly. "You must be nearly the same age."

"Never you mind how old I am," she said, surprising herself with her own pertness.

But it didn't take him aback—on the contrary, he laughed. "That will teach me to get personal this early in the morning. Well, I must get on. They like their meat by six o'clock up here, so the crew can get their breakfast, and the tourists can take home their kills in neat white packages."

So many questions crowded her tongue that she was rendered silent. He delivered meat each day by horse and wagon? Was he the butcher, then, whom Simon was to ask about the clothes? He must be. Or worked for one. Did that mean the Amish settlement was close enough for a horse to come here and back? Where they might get to church on a Sunday?

She would have to find out. About that, and a hundred other things she would need to learn if she planned to stay here. And she'd have to make up her mind about *that* in a hurry.

Probably by the end of the day.

There were four fishermen down in the meadow now, and the sun had cleared the mountains to glitter off the water and turn the grass on the creek banks an intense shade of green. It was just past six o'clock, but if Joshua King brought supplies for the staff breakfast, did that mean they ate before the guests? In which case, she might be late already.

Amanda turned back toward the big house. And as she did, the sun broke free of the mountain, so warm and so brilliant she had to shade her eyes with her hand.

5

Joshua King didn't dare say a word about the young woman on the hillside, or his brothers would never let him hear the end of it. They'd tell Mamm and Dat, and before you knew it, the entire church would know there was someone new in town and he had taken notice.

It was bad enough that he was one of only a handful of single men in the district, and the current population of hopeful young women was probably triple that. The Amish churches were growing, no doubt about it. There were churches at Westcliffe, and Hillside, and recently they had formed a new district out here in the hills, in the tiny town of Amistad.

One of the Latino guys who bought sausage at the shop said that meant *amity* in Spanish. Joshua figured it was a pretty good name for a town. More appropriate—and certainly more musical—than the name of the place in Kansas his family had left behind when they'd lost the farm in the recession. Mamm missed Kansas, but Joshua knew in his bones that God had led him right here to the most beautiful place in the world, doing work that was useful even if it wasn't farming.

The Amish meat processing plant down near Westcliffe had all the work it could handle. There was definitely a need for a second one, so the King men had stepped up to fill that place. A year's work in Westcliffe had educated them both—and the boys too—and now they were on their own. Dat still kept a few beef cattle on their acres, but since farming in the valley was a lot different than it had been in Kansas, many of the Amish had chosen service industries in which to make their living. A bakery, the butcher shop, the furniture store in Westcliffe, the dented grocery over near Monte Vista ... their folks had seen a need and quietly gone about filling it, and the *gut Gott* had provided them with customers.

Like the Gundersons, for example, whom Joshua sometimes thought could keep the King family in business all by themselves. Every morning he delivered sausage Mamm and Grace Ann made by combining pork and herbs and spices. Teresa the head cook would give him a list every Monday of the meals she planned for the upcoming week, and he'd bring everything from pork roasts to beef steaks to eggs by the dozen. A goodly number of the families kept hens and sold the eggs to the Lost Creek Ranch in summer. In the winter, when the hens stopped laying, they couldn't supply that many, but the number of guests dropped quite a lot, anyhow, and the ranch's chickens gave what was needed. The menu might change to waffles and pancakes and Teresa's excellent burritos.

They didn't make *those* on the farm in Kansas.

He'd never heard of a place that served up what the guests caught in the creek, either, but they did that here. He'd seen many a boy bursting with pride to have his catch featured on the menu. Teresa was pretty smart. Selling wild game and fish wasn't legal, but cooking up what the guests supplied was a good way to save a dollar and delight them all at the same time.

And now it was June and the summer staff were beginning to arrive. That meant Amish folks would be coming on trains and buses, too. It always made him happy to meet new people, to welcome young men and women here to work and for the ones God chose, maybe to stay. It was how the church districts were able to grow so quickly, how a man might find the woman God meant him to marry, how a community thrived with life while its children grew up.

And now, smiling up there on the hillside and looking as though she'd been raised up out of the land itself, was Amanda Yoder. He hadn't missed the sight of the sun, cresting the mountain at just that moment and touching her like the hand of a friend and making her hair and her *Kapp* glow.

Oh *ja*, now he was getting pretty fanciful. But the smile of a woman could do that to a man. Wasn't that what Dat always said as he touched Mamm's cheek and made her blush?

"Whoa." He pulled the horse to a stop outside the delivery door in the courtyard, well away from cars coming down the hill from the car park. Josie was a strong animal, a Percheron whose specialty was pulling heavy loads, but she had a thing about those loud sports cars. Most of the time she was just fine on the highway, and then somebody who hadn't had his muffler fixed would roar past her and make her skitter to one side before a man could get her pulled up and calmed down.

He climbed out and patted her neck. "That's my girl. You just stand and we'll have all this unloaded in a minute."

Peter and Moses were already busy with the tarp, which

was lashed down on all four sides to keep the dust off. Inside the wagon bed were eight coolers full of meat and eggs, the meat aged to perfection and the eggs fresh yesterday. He had a nice big trout that his neighbor had caught in Lost Creek, too, and given him this morning on the way up, but he'd fillet that later at the shop and his family would have it for a meal today.

Teresa appeared in the door of the industrial pantry when she heard him and the boys lugging the coolers in. "Morning, Joshua."

"Morning, Teresa. Another fine day for you folks."

"And for the rest of the valley, I hope." She dimpled. "I have news for you. Simon Yoder is back, and he brought some friends with him."

Joshua wondered whether it would be better to keep that news to himself when he went home, or if—

But that was none of his business. Better to leave that to the Lord than to stick his nose in where it didn't belong.

He opened the next cooler and the boys began to stock the fridges with neat packages. The guests' meat went in a separate freezer for shipping when they went home.

"I saw one of them—his aunt? Up on the hill just now."

Teresa's brows rose. "What was she doing up there?"

"Watching the sun come up," Peter said. "Or taking a walk. She's from Lancaster County too, isn't she?"

"Yes. She lives quite close to Simon, in fact, from what he tells me. But I'm not too sure her friends are going to last."

"You know this already?" Joshua hefted the last cooler down on the smooth cement floor and began to put the contents away. "Didn't they only get here yesterday?"

"Mrs. Gunderson was pretty put out. It's clear that three of them aren't Amish, and she hired them specifically because they said they were."

Joshua stopped his work altogether, two packages of sausage labeled *pork with rosemary and sun-dried tomato* cold in his hands. "They said they were Amish and they aren't? Why would anybody do that?"

He'd heard of Amish kids pretending they were *Englisch* while they were on *Rumspringe*, but never the other way around. He couldn't imagine how that would even be possible.

"Maybe times are tough in Lancaster County and they just needed the work." Teresa shrugged. "Not my problem until Mrs. Gunderson says it is. No matter what they are, the beds still have to be made and the bathrooms cleaned."

He nodded, and then with a tilt of his head, indicated that the boys could take the empty coolers out to the wagon. When he finished up, he found Teresa in her office, as usual.

"I was given a nice trout this morning by one of our folk," he said, leaning on the doorframe while she settled up for last week. "How are they biting here?"

She smiled again and held out the check. "Our trout might be smart, but not against four determined anglers. I'm expecting to have to gut fish within the hour. Enjoy yours, Joshua."

Tucking the check into his pants pocket, he said, "I'll do that. And..." How to say this without looking as though he was interested?

"Yes?"

"Maybe I could leave a message with you for Simon and his aunt. If they'd like to go to church a week from Sunday, someone from Amistad could come get them."

"That's kind of you. I'll be sure to pass it along."

Gut. He hadn't made it sound interesting, and as long as the boys hadn't heard, nobody would be the wiser.

"If you happen to see Amanda again outside, can you send her in to see me?"

"*Ja*, I surely will."

"Thanks, Joshua. See you tomorrow."

The boys had already put the empty coolers in the wagon and lashed down the tarp, so there was nothing to hold them back from rolling out of the courtyard and down the hill.

But Amanda was nowhere to be seen.

And for a man who wasn't interested, he was awfully disappointed about that.

❧

AMANDA SLIPPED INTO THE CABIN, ANXIOUS TO TELL Hannah about the Kings and the possibility of their being close enough to a settlement to be able to get to church. She was there, all right—sound asleep and the other girls gone, leaving their beds neatly made.

What on earth? It was lucky she'd come back. If she'd gone straight in to breakfast, poor Hannah would have been left to go hungry until lunch. And she'd probably have been late for work.

Which was just plain mean of Bonita. Jenny had seemed nicer—trying to be a peacemaker. But when she was alone with Bonita, did she just do as the other girl said? But despite the face that the morning would have gone better if she'd been here instead of rambling around on the hillside, she couldn't regret it.

Not the moment of joy when the sun came up. Nor meeting Joshua King and his brothers.

She shook the lump under the covers until Hannah stirred and rolled over. "Wha—? 'Manda?"

"Get up. It's time for breakfast. I'm told that the staff eat before the guests do."

"Time izzit?"

"Twenty past six."

Hannah groaned and pushed herself upright. She glanced at the bed opposite and even half asleep took in the neat blankets precisely tucked under the mattress on the top bunk. "Did they leave without waking me?"

"I think we'd best get in the habit of waking ourselves. Come on, hurry. I can smell cooking."

Hannah splashed her face and brushed her teeth, then pulled on her Amish clothes. Amanda did her friend's hair, tucking out of sight the ends that were still purple. With her *Kapp* pinned in place and her bib apron tied in a neat knot behind, she looked as Amish as Amanda herself.

Now both of them were lying for Mrs. Gunderson's benefit. Hannah, because she wasn't a member of the Amish church. And Amanda, because she was allowing the symbols of her faith to be used for advertising. How could lies like this last out the day? They couldn't possibly please the Lord.

Amanda's stomach rolled a little uneasily. The last thing she wanted was to be out of fellowship with her Savior.

Please, Father, guide me in the way I should go ... even if that's all the way back to Whinburg Township.

They descended the path to the courtyard and went into the staff dining room. Bonita and Jenny were already drinking coffee and joking with three boys whose cowboy hats hung on the pegs. Two older men were talking seriously over their own coffee, lifting their chins in greeting as the girls walked in.

"Oh, you're here," Jenny said, and waved toward a silver carafe at their end of the table. "Here's the coffee. And the cream, if you take it."

"Looks like I'll have to remember to set my alarm," Hannah said, pouring a cup and offering it to Amanda before she poured her own. "I didn't hear you girls leave."

"Good thing you have Amanda," Bonita observed. "She was up before all of us and didn't bother to wake anyone." Hannah's gaze could have blistered the paint off a barn, but Bonita only looked innocent and turned back to the cowboys with a smile.

So that was how it was. A little retribution for what they thought was her getting them back for last night. Was this how it was going to be all summer? An endless game of one-upmanship and paybacks that she didn't know how to play? Amanda felt tired already.

On the bright side, the coffee was really good. The dawn had been amazing. And it had been nice to make a new acquaintance. So despite everything, *der Herr* in His mercy had put three little gifts in her day. She needed to be thankful for that—and be vigilant for the sound of His voice telling her His will.

They all heard an exclamation that could have been a bad word and the sound of a crash from the kitchen behind the swinging door. Amanda and Hannah looked at each other. *Uh-oh.* In the next moment, Teresa pushed the door open and gripped it as though trying not to slam it, pushing her curly bangs under her chef's toque with an impatient hand.

"Who knows their way around a kitchen?" she demanded.

"Something happen, boss?" one of the cowboys asked.

Before she could answer, Simon, Ben, and Samuel came in from the bunkhouse and froze just inside the door, like deer scenting danger. Teresa glared at them as though they were late. Which they weren't. Breakfast, it seemed, was at six thirty.

"My prep cook must have decided last night would be a good night to tie one on, and is completely AWOL this morning. I need some help in here, and I need it now before the guests are up. So, one of you is going to volunteer."

"I can't cook," Bonita said.

"Me either." Jenny's eyes had widened at the prospect, as though Teresa were holding a meat cleaver.

"Don't look at us, boss." The cowboys shook their heads.

"Amanda can cook," Simon said easily. "Her pies and chicken and dumplings are the best I ever tasted."

"Dumplings?" Two of the cowboys actually looked at her as though they saw her, and Amanda felt hot blood stain her cheeks at being noticed by worldly men. She'd been taught to pass through the world humbly, without bringing attention to herself. It was difficult to behave as though sudden notice was normal.

"Well, Amanda?" Teresa said. "Yes or no?"

"I—well—won't you need me on the housekeeping staff?"

"It's only for today. Bonita can make do with Jenny and Hannah, and start your training tomorrow." Teresa jerked her chin in the direction of the kitchen behind her. "Come on."

Without another word, Amanda put down her mug and followed Teresa into the kitchen, the door swinging closed and cutting off the conversation that had risen around the table. The first thing she saw was what had made the crash—a big stainless steel mixing bowl full of eggs that were now splattered all over floor, cupboards, and up the side of the dishwasher.

"Where do you keep the mop?" she asked.

"Utility closet, there. But never mind. You fry up these sausages Joshua King brought, and the spuds and onions, and I'll clean up my own mess. I was trying to do too many things at once and knocked it off the worktable with my big backside. Here's an apron."

"I'm already wearing one." She was glad she hadn't put on her cape and belt apron. This one was appropriate for indoor work, and the other would be clean for Sundays.

"Oh. So you are. I thought that was just part of your dress." Teresa handed her a spatula and headed for the utility closet, leaving Amanda in charge of the huge commercial range.

At least it was gas, and she knew what to do with that. Turning the spitting sausages and frying the spuds and vegetables—she tossed in the chopped red pepper waiting on the cutting board too—was like a familiar dance. Not that she had ever danced, but it was a matter of timing and observation, and she'd been doing it since she was ten years old under Mamm's watchful eye.

When everything was cooked, she found the serving platters in the china cupboard and dished it up as attractively as she knew how, with the sausages arranged on a nest of potatoes and vegetables. Teresa, meanwhile, had mixed a new batch of eggs and turned them into the cast-iron skillet.

"Do you want biscuits?" she asked Teresa as she put the platters in the warming oven, the lower of the two set into the wall.

"If you can do them fast."

"Oh *ja.* No problem." Biscuits were easy, and fifteen minutes later she was pulling them out of the top oven. They were a tiny bit too brown, but tomorrow she'd remember that an electric oven behaved differently than a gas one.

"Nicely done, Amanda. And never mind about their being a bit well done. It's the altitude. Cook times will be different from what you're used to. Come on, help me get all this in there and then you can eat with your friends."

"What about you?"

"Me, too. I'll fill the coffee carafes first. Those boys go through one each, I swear."

She and Teresa carried in the food and set it down on the long table whose every chair was now occupied. All conversation went quiet. "They don't say grace in the guest dining room," Teresa said to Amanda as she took her seat, "but we do down here." And she proceeded to say a short grace aloud, much to Amanda's surprise. Should she say her own, silently? But then someone was passing her the potatoes, and the time for grace—and for thinking—was over as everyone dug in.

"Biscuits," one of the older men said with satisfaction as he buttered one and bit off half of it. "Haven't had one of these in a long time."

"What did I tell you?" Simon said to no one in particular.

"Teresa, this girl is wasted on housekeeping," one of the cowboys said. Would there ever be a day when she knew all of their names? "I'm all for that chicken and dumplings Simon was talking about, and I ain't going to get it if she's cleaning toilets."

"Hush, Rob," Teresa told him, but it didn't sound like she was angry about him telling her how to do her job. "Mind your manners, or you'll be the one cleaning toilets."

Amanda was trying not to blush at the compliments, but it was impossible. So she ducked her head and ate as quickly as she could, because there would soon be twenty sets of dishes to do. It was like Thanksgiving or Christmas at home, with the dining table made longer with card tables for the *Kinner*, so that everyone could sit down at once. And there were always dishes. Once you got those done, it would be time to prepare for the next meal. She had no doubt it would be like that here, too—especially since there were guests to feed.

When she was finished, she rose and began to clear the dirty dishes nearest her.

"Amanda, thank you, but everyone busses their own." Teresa nodded at a plastic bins on the oak sideboard that ran down one side of the room, below the cupboards of dishes and condiments. "Dishes go in there, for those of you who are new. Carson and Mike, you'll need to get a move on and set the tables upstairs. We serve at eight."

"Yes, ma'am." One of the cowboys tipped his mug up to his nose to get the last drop of coffee, while the other shoveled in everything but the red peppers, which he picked out and pushed to the side of his plate.

The next hour was a frantic rush of making a second breakfast from scratch—a meal that was as different as could be from that of the staff. Each table had a daily menu card, which was tacked to the bulletin board by the door in the kitchen.

WELCOME TO LOST CREEK RANCH
BREAKFAST MENU

Self Serve
Granola with fruit and yogurt
Toasted English muffins and homemade jelly
Cheese and cold meat platters

First Course
Cinnamon roll with seasonal fruit and custard

Second Course (choose one)
Fresh caught brook trout with country potatoes
Quiche with Neufchatel cheese, spinach, red peppers
Crepes bananas Foster

Selection of juices
Coffee or tea

"It's different every day, and we rotate through a seasonal menu," Teresa explained as she slid a pan of individual quiches into the oven.

"Isn't it a lot of work for you?" Amanda could hardly imagine how Teresa managed all this and looked after the staff as well. "Are the other meals as complicated? And what are crepes bananas Foster?"

Teresa laughed. "Crepes with bananas inside and pineapple sauce with rum on top, lit on fire tableside."

Lit on fire? Amanda's eyes widened, which only made Teresa smile again. "Lunch is cold and self-serve, but it still has to be prepared and set out. Dinner is hot and served family style at seven o'clock. I have help down here usually, but Jackson—the prep cook with the poor timing—is probably getting fired whenever he gets his sorry behind in here. Gotta solve that problem pronto, after I speak to Mrs. Gunderson. Two of the boys—Carson and Mike—they're the waiters. Mrs. G. likes them because they know their way around a place setting, yet they look like cowboys. And it doesn't hurt that they're easy on the eyes."

"How many guests are here?" And how many would want their breakfast lit on fire on purpose?

"It's early yet. We have a group of four fishermen who will be leaving on a pack trip tomorrow, a pair of honeymooners who get breakfast-in-bed service at their cabin, and an older couple. So pretty light."

Eight people. Amanda could handle that, if it didn't involve lighting food on fire. There was still the staff breakfast to clean up first. Teresa had showed her how to load and start the industrial dishwasher, but there were the baking sheets and cast iron pans to wash, all before she could start work on the guests' food.

But still, despite the work and the pace, she felt in her element, doing what she knew how to do—making someone else's job easier. As it turned out, she wasn't expected to do anything with the crepes bananas Foster. Teresa created the dishes and she followed along behind, quietly removing batter bowls and wrapping excess meat to go back in the refrigerator. More biscuits were easy to make, and the quiches and cinnamon rolls came from the local Amish bakery, ready to go in the oven. The kitchen looked like utter chaos, but behind it all was a system of order. Once you got the hang of it, it was like taking a boat into a current and using it to travel downstream. You just had to keep ahead of the current, was all.

It wasn't until Carson and Mike began to bring the bins of guest dishes back and Amanda had to scrape them into what Teresa called the chicken bin that she got her first surprise.

There was a lot of food left on the plates.

The biscuits were pretty popular—Amanda had never met anyone who didn't like biscuits, but no one had ordered the crepes. The quiches had just been picked at, and nobody except the older couple had ordered the trout.

"I wonder why the fishermen didn't eat their own trout?"

Teresa gave a snort. "I've never met a fly fisherman who actually does. Our stream isn't catch and release, but most of the anglers still use barbless hooks. The guest in cabin twelve caught that one, but he donated it to the menu without promising to have any."

"Maybe we should just serve sausage and eggs, like we do for the staff," Amanda said a little hesitantly. "It seems an awful waste for so much work."

"Amanda, Mrs. Gunderson sets the menu, except if someone catches a fish. It's not your business to have an opinion. It's your business to help me cook."

6

Amanda felt as though the woman had put a hand on her chest and pushed her away. Tears pricked her eyelids and the inevitable blush of shame at having spoken up when it wasn't her place burned her cheeks.

"Amanda?"

She concentrated on scraping a half-eaten quiche into the chicken bin. "Yes?" she managed through a tight throat.

"I didn't mean that the way it sounded. I'm sorry. What I meant was that while I appreciate input—and I agree with it—it's not up to me or you. Mrs. Gunderson makes those decisions."

"I understand."

"Do you have chickens at home?"

The change of subject was a welcome relief. "Yes. We have them for eggs, and meat in the winter. Though I have to say I do get attached. My mother has been very patient with me making pets out of some of them."

"They're all pets here. If the kids who come in the summer

knew we butchered the chickens they hand feed, you can bet the reviews would change for the worse."

"Reviews?"

"On the Internet. Mrs. Gunderson takes her Travelers' Choice award on TripAdvisor very seriously. Everything we do gets measured by that standard."

Amanda had no idea what that meant, but an award sounded serious. "I see. Well, I have to say I'm glad about the chickens. I like them."

"Good. You can take the bin out, then. I'll finish up here."

The *Hinkelhaus* and yard was just as picturesque as the rest of the property—and as spotless as many a kitchen might be. As a dozen hens and two roosters crowded around her, Amanda wondered who had the job of keeping the grassy enclosure so clean. The chickens made short work of the leftovers, and once she'd made sure the latch on the gate was securely closed, she stood for a moment watching them.

She was so absorbed in the birds' happy industry that when someone called her name, she jumped. But it was only Simon, moseying along the fence line toward her.

"Want me to give you a tour?" He was wearing his straw hat and looked as Amish as though he'd climbed out of Joshua King's wagon that moment. "Come and see the bunkhouse."

A little shocked, she shook her head. "I can't go into the men's quarters, Simon."

"Sure you can. We do our own housekeeping, but someone brings clean towels and toilet paper, and that would be one of you girls. Besides, no one is up there now. Everyone has gone to work."

That would be all right, then. And if it was true that the housekeeping staff stocked the supplies, it would be good for her to know where everything went.

She leaned the bin on the side of the chicken house and fell into step beside him, heading down the slope to the barn, the stable, and the bunkhouse that lay on the far side of the road, with the creek and the meadows beyond them. "Everyone has gone to work? What about you?"

He grinned that charming grin that got around everybody except his family. "I am at work. I'm showing you the ropes."

"Simon. What would you be doing if you hadn't seen me?"

"Making sure the horses were ready for the pack trip tomorrow, their tack was in perfect shape, that kind of thing."

She ought to shoo him off to his duties, but she was curious. "Do the horses carry everything? Food and cookstove and all of that?"

"No. Not here. There are what we'd call shepherds' huts and what they call rest stops along the river and up farther in the mountains, where the hunters go in the autumn. Supplies go up on four-by-fours and are stored in the huts, so that everything is waiting when the pack train gets there."

"Isn't that cheating?"

He paused at the bottom of a steep wooden staircase that ran up the wall of a barnlike building. "They pay for the experience of being out in the wilderness. They pay to catch fish, or shoot an elk, or ride on horseback. They don't pay to make their own meals unless they want to, though they do set up the tents and carry their sleeping bags on their horses. Come on. It's steep, so watch your step."

It was no steeper than the ladder up to the hayloft at home. But the cowboys' sleeping quarters here bore no relation to a hayloft at all.

"My goodness, Simon!" she exclaimed. There were beds in different configurations, enough to sleep sixteen men. Some ordinary beds, some bunk beds, and some built into the corners in an ingenious arrangement of two up and two down that somehow incorporated bookcases and a worktable. Big windows let in the light, and a normal sized kitchen filled the end where they stood. Doors led to what she assumed were toilets and showers.

"Rob Lozano, who gave you that nice compliment this morning, he built those outfits in the corners. He used to be a design engineer before he retired."

"It looks very complicated—and very comfortable, too."

"He's a good man. Nice to talk to." He glanced at her. "Good to have on your side. Jose Rodriguez is second foreman, and Jim Strever is in charge of horses and livestock, but Rob is pretty much in charge of all the other operations."

"What about Mr. Gunderson? Isn't he in charge?"

Simon shrugged. "He doesn't have much to do with the actual running of the place. He's more like the guy at the front door, greeting everyone and making them feel like cowboys for a week."

"Oh. I haven't even seen him. Do he and Mrs. Gunderson eat with the guests?"

He nodded. "Come on. I don't want to keep you from your work. Especially since it involves food."

"It's only for today." She led the way down the stairs. "Teresa keeps saying she's going to fire the prep cook, but I don't see how she can. There is so much work she could hire three more and she'd be just as busy."

"Food matters in a place like this." Which kind of sounded like agreement.

"You'd think so. But the menu is awfully fancy. City cowboys don't eat crepes bananas Foster. At least, I don't think they do."

She'd surprised a laugh out of him. "What does that even mean?"

She told him about the item on the menu, and about lighting it on fire, and how no one ordered it.

"I can see why. Bad enough your breakfast gets burned by accident. Who wants it burned on purpose?" He waved and headed off, but instead of going to the barn the way she expected, he circled around to the staff entrance under the deck.

That Simon. Amanda shook her head, half amused and half wondering if this constituted "watching out for him," the way she'd promised his mother. But you couldn't watch a man the way you watched a toddler, to make sure they didn't hurt themselves. A man had to take the consequences of his own actions, and while that might hurt, it also helped him learn. Maybe he'd come with them to the ranch because working here was good for him. Maybe he'd found that doing productive work was satisfying, and he'd wanted more of it. It was one of the steps a person took to growing up.

Amanda was just retrieving the chicken bin from where she'd stashed it when she saw a spiraling plume of dust above the trees. A vehicle, heading up the long gravel road from the highway. New guests? Should she go and inform Teresa that there might be a higher head count for lunch than they'd expected?

But of course guests would be expected. They made reservations and paid in advance. They didn't simply turn in through the gate, drive three miles up into the hills, and ask if there was room available, as though this were a motel.

In a moment she heard the growl of an engine, and a black and white pickup truck with the insignia of the county sheriff pulled in. Amanda's first instinct was to slip behind the chicken house out of sight—not because she felt guilty of anything, but because a man in a khaki uniform usually meant trouble.

But that was silly. For all she knew, the local sheriff and Mr. Gunderson were the best of friends, and he was dropping in for coffee.

It seemed the latter option might be the case, for the massive front doors of the house opened and a big man with an equally impressive white cowboy hat—one she would bet had never seen so much as a speck of horse manure or mud—loped down the stone steps to greet the sheriff.

"Tanner!" Mr. Gunderson boomed. "Good to see you. Coffee pot's on if you've got some time."

Amanda made her way under the deck to the staff door as the men climbed the stone steps up on to it.

"I'm not here on a social call, much as I enjoy your wife's coffee. I'm afraid I'm here on business."

And standing here listening was none of hers.

But Amanda couldn't help herself. Had there been an accident? Maybe something more serious than too much beer had happened to the prep cook. She gripped the plastic rim of the chicken bin and didn't move.

"That sounds too serious for such a beautiful morning. What's happened?"

"I'm not sure you're aware of this, but it seems there's some poaching on your thousand acres."

"Poaching! Not on my ranch, Oliver. You know everything at Lost Creek is above board. Why, even the fishermen are ferried into town to get their licenses before they're allowed to wet a line."

"This is more than a few brookies. We got a report of

gunshots up on the BLM land, and when we went up there this morning—"

"Up where?"

"Broken Ridge. South side, five hundred yards from the summit, on your land. Found two yearling bucks with hollow point wounds, right through the side."

In the silence that followed, Amanda heard the skreeling of a hawk, far above, as though nature itself had cried out in distress.

"You're going to have to show me." Mr. Gunderson's voice had gone dangerously quiet.

"Back of the truck."

Heavy footsteps clunked down the stairs, and Amanda jumped as though a bullet had whistled past her own ear. She ducked through the sliding glass door and hurried through the empty recreation room to the staff dining room, also empty.

From the wide window over the sink, Teresa had already seen the sheriff's truck arrive. "What took you?" Amanda opened her mouth to answer, but Teresa went on, "What's he here for?"

"There's been poaching," Amanda said. "I think he has two deer in the back of the truck."

Teresa sucked in a breath, and actually stopped moving for five seconds. "Run and get Rob Lozano and Jim Strever. They'll be in the horse barn, checking over the horses for the trip tomorrow. Go on—quick. The boss will want them."

Amanda dropped the bin in its place and obeyed. Her skirts bunched in one hand, her *Kapp* strings flying out behind her, she ran down to the barn and through the doors. It didn't resemble the barn at home at all, what with two vans and a four-wheel-drive truck all bearing the ranch name parked in it.

She only got a vague impression of tall timbers and neat floors before she stopped, panting. The smell wasn't right.

No horses.

The *horse* barn, Teresa had said. Amanda dashed back outside and ran to the next building, where the familiar scent of horses and tack and clean hay met her at the doors. And there was Rob Lozano's head above the slats of a stall, where he and Jim Strever were rubbing down an Appaloosa mare, clearly checking for sores or hurt muscles—anything that might prevent her going on the trip tomorrow.

"Rob—Jim," she gasped. "Teresa says to come up to the house quick. The sheriff is here. He says there's been poaching, and he has two deer in the back of his truck."

Without a word, Lozano came out of the stall and latched it behind him. "Does the boss know?"

"He's with him. But Teresa asked me to come get you."

"Smart woman, Teresa. Ten to one it means we'll be taking more than rods with us tomorrow."

"What?"

But he didn't reply, and his long stride soon left the shorter Jim to catch up at a run. Which was fine with Amanda. There were things that men took care of, and things that women did, and that was the way of it. She wouldn't want the responsibility of finding out who the culprits were. In country this big, how was anyone to know who had shot game illegally unless they caught them red-handed? To her mind, the bigger issue was men running around with guns when the pack train was heading up the mountain trails to the lake. She hoped they could tell the difference between a horse and a deer.

By lunchtime, every member of staff had heard that the sheriff had been there, and why. Speculation ran rife at the table over who it could have been and what the boss was going to do about it, but Rob Lozano soon hushed the talk.

"You kids never mind," he said gruffly. "This ain't the Wild West and you all ain't Wyatt Earp. It's the sheriff's job to find out who's being stupid and wasteful up there, and our job to keep our eyes open in case we see something that will help him in his investigation."

No wonder he had so much responsibility around here. He clearly was a sensible man with his head on straight—a man who wouldn't let Simon and Ben and Samuel come to any harm.

After the staff lunch was over, she and Teresa plunged straight into preparing the guest lunch, which was available starting at noon. It wasn't quite as complicated as breakfast, but still, everything had to be fresh and laid out nicely. Teresa showed her how to arrange the sandwiches so that they formed little towers, and the bowls of fruit and tureens of hot soup were presented in china as pretty as Mamm's wedding set at home.

The honeymooning couple wandered in hand in hand to take their meal with the others, which made two more sets of dishes for Carson and Mike to bring down afterward. While Amanda was loading the dishwasher for the fifth time since she'd started work this morning, a stranger ducked into the kitchen and slipped off his jacket.

"Sorry I'm late, Teresa."

Teresa finished sliding that evening's pot roast into the oven, closed the door, and straightened slowly. "Nice of you to join us. Did you get any of my phone messages?"

"Battery was dead. I see you have help." He nodded toward Amanda.

She wasn't sure what to do. Nod back? Introduce herself? Was this the missing prep cook?

"It's a good thing I do, because we'd have had a catastrophe of major proportions today without her. This is Amanda Yoder. Simon's aunt."

Did every introduction have to be in terms of her relationship to Simon? Just what kind of an impression had he made last summer that everyone on the place knew him by name? Most Amish men working for an *Englisch* outfit did their work and kept to themselves. But Simon, she supposed, wasn't like most Amish men.

"Hello," she offered for want of anything else to say. She didn't even know his name.

"Well, guess I'd better get to work then." He had unfastened two of the buttons on his jacket when Teresa seemed to make up her mind.

"Jackson Phelps, when you hired on here, it was with the understanding that you'd work a split shift. Six to ten, and then dinner from four to eight. Of the ten days you've been here, I've gotten only six days of work out of you. I don't know about you, but that's not what I signed up for."

Oh dear. Amanda sidled toward the dining room door. She had no business watching a man being shamed.

"I know, Teresa, and I'm sorry. My truck was broke down two days and I couldn't beg, borrow, or steal anything else to save myself. Then my sister and her five kids landed on me. She left last night, and—"

"And you went on a bender to celebrate."

"Well, yeah. If you knew my sister, you'd understand."

"I'm a pretty understanding person, but this is the bottom line. I need people I can depend on, and I can't depend on you. I'm afraid we're going to have to let you go, Jackson. If you'll wait, I'll ask Mrs. Gunderson to cut you a check."

He stared at her, a man who could have been anywhere from twenty to thirty, his face unshaven and his eyes still red though it was two in the afternoon.

"I said I was sorry, and I am. It won't happen again. Sherry's gone, and the truck's running fine."

"I can't take the chance. I'm sorry, too."

"But I need the work. It's not easy getting a job around here."

"Don't I know it."

"I've noticed lately there are certain new folks who don't have that trouble, both here and in town." His face was beginning to flush, and Amanda had the uncomfortable feeling she ought to have moved toward the door a little faster, because he was glaring at her as though he was angry she was witnessing this. Angry that she was there at all. Maybe an Amish person had beat him for a job at one time, and he was angry about that, too?

"I'll just see if there's anything left in the dining room," she whispered, and escaped out the door.

Voices rose, and too late she realized she shouldn't have been heading for the staff dining room, but for the service stairs up to the main floor. Well, she wasn't about to go back into the kitchen now, so she went outside and up the main set of stone steps to the big deck. She could go in through one of the sliding doors.

But the moment she stepped onto the deck, the view out over the valley stunned her all over again. Forgotten were the angry voices, and the poaching, and the niggling worry about Simon and her promise to his mother. Instead, she gripped the carved wood rail and breathed in the pine-scented air, letting it and God's creation cleanse her mind.

God had given her this gift to lift her out of her worries, and her soul rose in thanks to Him.

Dear Lord, thank You for bringing me to this beautiful place. While Sarah may want me to keep an eye on Simon—if that's even possible—I believe You have a greater purpose for me, more than just being advertising for Mrs. Gunderson. If it is Your will, reveal it to me in time. Help me to be obedient whatever happens, and please, Lord, make a way in the wilderness so that we might enjoy fellowship with the church while we're here.

She drew another deep breath and opened her eyes.

Only to jump nearly out of her skin when she saw an *Englisch* woman standing at the rail next to her.

"Sorry, I didn't mean to startle you." The woman smiled and clasped her hands, leaning both elbows on the railing and gazing out into the view.

Amanda took another breath to calm her heart rate. "I didn't know anyone was there."

"I could see that. Your eyes were closed. Were you praying? I understand that's why you wear the prayer covering—so you can pray at any time with your head covered, right?"

Goodness, what was she to say to that? Did everyone out West ask such personal questions of strangers?

"I—yes. I was. I was thanking God for His beautiful creation."

She wasn't sure what she expected, but it wasn't the delight that suffused the woman's face. "I knew it! I said to Jimson—that's my husband, over there at the window—I said, look at that Amish girl. I bet she's praying. And you were, just like on that TV show."

Amanda hardly knew where to look. It was one thing to

share your prayer life with your family. It was another altogether to talk about something so intimate with a stranger, right out in public.

"What TV show?" she finally managed, to get the woman talking about something else.

"Oh, you know. *Shunning Amish*. Too bad they haven't renewed it for next season. I loved that show. Especially the one about those quilters. And also the boy who was kicked out for not joining the church, and that Mennonite lady found him in her shed and gave him a job."

Amanda had seen the film crew at Englisch Henry's farm before he'd married Sarah. The whole district knew they'd wanted Henry to be in an episode and he'd finally refused for the sake of his Amish relatives' privacy, even though it had cost him a lucrative contract for custom pottery with a big department store.

It took Amanda a moment to realize she actually knew what boy this lady was talking about. "You mean Jesse Riehl?"

If she had been delighted before, the woman was practically awestruck now. "You *know* him?"

"I did," she said cautiously. "Before he moved to Australia."

"Australia! Well, wonders never cease. To think I'm talking to an Amish girl who actually knows a reality-TV star."

She'd best keep to herself the fact that she and Jesse had briefly been a couple. The woman might hyperventilate from sheer joy.

"I'm so glad we picked Lost Creek Ranch for our holiday. When we read on TripAdvisor that there were Amish folks working here, I said, Jimson, I said, we're going to Colorado this spring instead of on another boring cruise. I might never get to Pennsylvania and this is only two states away." She stuck out her hand. "Marlene Schuler, from Texas. I'm so happy to meet you."

Amanda shook her hand, feeling a little dazed. "Amanda Yoder."

Mrs. Schuler shook her hand as though it were a pump handle. "You know Jesse Riehl. That must mean you're from Whinburg Township. I'd ask for a selfie with you, but I've read enough Amish books to know you folks don't have your pictures taken. You won't ever have to worry about me trying to make a graven image out of you."

"Thank you."

"How do you say that in Amish?"

She really needed to get back to the kitchen. But on the other hand, wasn't this why Mrs. Gunderson had hired her? Because she wanted the tourists to come? And the tourists wouldn't come unless the staff were pleasant and welcoming.

"We say *denki*. Our language is called *Deitsch*. You say Pennsylvania Dutch, but people who aren't Amish speak that, too."

"Denki." Her pronunciation was good. *"Denki,* Amanda."

"When we see each other tomorrow, we'll say *guder mariye*. That means good morning, or good day."

"Guder mariye. Oh, I have to write this down." She pulled her little phone out of her pocket and typed something on the screen with both thumbs. "Just think, by the time we leave on Monday I'll be able to speak *Deitsch*!"

Amanda smiled. There was something of the spirit of a little child in this woman, so easily made happy with the gift of a few words. What must it be like, watching the lives of others on the television and crossing two states to see what you read about in books? She wished she had a way to tell Jesse Riehl about this. He had been more intent on the money the TV man would pay him when Englisch Henry Byler had refused to be on the program, but maybe it would please him to know he was remembered.

"I should be getting back to work, Mrs. Schuler."

"Oh, call me Marlene, please. What do you do here?"

"I was supposed to be on the housekeeping staff, but today I've been in the kitchen, helping the cook."

"Oh!" Plump fingers went to her mouth, where most of her lipstick had been licked off during lunch. "I guess I'd better watch what I say, then."

"Why would you do that? Do you like the food?"

"Oh, sure. The food is amazing. But I was just telling Jimson, I said, after a few days you get tired of amazing and just want something plain. Plain!" She laughed at herself. "I've heard about Amish food and how good it is ever since I joined a GoodReads group of quilters. I don't suppose there's any chance of some good Amish dishes on those little menus they put on all the tables, is there? Some shoo-fly pie, maybe? Or I know! Whoopie pies. I've always wanted to try a whoopie pie."

"I don't know, Mrs.—Marlene. I only got here yesterday and I have a lot to learn. But I do know that the menus are set a week in advance. Even if they did make a change, you might not see it if you're leaving before Monday."

Marlene pouted. "Hm. Well, they have those satisfaction survey cards in our room. I'll fill one out. You can't have an Amish woman in the kitchen and no Amish food on the table, now, can you?"

Amanda had to laugh. "My mother would agree with you. She made sure I knew how to cook. I was the youngest, with three older brothers, so I spent a lot of time in the kitchen."

"Well, then," Marlene said, as if that settled it. "I'll let you get back to work. I hope to see you again, Amanda. I want to increase my vocabulary."

With a nod and a smile, Amanda crossed to the sliding glass door and let herself in. Was it the ultimate in *hochmut*—pride—to like someone who seemed delighted by her very existence, with or without whoopie pies?

From his seat at the table by the window, Jimson Schuler nodded, and she smiled back, then set to work rearranging the sandwiches on the serving platters and checking to see if the soup tureen needed a refill.

It didn't. Possibly other guests besides the Schulers preferred something a little more down-to-earth than cream of asparagus with sun-dried tomatoes. Maybe she'd mention what Marlene had said the next time she and Teresa got a minute to talk.

Though she hadn't heard Jackson leave, it must be safe to go downstairs by now.

Safe.

Amanda had not realized before that, no matter how busy it was at home in Whinburg Township, no matter how many people filled the rooms for church or family gatherings, there was always a sense of peace and safety there. She was beginning to get the feeling that no matter how much money was poured into a place, peace was not as common as she used to think.

7

Only illness or being on one's deathbed would prevent an Amish person's getting to church, so with the next day a church Sunday, Amanda couldn't wait any longer to find out whether or not she and Simon—and maybe Hannah, too—would be allowed to go. If they were, they had to find a way to get into Amistad that didn't involve rolling up to an Amish home in a car instead of a buggy. Somehow she'd managed to miss Joshua King this morning, despite her vigilance—or maybe he didn't come at all on Saturdays. She was back on housekeeping duties after her brief stint in the kitchen on Thursday, so even though she knew he came at six, when she didn't see him, she still found herself scanning the courtyard and the road every time she finished her duties in a room and walked outside to the cleaning cart.

The road remained frustratingly empty, and her need to see this question resolved rose.

After lunch, she slipped into the kitchen to talk to Teresa, earning herself a glare from Bonita as she, Jenny, and Hannah left to work on the rooms upstairs. "I meant to ask you," Amanda said, "if you could tell me whether the housekeeping staff works on Sundays?"

"Gosh, did I forget that in my briefing when you first came?" Teresa turned from loading the dishwasher and dried her hands. "There are four of you, so the weekends are a trade-off, usually. Two take Saturday off, and two on Sunday, plus one other day. You guys decide which two are off on which days."

"I would like Sundays off," she said. "And so would Hannah, I expect. And Simon. For church."

"Right, I remember last summer Simon had Sundays off. Though most of the time, he was on pack trips that went over a weekend. I don't remember anyone coming to get him and Joe when they were here—or them asking for a ride down. And then when he was injured, of course, he had to stay put."

Simon wasn't much of a letter writer, but Amanda remembered all too well his mother's concern about his not getting to church very often. Had these been the reasons why? It was pretty hard to get down from the mountains in the middle of a pack trip, or when you couldn't walk.

"Tell you what," Teresa said. "It's fine with me, but Mrs. Gunderson has the final say. She's probably in her office, so if you get her okay, then we're good to go."

"Thank you. I'll go right now."

She ran up the stairs and into the main part of the house. Was it really only four days ago that they'd arrived and been awestruck by its grandeur? It was grand, all right, but after you cleaned something, somehow that cut it down to size. Or maybe focusing on a small part made the whole thing more manageable, like that old joke about how a person ate an elephant.

She heard the girls' voices from the great room as they

dusted and swept. She'd go join them as soon as she spoke with Mrs. Gunderson.

Voices came from her employer's office down the corridor because the door stood a little ajar. Amanda hesitated, not wanting to eavesdrop, until she recognized one of the voices.

Simon. Goodness, was he asking permission to go to church, too? Why hadn't he told her that was his plan? She put her hand on the doorknob and then stopped cold.

"—don't see how that's possible," Mrs. Gunderson was saying. "You asked me for a job. Fine. You've got one. But that doesn't come with any privileges."

"You didn't think that way last year."

"Last year is in the past, and if you bring it up, it may be we won't need you after all."

"Are you firing me?"

"Look, Simon. Our memories of what happened last year are so different one of us must be hallucinating. You're overstepping your place, and for a man who says he's Amish, that surprises me."

"You don't know anything about being Amish, Silvia."

"Mrs. Gunderson, please. Any more familiarities and you'll be dealing with my husband. Is that clear?"

"Mr. Gunderson's voice is loud and clear."

"I'm glad we understand one another. Good afternoon. If I don't see you before Monday, enjoy the pack trip."

Amanda stepped out of the way just in time. The door swung open and Simon strode through it so fast she felt a breeze on her face. In seconds he was out of sight down the staircase. What on earth had that been about? It sounded as though he had been dangerously presumptuous, to the point where he'd nearly lost his job.

Did he want to have to go home months early?

Cautiously, she peeked around the door to see Mrs. Gunderson standing at the window, hands on her hips. The blond woman's jeans fit like a glove, and she wore a lacy cotton blouse and as she turned, Amanda saw a silver coin on a leather thong around her neck. The silver medallions they called *conchas* formed a belt around her slim hips.

"Mrs. Gunderson, excuse me," Amanda said hesitantly. "Is this a good time?"

The woman looked up, and her frown smoothed itself away into a face so calm it could have been a mask. "Amanda, is it?"

"Yes. I wondered if I might speak to you?"

"I'm not in the best frame of mind for a conversation, but that's not your fault." She beckoned Amanda in. Neither of them sat—Mrs. Gunderson because she was pacing back and forth in front of the window, and Amanda because she thought she would appear rude if she did. Besides, the other woman's energy made her nervous. She was like a cat switching her tail, and at any moment she might scratch.

"What is it, Amanda?"

Oh, how she wanted to know what Simon had been talking with her about! What privileges had he asked for? And who was hallucinating about what? But she didn't dare. She'd be scratched for sure.

"Teresa suggested I come up and confirm with you that it would be all right for Simon and me and maybe Hannah to have Sundays off for church, if we can find a way to get to Amistad without inconveniencing anyone."

Mrs. Gunderson stopped dead on the carpet and stared at her. "Did you just talk to that boy?"

Boy? "I'm sorry—who?"

"Simon. He was just in here asking me the very same thing."

"He was?" Going to church was the privilege? Now she really wished she'd thought to go to him first, and do this together. Because clearly the answer had been no. Maybe it wouldn't have been if he hadn't made her angry about whatever had—or hadn't—happened last year.

"You must have seen him in the hallway. But no matter. I understand there's a service tomorrow, but with no notice I can't let three of my staff disappear with no one on hand to replace them."

"Teresa says it's all right with her," Amanda faltered. "We're supposed to have two days off and—"

"Teresa doesn't know the bigger picture. Tomorrow is out. You can take your two days during the week, while the fishermen are away on their pack trip. And on a different subject, I told Simon the cost of clothes for the other boys will have to come out of their first paychecks. I won't pay to fix a situation that never should have come up in the first place. Not when I was told the five of you were Amish."

Even if she'd wanted to, Amanda wouldn't have dared to argue. "So we're to stay on?"

"Yes, if that's agreeable to you all. And there's something else."

Amanda wasn't sure she wanted to know what else. She wanted to run away up into the trees and mourn the fact that she wouldn't be able to go to church, and meet the people here, and maybe even see Joshua King again.

"Come with me. I want Teresa in on this."

Amanda followed her employer back down to the kitchen, where Teresa came out of the pantry at the sound of her name. "Mrs. Gunderson. Oh good, Amanda found you."

"Yes, she did. How long have you been without a prep cook?"

Teresa blinked, as if this was not what she'd been expecting. "Not long—since Thursday. I couldn't depend on Jackson, so I let him go. Once we get into the summer season, I need someone who doesn't go on a bender every time he's under stress."

"How have you managed?" Mrs. Gunderson flicked the menu card, then the other notices hanging on the bulletin board by the door, as if she was looking for something. "Do you have a listing up online?"

"No, I haven't had time to post it. Luckily, we're not full. The fishermen will be gone for a week, and the honeymooners leave tomorrow. The Schulers checked out this morning, as you know, and promised they'd be back next year. I like happy campers."

Mrs. Gunderson was not the kind of woman who could be deflected that easily. "Regardless, you can't operate in here alone. Amanda, Teresa had good things to say about your performance in the kitchen on Thursday. Maybe I can make up for your missing church. I'd like to take you off housekeeping and promote you to sous-chef. Would you agree to that? It's four dollars more an hour."

Four dollars more! Amanda had never made so much money in her life—though the likelihood of its making up for not getting Sundays off was pretty low. "Mrs. Gunderson, thank you very much. But I really don't know anything about being a ... sous-chef."

"I wouldn't say that," Teresa said. "You did great in here."

"That was mostly just breakfast. At home I cook for my family every morning. It wasn't so different."

"I like to think that the guests here are like family," Mrs. Gunderson said. "So that's a point in the plus column as far as I'm concerned."

"I'm all for it, if you agree, Amanda," Teresa told her.

"But—well—"

"What?" Now Mrs. Gunderson's gaze made Amanda think not of a cat, but of a hawk, tilting in the updraft and watching the meadows far below for just one small creature to move. "Is it the money?"

"Oh, no, not at all. The money is very generous. It's just—I'm thinking of Sundays. I'd still want them off, just not tomorrow." Goodness, was she crazy, speaking up like this? Mrs. Gunderson could take back her offer and fire her on top of it. "And meals then," she finished lamely.

"Sundays again." Mrs. Gunderson gazed at her, those blue eyes unflinching. "You're persistent, I'll give you that. What time is church?"

"Eight, if it's the same as at home. I can find out for sure."

"And you'd be back when?"

"At home the service goes until eleven thirty, and then we have the fellowship meal, and then everyone visits during the afternoon. Sometimes there's another meal before the *Young*—er, the young people go off to singing." She slowed to a stop as her employer's eyebrows, shaped like a butterfly's feelers, rose under her perfectly cut bangs with every word she said. "That's at home, though," she whispered. "I don't know if it's the same here."

"If it is, you're saying you won't be available on Sundays at all. That's what Simon said, too."

As Mamm might say, she was in the deep end now. She might as well try to swim her way to shore. Sheltered in her own home, she had never had to stand up for what she believed in. Now was the time for drawing the line and sticking to it, no matter what happened afterward.

She moistened lips that had gone dry despite her attempts

at encouraging herself. "Sundays are our day of rest. We don't do business on that day."

"Meaning you don't work."

"I—well, other than making meals for the family, no. Some don't even do that. They prepare food ahead, that doesn't have to be cooked."

"But isn't church every other week?" Teresa asked. "Seems to me I heard that somewhere. Joshua King, probably."

"It is, but Sunday is still a day of rest." Simon had got nowhere with Mrs. Gunderson. Amanda could see the job in the kitchen receding farther into impossibility with every word she said. Maybe even her job in housekeeping. Well, if it was God's will that she had to leave because she'd obeyed His commandments, then she would.

"She is entitled to a day off, Mrs. G." Teresa shrugged. "I can manage. I've been hauling one of the boys in here to flip sausages. Tyler. He's got quite a talent for it."

"We don't have sausages upstairs." The words were enunciated with precision. "Our meals could be photographed for *Travel and Leisure*. One day I hope they will be."

Amanda had never heard of a meal being judged on its looks rather than its taste or nutrition. That was just crazy.

"So let me get this straight," her employer said, returning that clear blue gaze to Amanda. "Even on alternate Sundays, you won't be available? You won't take Saturday instead?"

"It wouldn't be right, Mrs. Gunderson." Any minute now she would be fired, but the words had to be said. "But I'm happy to work anywhere you want me on the other six days."

"You get two days off by law," Teresa reminded her. "It doesn't matter which two days. Things are a little relaxed right now because the season hasn't really started."

"I don't mind working six days if I can have Sundays off,"

she said. "Truly, I don't." She worked every day at home, didn't she? Doing essentially the same things?

"We're not that kind of outfit," Mrs. Gunderson said. "But I can't have Teresa on her own every weekend. That's not fair to her. Ideally, you'd fill in on her days off, and vice versa."

"Cook for the whole ranch?" Amanda's eyes widened. "Those fancy menus?"

"Not right away." Teresa smiled at her. "We'll find a solution. And I'll teach you the menus."

Mrs. Gunderson still hadn't said it would be all right. "You did want Amish staff," Amanda ventured. Maybe she needed to be reminded of what she'd wanted in the first place. "All of us will need Sundays off. It's our way."

Mrs. Gunderson gazed at her, then one corner of her mouth twitched, as though she realized she couldn't argue with that. "I did, didn't I? I guess that's the price I pay. Hopefully we'll make it up in more bookings. All right, then. Every Sunday off for all the Amish staff, including Ben and Samuel, and a day during the week to be agreed on with Teresa. And you'll accept the sous-chef job?"

"Ja," Amanda said promptly. She was taking no chances, now that everyone had the same understanding. "I mean, yes."

"Good. All right." Their employer turned away. "Oh, Teresa, one more thing. We got a corporate booking for the July Fourth weekend. Ten executives for an overnight team-building trail ride, and exclusive use of the conference room on the Monday."

"Great!" Teresa said. "Quilters next week and suits after that. I love it. Will they need an obstacle course like the Japanese company last year?"

"I don't think so. Trail ride and archery practice is what

they said. Let Jose know, will you, before he takes the fishermen out?"

"I sure will."

Their employer left, moving with feline grace, and Teresa waited a moment until the door closed. Then she glanced at Amanda. "Prep cook, huh? Are you up for it?"

"I think so." Amanda couldn't help but smile at the twinkle in Teresa's eyes. "I like to cook a lot better than I like cleaning toilets and making beds. Or being fired."

"That makes two of us," Teresa said. "And there was never any danger of you being fired, Amanda. What made you think that?"

If she'd had half Teresa's confidence, maybe she wouldn't have thought those things. But never mind. God had arranged everything perfectly, and given her words to speak in time of need. "Will the Sundays off be a problem for you?"

She shook her head. "We'll work it out. We always do. Come on. Time to get supper going—your new job starts now."

It wasn't until they had the fancy cut of beef wrapped in its pastry covering that Amanda realized one more thing she should have thought of before.

If she was in the kitchen now instead of up the hill cleaning the guest cabins, she would see Joshua King every single day.

❧

When Hannah heard from Amanda that she, Ben, and Samuel were allowed to stay, but the boys' Amish clothes had to come out of their first check, she said, "I'll tell them," and hustled off down the slope toward the bunkhouse before anyone could tell her not to.

"Hey, Reese," she greeted the cowboy who had come to pick them up ... was it only last week? It seemed like half the summer already. "Have you seen Ben or Sam?"

She really wanted Ben, but he didn't need to know that.

"Haven't seen Ben, but Sam's in the horse barn. Pack trip is leaving Monday at six sharp, so he's checking the supply lists for the animals."

"Thanks." If she'd been alone, she'd have gone up into the bunkhouse and had a peek inside, but who knew what horrors she'd see there? Cowboys in their underwear, yikes.

She found Sam in the tackroom with a sheet of paper in one hand, going over harness, bridles, and saddles with the care he might have given to Dat's buggy horse's much more complicated outfit. Some things, she supposed, you just never forgot.

"Hey," she said, bumping his shoulder with hers.

"Hey," he said in surprise. "What are you doing out here?"

"I came out to give you and Ben a message. He's not around?"

"Haven't seen him in half an hour or so, but that doesn't mean anything. Jose has us running all over getting things ready for Monday. He might even have gone to town with one of the guys."

She made herself comfortable on a chair that might have come with the old buildings down in the meadow. "Mrs. G. says we can stay even if we're not technically Amish, as long as we dress the part. But—news flash—when you get your clothes, the cost of them comes out of your first paycheck."

He nodded as though she'd confirmed what he'd already

figured would happen. "I hope they don't cost very much. Guess I shouldn't have given away my shirts and stuff when I left home—but I never would have predicted I'd need them again. In October maybe I'll leave them here for the next fence jumper she wants looking Amish. It might even be me, next year."

It sounded like her brother wasn't so easygoing about the dress code here—or about fence jumping—as she'd thought. "We don't exactly have a choice if we want to keep working here. You're still planning on going home in October, though, right?"

His gaze was puzzled. "Why wouldn't I?"

"Have you talked to Ben about it?"

"Ben doesn't talk about things, if you noticed."

"He said on the train he wanted to just keep on going," she told him, hearing the wistfulness in her own voice. "I can't tell if he means it or not. Which is why I asked."

"He probably doesn't mean it. What would he do?"

"I don't know. Do they have RV factories out there?"

Samuel shook his head. "Part of coming to Colorado was to find out if there was something different to do. I ain't going back to the factory, that's for sure. But Ben didn't give up the lease on the trailer, did he? So in my mind, that means he's planning to go back."

That sounded reasonable. "If he didn't mean to go home with us, we'd have driven out here in his car, wouldn't we?"

Samuel laughed—a rare thing, in her experience. "That old wreck? If it made it to the county line I'd have been surprised. It's good for going back and forth to work, but I wouldn't trust it out on a real highway. It probably couldn't even get up to the speed limit without parts falling off."

"Poor car. Don't speak ill of the nearly dead."

Which got her another smile. Then he gave her a glance up under his bangs. "So are you guys pretty serious?"

She lifted one shoulder in a half shrug. "I think so. We like the same things—and we're kind of in the same position. You know, in life."

He moved to the saddles on their wooden supports. "Are you? You've been thinking about joining church, right? Or not?"

"Aren't we all?" She sounded flippant, but she wasn't. Not really. "It's not like there's a time limit on it, right? Mamm and Dat will still be there."

"Waiting. I know," he admitted. "But isn't it kinder to make a permanent decision? To make them happy or ..."

"What? Pretend we've died?"

"They'd never do that. Even when you were gone, they never believed you were dead. They hoped, every single day. Mamm had that lamp in the kitchen window to prove it. To guide you in, in case you came home at night."

In spite of herself, Hannah found her throat closing up at the thought of it. Of Mamm, never giving up on her even as year after year passed, struggling not to give up hope. Could she really just walk away from that kind of love?

Even for Ben?

No, she couldn't make that choice. The Amish lifestyle was one thing—saying a permanent good-bye to her cell phone, never hearing from any of her gamer friends again, living without electricity and having a life of home and babies to look forward to. Not that those were a bad thing. Eventually she wanted a place of her own. And a baby, too, once she got it together enough to make the kind of mother a baby deserved. But to a worldly girl, those things were a choice. To an Amish girl, that was like the only future there was. If you didn't choose that, you were an old maid who looked after your elderly parents until you got so old someone had to look after you.

"What kind of thoughts are giving you that kind of face?" Samuel asked, pausing in his examination of the bridles to look her over just as carefully.

"I'm just thinking about a woman's options in the church," she admitted. "You know, marriage and kids or staying an old maid the rest of your life. Oh joy."

"Nothing wrong with marriage and kids," he said. "As long as Ben thinks the same."

She didn't know if he did or not. "I'm only nineteen. It's too early to give someone the *what are your intentions* questionnaire."

She thought he might laugh, but he only shrugged. "Helps to know, though," he said. "Why invest years in a person who doesn't have the same plans as you?"

"Plans? Neither of us has plans. We're here for now, and that's good enough for me." She got up and shocked him by giving him a hug. "That's in case there's a whole herd of people around when you guys leave on Monday."

To her surprise, he gathered her in and hugged her back. *"Meine kleine schweschder,"* he said. *My little sister.* "You take care of yourself while we're gone."

"Oh, I will." She crossed to the door. "And if I don't, you can guarantee that big sister Amanda will."

She knew she sounded flippant, but all the same, there was something comforting in knowing it was true.

8

At six o'clock on Monday morning, Samuel and Ben led the horses out for the fishermen's pack trip up to the lake in the mountains. Samuel hadn't figured out yet why four men needed four ranch employees to look after them, but he supposed it would come to him sooner or later.

Once the fishermen were mounted and their rods and equipment packed carefully in saddlebags or in backpacks, they moved out. Samuel's horse was a beautiful bay gelding that any Amish man would immediately consider as a buggy horse. But Caya wasn't a buggy horse. And he wasn't an Amish man.

Not on the inside, at least. Or on the outside, since there hadn't been time to do anything about the Amish clothes situation before they left. But Amanda had promised she'd see to it during the week they were gone. One other thing they'd discovered this morning was that with his raise in pay, Simon had been promoted to camp manager for trail rides, which meant he didn't have anything to do except enjoy the ride until they got to their camp spots, while Ben and Sam kept an eye out for the horses the whole time.

Joshua King had come early enough for Amanda Yoder to ask him about the shirts and hats before breakfast, beating him and Ben to it. And she'd seemed pretty happy about the chance to talk to Joshua, too. Samuel could see through a grindstone when it had a hole in it. Amanda was nice. Ordinary looking, and not very exciting, but steady, and good in the kitchen. In Samuel's opinion, Joshua could do a lot worse. Of course, with all of them going away at the end of the summer, and as shy as Amanda was, it wasn't likely the two of them would get anything started, so he hoped Amanda wouldn't go getting her expectations up.

The scent of sage and dust filled his nose and he relaxed a little. The horses seemed to realize where they were going; they'd probably all done this trek fifty times. But it was new to him. New and exciting and the closest thing to an adventure he'd probably ever get.

By the time lunch rolled around, Samuel had begun to wonder if he couldn't have chosen an adventure that didn't involve sore muscles in his legs and rear end. The high altitude meant he had sunburn on the parts of him that weren't covered by sleeves and his borrowed straw Stetson. He knew all about caring for horses, tacking them up, and even doctoring them a little when they were sick. But riding for pleasure had been forbidden by the *Ordnung* at home. Horses were for work, out in front of a discer or a market wagon or a buggy. Just one of the many things that didn't make sense to him about the Amish life. The *Ordnung* in Amistad probably had as many inconsistencies—though at least they allowed people to use cell phones, because the distances between farms was so great that they had to carry them for their own safety.

"Maybe that's the good thing about starting up a community from scratch," Ben said when Samuel mentioned this at the lunch stop. Teresa had packed sandwiches, fruit, cookies, and a drink for everyone, so once the fishermen had what they needed and the horses were fed and watered, Ben and Samuel could relax under a pine and eat and talk. "You get to set rules that make sense for where you live."

"And not rules that have been in place for two hundred years," Samuel agreed, his mouth full of cold roast beef and tomato and lettuce. And horseradish so good it made his eyes water.

"Still don't want to submit to them," Ben said around his own sandwich.

"It might not be so bad out here." Samuel plucked up his courage. Ben wasn't much for sharing personal stuff, but his conversation with Hannah the other day was still on his mind. "What are you going to do if Hannah decides to join church? I mean, have you seen her? She looks as Amish as Amanda."

"And as soon as she opens her mouth to that Bonita girl, anyone can tell she isn't." Ben chewed his beef for a moment. "Not a lot of love lost there. I hope she gets past it, or it's going to be a long summer."

"So you don't think Hannah will?"

"I've got no way to know."

"Don't you talk about it?"

"Maybe. But the few minutes we get together I hate to waste on talking." Ben grinned, and Samuel rolled his eyes.

"Thanks to Amanda, we get Sundays off. You going to go to church?"

"Not me. You go if you want to. Someone has to take the girls, and you have a driver's license, too."

Samuel made a noise that was half chuckle, and it turned into a snort when the horseradish went up his nose. When the coughing stopped, he gasped, "I can just see the girls getting out of the car instead of a buggy. The bishop would run us off the place. Besides, it's not likely Rob would let me take the ranch van, or one of the trucks."

"Maybe they have a tractor. You could pull a wagon with the girls on it."

This made Samuel laugh again—more cautiously this time, and not with his mouth full. And then Simon was giving them the high sign, and it was time to pack up, put away the trash from lunch to be burned in the campfire later, and mount up again.

Simon guided his horse over to theirs. "Don't worry," he said in a low voice as Samuel swung himself into the saddle. "Saddle sores'll be gone by the time we get back to the ranch."

A week from now. Samuel just grinned and bore it. The last thing a man wanted to do was show weakness, or give Simon Yoder anything to tease about. He never missed a trick, and while some people found his comments funny, Samuel had discovered on the trip out here that a little went a very long way. Teasing and joking was one thing. Even Dat appreciated a good joke, and that took some doing for such a serious-minded man. But Simon's teasing always had a little prick in it, like the nettles that came up in spring. And like the nettles, the sting took a while to fade.

The first night's camp was in a meadow that had filled in a notch between two big rocks. Here a stream trickled out of the ground, but it was only good for watering horses. They carried water for cooking—or rather, the four-by-four that had been up yesterday carried it.

After he and Ben had unsaddled all nine horses, curried them, and taken care of the tack, Simon set them to work setting up the tents that had been left there in a weatherproof bin. The fishermen inspected the little stream, but even they admitted there was hardly enough water in it to keep a frog dry, never mind sustain fish. So they helped with the tents, too, and one of them even volunteered to barbecue the ribs that were on the first day's menu.

Jose Rodriguez, Teresa's husband, was the trail boss and even though he was in charge of the camp kitchen, he nodded and let the guest go to it.

Turned out the man knew what he was doing, with a little extra heat in the form of a chile sauce supplied by Jose that he said was made and bottled right in Amistad by one of the Amish families.

If that wasn't adaptability, Samuel didn't know what was. "A man could make a living out here, where things are so different," he said to Ben as they bedded down for the night.

"Maybe he could, whether he joined church or not." Ben was like that, able to pick up a conversation right where you left off hours before. When he was in the mood to converse, anyway. "Are you thinking about it?"

"It deserves a lot of thought. It's a big step."

And if his unwillingness to join church was going to separate him from his family whether he lived here or in Pennsylvania, what difference did it make if they were separated by half the country, too?

The only ones who would care were Mamm and Barbie, and they would write him letters.

"What's a big step?" Simon pushed open the tent flaps and crawled into his spot at the back. The remaining camp pad was for Jose, who had been having a beer with the fishermen, but from the footsteps outside and the swing of the flashlight beam, was now making the rounds to ensure everything was buttoned up for the night.

"Nothing." Samuel pulled the sleeping bag up around his shoulders. It got chilly up here at night, though the sunburn was keeping him plenty warm despite the aloe Jose had given him.

"Maybe you're thinking about joining church out here," Simon speculated as he shucked his clothes.

"Maybe I'm not. And don't you go preaching at me. I have a mother and father for that."

"Not my job," Simon told him. He climbed into his sleeping bag. "But it's sure tempting to stay after the summer season. Jose says winters aren't as bad as you'd think. It's just a matter of getting work that pays enough to make the bank pay attention to you when you want to buy land."

That problem had to be dealt with no matter where you lived. "It's not like there's affordable land in Whinburg Township either. Even if you are the eldest son."

"Mamm and Englisch Henry are *im e Familye weg* so even if I did eventually get my father's original piece of land, the rest would probably go to the new baby. That leaves Caleb on his own."

The practicalities of willing a farm to the eldest son, leaving all the other boys in a big family to make their own way, were familiar topics to any Amish man. And now that Samuel had jumped the fence, he supposed that the twins would take up farming, and assume responsibility when it got too much for Dat. If they were inclined that way. If not, then Barbie would eventually get married and her husband might farm it. Because it didn't sound likely that Hannah, the eldest of his sisters, would be joining church and looking around her for a good Amish farmer anytime soon.

If you went home and joined church, you could farm with Dat and everything would be the way it's supposed to be. What he calls the right order of things. And then maybe Hannah would, too, and except for Leah, the whole family would be in fellowship again.

His stomach rolled, from unwillingness, and from guilt at being unwilling. Like he'd told his sister, he needed to settle to something better than building RVs. Working out here was supposed to help him do that. So here he was, lying between his friend Ben the other fence jumper, and Simon, who had joined church already. Halfway between, not knowing which way to roll.

When Jose came in and got ready for bed, it was almost a relief. Because none of them would say a word about anything but horses and fish in front of the *Englisch* man from New Mexico.

❧

THE NEXT DAY ON THE TRAIL WAS SIMILAR TO THE FIRST, except that they were gaining altitude and Samuel's muscles hurt worse than ever. On Wednesday morning, the day they'd reach the lake, Samuel woke with a start, chilled from forehead to chest where he'd pushed the sleeping bag down in his sleep and been exposed to the night air.

What had just happened?

He blinked up at the window in the lightweight tent, where the sky was the cold, clear gray of just before sunrise. A quick glance around the tent showed him Ben and Simon were gone, and had left him rolled up like a caterpillar in his bag. Had the sound of their leaving been what had awakened him? Or had one of the fishermen got up early and knocked something over? In which case, if the other two weren't there, it was his job to go out and supply whatever it was the guest needed.

Jose Rodriguez stirred and sat up, and when he saw that Samuel's eyes were open, put a finger to his lips. He pulled on his clothes and Simon slid out of his bag and did the same. Getting his boots on in the cramped space took a bit of doing, but he managed it eventually. He pulled his denim jacket out of his pack and shivered into it.

He found Jose with his hands on his hips, gazing into the scrub forest close by and on the ridge opposite their camp. A deep gully lay between them and the ridge. "It woke you, too."

Samuel nodded, and said in a low tone, "I thought one of the others might have knocked over the coffee pot, but it's not out. It was definitely a loud noise, though. Simon and Ben?"

A sidelong glance told him he was off the mark. "I'd like to know where they are. How are you at tracking?"

There was nothing at home to track except maybe the cows if they broke through a fence. "I've never done it. You're not going after my friends, are you?" Why would he? They were probably scouting up the trail, or looking for a creek to fish for breakfast.

"Not right now," Jose assured him. "It's animals I'm concerned about. Stay behind me, and make as little noise as you can." Quietly, he opened one of the weatherproof bins in the supply shed and collected a rifle. Pocketing a handful of bullets from a second bin, he loaded the gun and led the way past the big rocks and down into the trees.

The dry grass helped to keep their progress fairly quiet,

especially after Jose directed him to step in his footprints, but Samuel still felt like the proverbial bull in a china shop. Every time he stepped outside Jose's trail and his boot landed on a stick he hadn't seen in the gray light, he winced. And as they made their way farther down the slope, he realized what Jose was doing. Heading for the nearest watercourse, at the bottom of the fold between the two ridges. It was a different creek from the one they'd camped next to up on the flat, and its banks were soft and pocked with animal prints. Deer, and coyotes, and cats. Big ones.

Jose pointed as he bent to examine the track. "Mountain lion. Too big for a bobcat."

And there was a splash of blood.

Samuel hadn't wanted to speculate before, but now he knew for sure why Jose had brought the rifle. And what the sound had been that had awakened him.

A gunshot.

He pointed at the splash with tufts of hair stuck in it, and Jose nodded his approval. He pulled out his cell phone and took a couple of pictures, then shook out his hanky and carefully collected some of the bloody hair. Maybe the game warden would want it. They changed direction now, looking for broken branches and displaced rocks as the wounded creature tried to find cover. A deer, from the size of the hoof prints. Not an elk.

Jose cursed at the idiot who would shoot something out of season. Worse, shoot it and not make sure the job was done and the animal dispatched humanely.

Thirty minutes later the sky had brightened to a clear yellow and the first hawk had launched itself into the air to skim the treetops. Thirty minutes where Samuel kept wondering where Simon and Ben were, with a poacher somewhere out there. Thirty minutes of hoping his friends hadn't done something massively, criminally stupid.

And there in a clump of sage next to a granite outcrop was a two-year-old mule deer, his antlers in velvet, lying on his side and thrashing convulsively, unable to go any farther. His eyes rolled in terror as they approached, and they could both see the wound in his side.

Samuel's heart clutched with pity that such a beautiful animal should be reduced to this for no reason at all. For the shooter wasn't tracking it for food. There was no sign of anyone but themselves, tracking it for mercy. In moments, Jose had put the creature out of its misery, and stood, head bowed, as though acknowledging its passing while gritting his teeth in anger at the necessity of it.

"Can we carry it out of here?" Samuel asked quietly. "For the warden? It'll take two of us."

But Jose was examining the carcass. "Small-gauge bullet, same as the animals in the sheriff's truck the other day."

He pulled his phone out again and took pictures of the scene, including a couple of close-ups of the wound. He touched the antlers gently. "He's in velvet. Maybe he wasn't shot for food, but for these. We beat whoever did it down here, and they'll come looking for him."

"Why those?" Samuel couldn't understand it. What would anyone want with antlers in velvet? Everyone knew that trophy hunters went after the eight-pointers, not young animals like this.

"Same reason criminals shoot rhinos, or bears. There are folks who believe the velvet, the rhino horn, and the bear's gall bladder are aphrodisiacs. The things a man will do to prove himself better than another man."

Samuel was struck speechless as he tried to sort out something so crazy.

Into the silence, Jose said, "Best I call the Wildlife warden. We'll take this animal back to camp and then we'll split up."

"You and me?"

"No, the group. Simon can manage the pack trip, and with at least one cook along among the guests, they won't go hungry. Ben can look after the horses by himself. I need you to backtrack and find out where this deer was shot. It wasn't in the creek bottom where we found those cat prints. And then see if you can find out where the poacher shot from. He might have left something behind."

"Me?" Samuel sucked in a breath. When he said he'd never tracked anything before, he'd meant it. "I don't think that's a good idea."

"You afraid?"

"That wasn't what I meant." Samuel scanned the ridgeline. "They could still be out there. Like you said, they still might come looking for him. What if everyone heads off and you're in camp alone when they show up?"

Jose slung the rifle over his shoulder. "I'm not too worried. One of the boys from the paddock can come up in the four-wheeler and take this animal down to the house. I'll ride down with him and talk to the Wildlife warden. Then I'll come back and meet you at the lake."

"I don't like this. Any of it."

"I don't either, but remember what the boss said. We're to keep our eyes open. Now that we have proof there are poachers on Lost Creek land, not BLM land, it's even more important that we let the warden know."

"And the first thing he'll ask is where the animal was shot." Samuel had to acknowledge the truth of it. They had to split up, and each do a task they didn't care for in the name of what was right.

"Come on." Briefly, Jose's hand lay warm on Samuel's shoulder. "Let's see if we can get him up to camp. The four-wheeler could do it, but not without tearing up the hillside."

Though the animal wasn't full grown, it was still a struggle to get nearly two hundred pounds of dead weight down into the creek and then up the steep slope on the other side. And when they reached camp, they found Samuel and Ben back and the others getting ready to send out a search party.

Jose told them briefly what had happened, and let them know the plan. "I'm going to hike up to the fire spotting tower on the ridge behind us, where there's a signal, and call down to the house." He glanced at Simon. "You okay with going on ahead?"

Simon nodded, his gaze clear and steady. "I did four fishing trips last summer. I remember the way."

"Good. If everyone keeps an eye out—especially around the lake at dawn and dusk, when you'll be fishing and the animals will come to drink, you might spot something. Just be careful, and wear your vests when you're outside camp."

They'd all been given bright reflective vests to wear in case they got separated. Samuel hadn't expected to use them the way hunters wore blaze orange, though—to let another hunter know not to shoot. Not at this time of year. Not on ranch property.

"Everyone okay with going on?" Simon asked the fishermen. "The poachers didn't get what they wanted. But they won't stop you getting the fishing you came for."

With a glance at one another, every man nodded in agreement. Because who would say no, and go back to the house empty-handed and days early? After that, the sensible thing to do was make coffee and breakfast, and then break camp to head out.

As the others made their way across the little meadow on the trail, Samuel calmed Caya, who couldn't understand why she wasn't going with the rest of the string. "Easy, girl," he murmured, stroking her nose. "We'll join them just as soon as I get my job done."

He shrugged on his reflective vest. He was doing the right thing, gathering information for the warden. When he got back, everyone would be okay. But it didn't make him feel any less vulnerable as he chose a rifle from the box, slid some bullets into his pocket, and headed down the slope.

AT THIS ALTITUDE, THE SNOW THAT CROWNED THE mountaintops was a lot closer, and Samuel felt its cool breath as he leaned over, his hands on his knees, examining the site he'd just found. He'd accomplished the first part of the task Jose had set him, anyway. A tracker who actually knew what he was doing might have got here faster, but sometimes the old proverb was true: Slow and steady won the race.

For here was the place the deer had been shot—the place where the blood trail began. Here were scrapes, blood and hair on the rocks where the animal had fallen and struggled to its feet again, a couple of the smaller stones knocked out of their beds in the dirt altogether.

And what was this?

Among the signs of a scuffle, and the tracks of other animals, was a Winston cigarette butt.

For a moment, Samuel's gut churned with anger at this callous disregard for the beauty of God's creation. A man didn't have to be Amish to take exception to that. But as he pulled out his phone and snapped pictures of the site, following Jose's example, he realized it didn't make sense. A deer could smell a man smoking from hundreds of yards away. The hunter wouldn't be that stupid.

But what if that wasn't what had happened?

He gazed at the trail, trying to imagine why a man would leave litter out here. Especially litter that smelled.

Deer were curious creatures—he'd learned that hunting with his father. Easily spooked and prey for just about everything, but intelligent and vigilant about their surroundings. What if that curiosity had been the animal's downfall? What if it had come upon a cigarette butt planted on purpose in the trail, and paused to sniff it just long enough for the poacher to take his shot?

Samuel pulled an empty sandwich bag from his lunch out of his pack and carefully, without touching the butt, rolled it into the bag. Then he shook out a used napkin and gingerly picked up some of the bloody hair. He didn't know what the warden would make of it, but best to be thorough and do what Jose had done. When he'd tucked the napkin into the bag and put it in his pocket, he uncapped his water bottle. He'd drunk nearly half of it. Altitude and dry air had made him all too aware that if he didn't stay hydrated, a search party would be coming for him next. He put the bottle in his pack, hitched the rifle strap up on his shoulder, and focused on his surroundings not from the point of view of the deer, which he'd been doing up until now, but of the hunter.

The deer had been on its way down to the creek in the draw half a mile or so away as the crow flew. The game trail, a faint path a couple of inches wide, meandered through the scrub and pines. So if he had been the hunter, where would he take up his vantage point?

The problem was, there were all too many good ones. Every ridge seemed to have natural blinds and hiding places, every slope a hollow where a hunter could conceal himself and simply wait for his prey to wander past.

Unbidden, a memory came of Dat teaching him how to shoot, out in the back pasture with a row of tin cans. He had to have been only eight or nine—long before Hannah and Leah had been taken away. Dat and Onkel Orland had been planning a hunting trip—and all his cousins his age were fizzing with excitement at being allowed to go too. But first, each boy had to learn how to treat the rifle with respect.

"The smaller the caliber, the closer you have to be to the cans," Dat had explained. "And the more you have to pay attention to things like the wind. Feel that?" He'd licked his finger and held it up, and Samuel had been quick to do the same. The breeze had cooled the side of his finger.

He didn't remember if he'd managed to hit one of the cans, but he supposed he must have, because he remembered that trip vividly. Then, after the girls had been ... After that, his father and Onkel Orland had taken him hunting again in Western Pennsylvania, just the three of them. With the benefit of a few years of hindsight, he realized now that the trip had been less about providing meat for winter and more about taking his father's mind off the awful situation their family had been in, just for a couple of days.

But now, Dat's words in his memory, he took a look around. If he drew a circle around the scraped rocks fifty feet out, that might be a starting point. He could keep widening the circle until he either found something or it got dark and he had to return to camp.

Of the two, he'd prefer the first option. The last thing he wanted was to disappoint Jose and come back with only a cigarette butt to show for his hours of hiking around.

Despite their dangerous task, he'd enjoyed partnering with Jose to find the deer. The man didn't treat him like grunt labor, and unlike the Amish crew at the RV factory, there was none of the not-so-unconscious separation he and Ben had to put up with on a daily basis. Oh, it wasn't like the Amish men back home were trying to exclude them. Not at all—they'd go out of their way to be friendly and welcoming. But every smile or kind word was meant to convey what they were missing every minute they weren't willing to join church. He and Ben had got in the habit of taking their lunch break out on the edge of the parking lot, behind the equipment sheds, just to get a break from it.

Enough woolgathering—back to work.

Even with the distraction of the cigarette, the deer hadn't been killed with a clean shot. It had been wounded in the front right quarter with a small-caliber gun, probably a .22 rifle. He could only hope that the poacher had intended to shoot it in the head at fifty yards, not deliberately draw out its death by a bullet in the body. Hunting game with a .22 was illegal for that very reason. If a hunter was going to bring down a deer, he used the appropriate caliber to minimize the animal's suffering. But poachers, Samuel guessed, didn't care about the law, or the rules of safe and humane hunting.

He paced out fifty feet and then headed south, drawing himself an imaginary circle on the slopes and picking out landmarks to guide himself with. He'd been blessed with good vision, so he swept from side to side of his circle as he walked. The first circuit took a good hour and another quarter of the water bottle, and netted nothing except a lot of startled lizards and a frightened grouse that beat up out of a clump of sage and scared Samuel sideways.

He expanded his circle by twenty feet and walked it again. The sun passed its high point and the shadows of the rocks and trees began to hint that maybe he ought to pick up his pace. But slow and steady, he heard Dat say again in his memory, won the race.

Another expansion, another twenty feet. Then another. And this time, on a broken slope where clearly a landslide had occurred during some wet spring long ago, he found moss scraped off a stone. It could be nothing—another deer, a falling rock. But there, just beyond the scree, was an outcrop of granite that would both hide a hunter and provide a place for him to brace his elbows while he took aim.

Careful where he put his feet, Samuel climbed over the scree and down to the rock.

Satisfaction gave him as warm a glow as exertion, as he gazed at the place where the poacher had waited. Waited, and left behind boot prints and a flattened area of grass. Had he only taken that one shot? Samuel hadn't heard more, but he'd been asleep. Now he had to find his brass, or there would be nothing to link the poacher to his victim.

More circles, tight ones, making sure he didn't miss a thing. And his vigilance was rewarded—there in a crevice in the rocks was a gleam of metal. A bullet casing, expelled from the rifle and not picked up the way Dat had taught Samuel all those years ago. Why would a man leave evidence like that behind? Had he been distracted, or in a hurry because he was afraid he'd get caught? Or was he simply not an experienced hunter? Any way you looked at it, that poor deer had paid the price.

Carefully, Samuel took pictures of this new location,

including a sight line down to where the deer had been hit. Then he collected the casing, placing it carefully in the sandwich bag with the cigarette butt and the napkin containing the deer's hair and blood.

There was nothing more he could do here. He took his bearings by his landmarks, and headed back to camp.

9

A week of Bonita James was enough to drive anyone right back to Whinburg Township. Thank goodness today was Wednesday, and Hannah could escape on an actual day off. She didn't quite know where she was going to escape to, mind you, but at this point, anywhere would do.

With a sense of relief, she pulled on her jeans and a clean T-shirt, brushed her hair so that the purple tips curled up a little bit, and followed Amanda down to the staff dining room. It wasn't that she hated dressing Amish. She didn't mind it. But she'd rather it was her choice instead of Mrs. Gunderson making decisions about what she put on in the morning.

"If anyone wants a ride into town, I'll head out about nine in the ranch van," Teresa said to everyone in the staff dining room. "I have some shopping to do, and some other errands that will take a couple of hours. I haven't heard anyone is going to town before the weekend, so grab your opportunity now, while you have it."

"What are you girls doing on the weekend?" One of the

cowboys who hadn't gone on the trail ride reached for a fluffy biscuit. "You plan to go to church?"

"Service is every other week," Amanda said shyly. "This Sunday is the off Sunday, so next week we'll go." Hannah knew she didn't talk to *Englisch* men very much, so every sentence was an exercise in bravery.

"You and Hannah?" Bonita asked Amanda now, sipping coffee.

"If she wants to. But I was thinking more of Simon and me. We're church members, you see."

"Is that so. How are you going to get there?" the cowboy asked. "Teresa might not have a shopping trip planned."

"You might ask Joshua next time he comes." Teresa brought in the last tray of bacon and Amanda handed it around. "He leaves three days' worth of meat on Friday because he doesn't come on Saturday or do business on Sunday, so you'd want to make arrangements before then. You missed him this morning, or you could have asked."

"Thank you. I will tomorrow."

At which point she blushed so hard she couldn't get out more than that, much to the amusement of Bonita and Jenny.

"So you're going, too?" Teresa said to Hannah. "You're not Amish—I mean, a church member—are you?" Her gaze flicked over Hannah's hair.

"No, I'm not." How had she gotten herself into this? She hadn't had any intention of going to church, and now she had to show some solidarity. It was all Bonita's fault. "But Mrs. Gunderson would want it, wouldn't she?"

"I don't know if she has any say in the staff's private life outside of work hours," Teresa said slowly, a pleat forming between her brows. "But that's none of my business, either. My business is getting my errands done. Nine o'clock, then, at the barn." And she sat down to her own breakfast.

What a relief it was to leave the table and not have to go and get the cleaning cart! Because Bonita, of course, had commandeered the job of changing out the towels, which was the best job of all. She rolled the fluffy white Turkish towels and made roses out of facecloths while Jenny soldiered through the rooms, vacuuming and stripping and making beds—king size, queen size, twin size, bunks. That left Hannah helping Jenny where she could and cleaning anything made of porcelain—shower, sink, and yup, toilets.

During her brief stint in housekeeping, Amanda, gentle but brilliant, had suggested that they rotate jobs every day. Jenny had backed her up, so at least Hannah didn't have a steady diet of toilets to look forward to all summer. But Bonita, as the senior member of the team, refused to rotate, and there was no one to make her. Teresa wouldn't help. As long as everything sparkled when she made her rounds, she left them to iron out their own differences.

But now Amanda was in the kitchen permanently, and Hannah just had to take a deep breath and tough it out. But today, Hannah didn't have to think about the eight guest cabins, and the suite and four double rooms in the main house (toilet total: fourteen). All she had to think about was going to town and maybe seeing something cute in one of the shops.

"Just think, for a couple of hours, I'm free of people telling me what to do and how to dress and how to act." She and Amanda rambled down toward the barn, stopping every now and again to take in the view. But while the mountains were beautiful and the sun felt good, any view that didn't have Ben in it was just a pretty hole waiting to be filled by the sight of him, as far as she was concerned.

After today, five more days to wait. She'd been spoiled traveling out here and having him at her side almost twenty-four seven. At home they saw one another every couple of days, because her father didn't like him coming around. Jonathan Riehl would never say so, because he was all too aware that she was still *Englisch*, but his frowny face told everyone in the house how he felt. So all those days on the train had been like her first taste of chocolate, and now that she was hooked, she wanted it every day.

"We need to find peace with Bonita," Amanda said. "Somehow."

"I don't think anyone finds peace with her. Not even Jenny. She just does what Bonita says to stop her carping."

"It's a form of peace, I guess."

"More like total surrender. Which isn't exactly peace."

Amanda leaned back on the warm, red-painted planks of the barn, and after a moment, Hannah did, too. Mornings were still pretty chilly, even in the first weeks of June. It didn't start to warm up properly until after nine.

"Standing up for yourself is one thing, but I heard what you said to her last night before we went to bed. Remember *Uffgeva*, Hannah."

The giving up of oneself. Putting others first. Well, that didn't apply to Bonita—she forced everyone around her to put her first. "Every woman has her limit."

"You're lucky she didn't tell Teresa."

"I don't care. It felt good to say what I thought, even if you're going to lecture me."

Amanda bit her lip, gazing across the field where the second string of horses grazed. Where the first string would be grazing when the boys got back. "I'm sorry if you think Im lecturing. I don't mean to come off as your teacher, or a big sister who's always right. I'm just trying to help you make Mrs. Gunderson happy, that's all."

"She was nowhere in sight. She never is, and you know it. She's always in the great room with the guests."

"I know. But she wants Amish girls on staff, so I'm just trying to help you be an Amish girl."

"Technically, I am one without help."

"But it's the actions that show it, as well as the clothes. Which I'm sure Ben would tell you if he were here."

"I wish he was. I miss him like crazy."

"When you're busy, the time will fly. But Hannah, I mean it. You can't say things like that to people. If you get sent home, what will happen to me?"

Rebellion bubbled up under her breastbone—what Amanda would probably call unwillingness. It seemed to be happening a lot lately—though why it should happen here and not at home under Jonathan's stern eye was something she hadn't figured out yet. Maybe because Jonathan and Rebecca didn't insist that she obey the *Ordnung*. Why should she have to when she wasn't Amish?

"I expect you'd stay here and finish out the summer. After all, you're what Mrs. Gunderson wants, right? The real deal."

"But I don't know if—"

One of the cowboys walked around the corner of the barn. "Hey, you girls. Teresa's loaded up and waiting."

And in the scramble to get into the van, there was no chance to speak about something so private. And talking about Mrs. Gunderson behind her back probably wasn't very smart, either.

It was only twenty minutes into Amistad, but fifteen of that was the long gravel road down from the ranch and out through the grassy hills to the highway. Before long they passed the sign that said AMISTAD: POPULATION 1856. Even before that Hannah saw two of the familiar yellow signs with the little black buggy icon on them. Just like at home, these warned people zipping past in trucks and cars at sixty miles an hour that there could be an Amish family over the next hill or turning out of a gravel road, filled with defenseless kids and pulled by a horse who might not have learned yet to ignore the horn.

When Teresa parked the van in front of the market, Hannah pointed at the two-sided shed at one end of the lot. "Look. Buggy parking."

Amanda smiled. "So it is. We should introduce ourselves to whoever is in the market, so that we know someone when we go to church."

"Someone other than Joshua King?" Hannah didn't know what made her say that. The minute Amanda looked away to hide her face, she wished she hadn't.

Shame made her cranky. But instead of apologizing, she changed the subject. "Come on. Let's get out of here before Jenny and Bonita decide they want to come with us."

"That's not very likely."

Teresa called after them, "Meet back here in two hours, okay?"

Hannah waved, and hustled Amanda up the street, protesting, "But I wanted to go into the market and meet those folks."

Bonita had been going in, and it would have taken a hailstorm to force Hannah in there once her nemesis set foot in the door. "There are lots of Amish folks here." She pointed down the quaint main street. "See?"

Amistad wasn't a very big place, but it was clear it had been there for a long time. Like a hundred years, maybe—the same age as the old tumbledown building in the meadow at the ranch. On one side, a row of shops with tall false fronts made it look like a movie set for a western, only they were painted colors like sage green and rose and gray. A black family buggy with an angled bottom was tied to a rail in front of one shop, its horse patiently waiting with one knee bent and its hoof tipped up. On the other side of the street, more modern buildings sat among the old ones. Hannah supposed there was some unwritten rule that a bank always had to look like a piece of polished granite. In front of it was another buggy, also black but with a square shape and a flat bottom. There was a tiny hamburger and ice cream drive-in, too, with a real neon sign that worked even in the daytime, forever pouring orange soda into a cup.

The next best thing to fast food. She liked Amistad already.

Other buggies were parked here and there. Every one seemed to be different. Not like in Whinburg Township, where the closed buggies were square and gray and all looked the same. Only the *Youngie* dressed theirs up a bit, with reflectors stuck on in patterns on the back, or a string of dingle-dangles hung across the storm front.

Was there no *Ordnung* here that dictated how buggies ought to be built? In Hannah's experience, that would be a first.

"Look, a quilt shop." Amanda took her elbow. "Let's go in."

"I wonder if the Amish own it? That buggy is parked right in front."

"The owner's is probably around back in a shed. A horse can't stand in the street all day—that one probably belongs to a customer."

A bell tinkled over the door as they pushed it open. The

Amish woman behind the counter looked up from the place mats she was sorting, and smiled—at which point she realized that Hannah and Amanda were together, and the smile became puzzled. "Good morning," she said, clearly splitting the difference and choosing English instead of *Deitsch*.

Another Amish woman was occupied in the fabric section, matching colors to a stack of bolts she'd already chosen.

"Guder mariye," Hannah said cheerfully. *"Wie geht's?"*

"Gut, denki," the woman returned after a surprised hesitation. *"Wilkumm in Amistad."*

"Thank you," Amanda said, offering her hand and speaking in English, which Hannah appreciated. Though she'd been trying to learn *Deitsch* since she'd been living with her Amish family, anything beyond greetings and basic nouns and verbs was a challenge still. It was hard to learn a language that wasn't written, only spoken. It meant you picked up verb conjugations by osmosis instead of memorizing them in a textbook, like Spanish. The woman would have discovered her limits pretty shortly after Hannah's bit of showing off.

"I am Amanda Yoder, from Whinburg Township in Pennsylvania. This is my friend Hannah Riehl. We're working at the Lost Creek Ranch this summer."

The woman shook her hand heartily, and offered her own to Hannah, too. She had a grip like a vise, but in a good way. Her eyes sparkled with interest. "I heard about you girls from Joshua King. We were all wondering when we'd get to meet you. There are some young men with you, too, I understand?"

"Ja, my nephew Simon Yoder, and Hannah's brother Samuel, and our friend Ben Troyer."

"That's quite a group." The woman was probably a little younger than Hannah's own mother, and her comfortable figure was likely the result of the same fondness for noodles and pie. She beamed at them. "I hope we'll be seeing you at church. It's always interesting to see the new ones coming each summer. Some of them stay, you know. Our district grows each fall—in fact, any more and we'll have to split the churches again."

"My nephew came last year and encouraged all of us to come back with him," Amanda said shyly.

"Simon Yoder, *ja.* We met him," the woman said. Hannah looked at her a little more closely, trying to figure out what her tone meant, but she moved away to adjust a quilt on the wall. "Are you girls quilters?"

"I am now," Hannah said. "I just finished my first one for the fire auction this spring. A Blooming Nine-Patch."

"I like that pattern." The woman's face warmed into a smile again.

What was that about? Did Simon have some history among the people here that he had managed not to mention for a whole year? Maybe Hannah would make it her mission to find out. After all, she'd already committed to going to church next Sunday.

"I like it, too," Amanda said. "It looks so complicated and goes so fast."

"Listen to me, talking away and not introducing myself." The woman touched her bucket-shaped pleated bonnet absently, as though making sure it was secure. "My name is Mariah Gingerich. My husband is Nathaniel, who has the feed store up at the east end of town. If you go out that way, you can't miss it."

"Are the shops here mostly owned by Amish folks?" Hannah asked. "There are rails in front of nearly all of them."

"*Neh*, maybe only a third are. But the town has been very welcoming. Those rails went in about three years ago, and a good thing it was, too, since I think we doubled in numbers in that time."

"I hear the tourists like it that you're here," Hannah said. "In fact, we—"

"Oh, Hannah, look at this beautiful Compass Rose," Amanda interrupted.

Hannah was so shocked at Amanda interrupting anybody that she meekly followed her over to look at the quilt on the display wall. "What?" she whispered.

"Later." In a normal tone, Amanda said over her shoulder to Mariah, "Did you make this?"

That lady laughed. "Not I. Too fussy, having to cut all those long triangles. No, that was Savilla King, Joshua's mother. She's laid up, you know. Quilting keeps her hands busy, and brings in some income for the family. Now that the *Englisch* schools are out and the tourists are coming, that one will go. I'm going to move it into the window on Monday."

"I'm sorry to hear she's not well," Amanda said.

"Her family and neighbors all help, and gladly. If you're working at Lost Creek, you must have met Joshua."

"Yes." Amanda said no more, so Hannah rushed in to fill the gap.

"Are there lots of *Youngie* here?" she asked.

"A fair number." Mariah nodded. "My *Dochder* Lizzy said there were twenty-one."

"That is a good number," Hannah said. "In our church I think there's maybe seventeen or eighteen, so the kids in the whole district—four churches—come to singing."

"In *your* church?" This time Mariah couldn't keep her curiosity under its lid of politeness.

As soon as the words had left her mouth, Hannah knew she was going to have to explain herself—standing there in her jeans and T-shirt. "Yes. I haven't joined church, but I still go with my family."

"Ah. You're on *Rumspringe*, then."

In a way. "Ja."

Mariah paused, as though something had just occurred to her. "Riehl. In Whinburg Township. Didn't I read something about that in *The Budget*? You're not the girl who was returned to her family after being—"

"Ja." Hannah cut off the rest of it. She hated the word *kidnapped*. Hated the fact that people recognized her not for herself, but for her *Englisch* parents' crime. Now it would be all over the district and going to church next week would be like running a gauntlet of people carefully trying not to make her feel uncomfortable. Of gentle kindness. Of constantly reminding her that she was not only not Amish, but not *Englisch*, either.

Never mind solidarity. Maybe she'd reconsider going.

"Well, I'll be. God's ways are mysterious, and here you are. I hope you'll enjoy working up at the ranch. And as for *Rumspringe*, this is a fine place for that." Mariah's smile was back as she turned the subject with all the skill of a man turning a six-mule hitch at the end of a row. "Everything is too far away to get into trouble. I think the worst our young folk get up to is a band hop in a field. Last year they did it in May and it snowed on them, and there hasn't been one since."

Even Amanda smiled, but Hannah couldn't tell if it was relief, or amusement at the story. "I guess the *gut Gott* showed them what He thought of that," Amanda said.

Which told Hannah what she thought of band hops.

"So He did."

The Amish customer brought her stack of bolts over, and Mariah introduced them, though it was hardly necessary, since she'd heard everything. Her prayer covering was identical to Mariah's. So how come the *Ordnung* said that *Kapps* had to look the same, but not buggies?

Once Mariah began to measure and cut the lengths of fabric, it seemed like a good time to say good-bye and fade out the door.

"Oh, before you go, you might let Teresa Rodriguez know the quilts that she asked for are ready to be picked up," Mariah said. "Apparently there are a bunch of quilters coming, and she thought we might be able to sell a few if they were on display at the big house."

"That's a good idea," Amanda said. "I'll be sure to tell her." Then she slipped out the door after Hannah, the bell jingling cheerfully.

"Not too many secrets in this town, is there?" Hannah said on a sigh as they looked into a window with a display of kitchen gadgets, china, and pretty bouquets of silk flowers sitting on flowered place mats.

"I'm sorry all that came up if it distresses you," Amanda said softly. Then she caught herself. "Of course it distresses you. That was stupid. I don't know what's the matter with me."

"Everyone throwing Joshua King in your face, for starters."

Amanda rolled her eyes. "We hardly said six sentences to each other. I don't know why people are making such a thing of it. Besides, every girl in the district is probably putting things in her hope chest with him in mind—to say nothing of the girls who come here to work."

"They don't have eyes as pretty as yours," Hannah said loyally, which only made Amanda look embarrassed. "I will say, girlfriend, that Colorado agrees with you—dry air, altitude, something. Do you know your skin is clearing up?"

"That's the cream Sarah gives me to put on it."

"Maybe. I think it's all the water they tell us to drink because of the altitude. Or the air. Me, I'm going to turn into a Gila monster by the Fourth of July. But your skin seems to like it."

"What on earth is a *hee-la* monster?"

When Hannah told her, Amanda laughed. Which made it seem like a good time to ask, "So what was bothering you earlier? You tried to say something when we were waiting for the van, and then you stopped me inside, when I was about to say something about Mrs. Gunderson's dress code."

A little park lay behind the drive-in, with a wide, shallow creek running through it that might even be fed by Lost Creek, miles up in the hills. Amanda nodded toward it. "Let's go over there."

"It's eleven. How about an ice cream on the way?"

"Good idea."

Once they had their soft ice cream cones, she and Amanda settled onto a bench in the sunshine to watch the creek chatter past. "Okay, spill," Hannah prompted her. "What's bugging you if it isn't Joshua King and it isn't Bonita?"

"It's what you call the dress code," Amanda said after a few moments of struggle.

"What, the fact that the women's *Kapps* here have to be the same, but every buggy you see looks different?"

Amanda stared at her. "What are you talking about? I'm talking about Mrs. Gunderson."

"Oh." Her ice cream was starting to melt, so she licked it faster. "Why would that bug you? If it bugs anybody, it should be me."

"It's all part of the same thing, I suppose. It just doesn't seem right."

"Like asking me to dress Amish when I'm not?"

"And asking me to dress Amish when I am. To bring the tourists in. Same with the quilts from Mariah's shop. So that Lost Creek Ranch has something nobody else does."

"Is that it?" It was almost a relief to know it was a question of ethics and nothing more serious. "I thought you wanted to go home."

"I thought *you* wanted to go home, the way you've been talking," Amanda replied. "But I almost wonder if we should. Because otherwise it seems like we're allowing ourselves to be used for ... for advertising."

"Everybody does that," Hannah objected, gesturing up the little hill toward the quilt shop, "when you get right down to it."

"I said it wrong. It seems like we're—I'm—allowing the expressions of my faith to be used for money."

"Oh." That put a different spin on it. "I get it now."

"I don't know what to do. I don't like being used, but at the same time, I couldn't earn as much as we do here if I were a *Maud* at home. I couldn't even be a *Maud*, and leave Mamm with all the work." She sighed. "So that makes me willing to go along with it."

She looked down at her melting ice cream, then got up and put it in the trash can chained to a nearby tree.

"Wow." Hannah felt as though she couldn't quite get a deep breath. "I don't know if I'd put it like that."

"It's the truth."

Whose truth? Not your average person's that was for sure. "Aren't you overthinking it just a bit, Mandy? It's just a job."

Amanda lifted one shoulder. "Maybe I am making too much of it. Of myself. Maybe I should just be glad I have a job when so many don't."

That you got because you wear a prayer covering and know how to cook. "People get jobs because they wear a suit and tie and know how to use a calculator, right?"

"It's not the same."

No, it wasn't. Not really. Calculators weren't a religious symbol—though with some people she'd met, you'd almost wonder. There didn't seem to be an answer to Amanda's dilemma, either. Not if they didn't want to get back on the train and go home. Which Hannah emphatically didn't want to do. She wanted to stay here, with Ben.

And make sure he stayed, too.

SOMEONE HAILED THEM FROM THE TOP OF THE GENTLE, sunlit slope. Someone speaking *Deitsch*. Anxious to welcome anything that wasn't another uncomfortable thought, Amanda turned on the bench to see Joshua King loping over the grass, surrounded by a flock of *Kinner*.

"Well, look who came to town," he said. "Amanda Yoder." His grip was warm and firm, and it was *gut* that he had Hannah to turn to or who knew how long she might have stood there grinning like a complete fool.

Amanda blushed at herself, and bent to a little girl with a small, bucket-shaped *Kapp* covering her curly brown hair. "And who might you be? I don't remember seeing you on the morning deliveries."

"I'm Mary Liza," the girl said shyly. "And that's my sister Rachel. She's twelve and I'm seven. We're getting supplies."

"I'm very happy to meet you, Mary Liza and Rachel. I'm Amanda and this is Hannah."

Rachel leaned against Amanda's green skirts and whispered, "Is that the girl who was kidnapped?"

Good grief. Did everyone in town read *The Budget* from cover to cover, even the little ones?

Praying that Hannah, who was joking with Peter and Moses, hadn't heard, Amanda whispered back in rapid *Deitsch*, "Yes, but it hurts her feelings if you say so. To us, she's just Hannah."

"Ja." The girl turned solemn eyes on Hannah, as though she'd just heard she was about to be called home to the Lord at any moment. "Why is her hair purple?"

"Because she's on *Rumspringe*." Thank goodness Mariah Gingerich had given them this handy reason. Hannah wasn't, really. *Rumspringe* was the season of experimenting, of exploring. The season for the *Youngie* who had grown up in the church to taste the *Englisch* world before they decided whether or not to be baptized. But Hannah had lived both lives, and she was no closer to choosing one than—than Ben Troyer. The problem with being in the place where two ways met was that if you didn't choose one—or allow the Lord to take the reins of your life—you never went anywhere.

"Boys, how about you take your sisters down to the creek and get your feet wet?" Joshua suggested. "First dip of the season is always the best one."

"I'll come with you." Hannah jumped up. "I work right next to Lost Creek and haven't had a single minute even to look at it. Last one in is a rotten egg!"

She chased the little girls down the slope, pulling off her sneakers as she went, while the older boys loped along behind.

Was it possible to actually die of embarrassment at being left alone with a single man on purpose? Amanda would have run down there with them—had half turned to do so—when Joshua settled onto the bench and crossed an ankle over his knee. It would be rude to leave him here to talk to himself. Oh, dear. Amanda sat on the very end of the bench, hoping he'd decide he wanted to wade, too, and leave her up here in the sun to recover.

"I didn't plan that." He twinkled at her. "Honest. I just remembered how good it felt with my feet in the cold water and my shoulders in the hot sun ... and the words came out."

"It's all right," she said softly. "It looks like Hannah is the rotten egg after all. She had to get her shoes off."

It was rare for Amish children to wear shoes anywhere except to church in the summer. The boys were older, and working, so their sneakers lay in the grass, but Hannah had had socks to deal with, too, and jeans to turn up into cuffs.

"So you have a day off, then, do you?" Joshua spoke as though he hadn't noticed the agonizing silence in which Amanda had struggled for something sensible to say.

"We do," she said softly. "We have Sundays for sure, and one during the week."

"Do you have a way to get to church?"

"No." Which he knew very well. "Teresa suggested I ask you what might be best."

"What I think best is that you ride with us." And before she could say a word, he went on, "It's just you and Simon, isn't it? We're a big bunch, but we can find room for two."

"But it's so far up the mountain and—and—Hannah might want to come as well."

"Is that so? Well, that's *gut*. For her to learn about our ways, I mean."

He read *The Budget*, too, it seemed. "Does everyone in the district know her story?"

"*Ja.* There was a letter in *The Budget* not long ago, and

unless there is more than one Hannah Riehl with purple hair in the world, everyone who has read it will remember it as soon as she says her name."

Poor Jesse. If only he had known he merely had to write a letter to *The Budget* to become famous, maybe he wouldn't have allowed himself to be filmed for *Shunning Amish*. Then again, that wasn't why he'd done it. He'd done it for the money. So he could leave and never come back.

"Did I say something wrong?" Joshua peered into her face, all the twinkle fading from his kind brown eyes. "You look sad all of a sudden."

She did her best to relax into a smile. "I was just thinking of someone back home."

"Oh." He got up and walked a few steps down the slope, settling his straw hat more firmly on his head, as though to keep the sun out of his eyes. "Someone special?" he said over his shoulder.

"A friend. Who has moved to Australia."

"Australia!" Sheer surprise brought him back to the bench. "Not Amish then, I take it."

"No, not Amish." Better leave it at that, in case he'd ever heard of *Shunning Amish*, like the Schulers.

"It will be no trouble coming to get you next Sunday." He picked up the reins of their conversation as though it had never taken such an odd swerve. "Church is at the Fischer place, which you probably passed on your way into town. Big place, log bottom, clapboard top?"

Amanda nodded. "We did see it. It's ... unusual."

He grinned as though pleased she'd noticed. "It is, at that, which is why Kentucky Zeke Fischer got the place. The previous owner had half a log home built when he ran out of money and the place went up for auction. Zeke's a carpenter, and so is his brother. They had a hybrid kind of house up in no time."

"I'll look forward to seeing the inside of it, then," she said. "And to meeting the Fischers. We met Mariah Gingerich in the quilt shop just now."

"A good friend of Mamm's, is Mariah. Stocks her quilts in such a way that the tourists can't help but buy them."

"I saw her Compass Rose. It's beautiful. Anyone would be lucky to have it in their home."

"I'll tell her you said so. We all do what we can to make a living here. The butcher shop does all right, but Mamm wants to do her bit since she can't do much around home. My sister Grace Ann has that to take care of."

"Is yours the only butcher shop in town?"

"In Amistad, yes. There's another Amish-run one in Westcliffe. We do retail, and I specialize in processing what the hunters bring in during the autumn. Or outside of it." He laughed.

"What do you mean?" The thought of the poachers came unbidden, bringing a kind of chill.

"Have you heard of the road-kill rule?"

"*Neh.* What is that?"

"Say a man hits a deer or an elk with his truck, accidentally. He can take it, gut it, and hang it, as long as he lets Colorado Wildlife know about it within forty-eight hours. Once the warden comes to inspect it and gives his okay, he can bring it to me to have it processed."

"I've never heard of such a thing. That would never happen in Whinburg Township. The Highways people come and remove animals like that."

"A waste of good meat, if you ask me. I don't get many, because a man doesn't want to risk the damage to his truck or car. But accidents happen—and they help to put a little in the till during the other months of the year."

"I'm glad, then. That you can make a living here. You seem to enjoy your life in the valley."

He glanced at her and seemed to be about to say something, but a shout from the creek made him change his mind. "Come on. Looks like we might have to play lifeguard if someone falls in."

Laughing, she ran down the slope after him, where Peter was having trouble keeping the little girls from trying to swim. It was like being at home again in Willow Creek, carefree and having fun and splashing one another. At this elevation, the air was thinner and the sun much hotter than she expected, and Amanda was forced to retreat under the trees when her face began to burn. If she hoped that Joshua might talk with her again, she was disappointed, and all too soon it was time to head back to the market at the other end of town, to meet Teresa at the van.

"It's back to work for us now. See you tomorrow," Joshua called as she and Hannah walked past the drive-in, where the horse waited patiently under a pine tree.

"Sounds good," Hannah called back, saving Amanda from having to reply. When they were out of sight and walking back along the old-fashioned raised-plank sidewalks of the downtown area, Hannah elbowed her. "That boy likes you."

Amanda snorted at the thought. "That *boy* has to be nearly thirty. And he does not."

"Does too. You were talking up there for ages."

"He was just being polite. And kind."

"Amanda Yoder, you take *Demut* to new depths. Anybody with eyes in their head can see he's interested. Guys don't sit on park benches talking with a girl just to be polite, especially when it's a warm day and everybody else is wading in the creek."

"And you're an expert on guys, are you?"

"No," she said breezily. "But I do have a little experience."

Amanda couldn't argue. Hannah had more than she did, that was for sure.

After delivering her message to Teresa about the quilts, and consequently making a stop at the quilt shop, Amanda spent the drive back to the ranch in a kind of daze. Riding in an *Englisch* car was like that anyway—everything went by so fast, and since you never had to drive, you didn't need to pay attention either. Her conversation with Joshua King played over and over in her mind, but no matter which way she turned it, she still couldn't see evidence that he liked her any more than he liked Teresa or Hannah or anybody else.

As she'd already concluded, he was just being polite and kind.

There was something to be said for kindness—not the sort that hoped there would be benefits to the things it did, but the sort that was simply part of a person. The sort that you could see in a man's eyes as well as his actions.

Never mind thinking about Joshua King in that way, she told herself sternly as they drove up the long gravel road to the ranch. With as many *Youngie* as there were in this valley, and more due to come soon, it was a sure route to the kind of humiliation she'd endured last year.

And one summer like that was enough to teach her the kind of lesson that lasted a very long time.

10

One of the many things for which Joshua gave thanks to *der Herr* each day was the fact that he and his father were able to provide for their family. Such a basic thing, but these days not everyone could say the same. Back in Kansas, there had been the farm, but even there, some years they were barely able to scrape by, even with the help of other family members. And finally it had failed altogether.

Here in Colorado, though, he'd been able to master a useful trade, and in time open up his own butcher shop. Dat kept the books and manned the retail register, while Joshua did the actual cutting and the deliveries. It was a system that suited them both, and being able to apprentice his brothers suited him even better. King Cuts and Meats had three restaurant accounts now, along with the Lost Creek Ranch, and those accounts were in a fair way to being able to cover the mortgage just on their own.

The boys jumped out of the family buggy and swung their sisters down, and then Joshua backed it into the barn and unhitched Rusty. *Pride of Rustico* had been his racing name, but now the black gelding's running was limited to the fields out back and the ground-eating trot that took him into town and to church.

"What do you think, Rusty?" he murmured as he curried the animal. "I should have done it when I saw her, shouldn't I? Should I phone up there now and invite our new friends to lunch on our off Sunday this week?"

Better he ask Grace Ann and Mamm than the horse. But somehow saying it out loud made it more possible that Amanda Yoder might agree to come. She had said she wanted to meet the folks in the district, so it would only be neighborly to give her an opportunity.

When he brought this up to Mamm and Grace Ann a little later on, when he looked in on his way over to the butcher shop at the front of the property, one stopped her stitching in the big chair while the other stopped rolling out pastry dough. He'd never realized before how identical their gazes were, how similar their eyes.

"Company for lunch on Sunday?" his sister repeated. "From Lost Creek?"

"You remember Simon Yoder," he said, trying for a casual air. "His aunt is there this year, along with..." He paused. "Hannah Riehl."

Grace Ann merely looked puzzled, but Mamm's eyebrows rose as realization hit. "Hannah Riehl, from out East—one of those girls who were kidnapped?"

"The very one. I'm not sure where her sister is, but the point is, it would be neighborly to have them down here for lunch and some fellowship."

"This aunt, then—she's some years older than Simon?" Mamm went on, clearly trying to recover from the surprise.

"What's she doing out here? Doesn't she have a family of her own?"

"I don't know." Mischief seized him as he realized both of them thought Amanda was some years older than she actually was. *Quite* some years. "You'll have to ask her. I'd like to telephone up there this afternoon."

"But this Hannah, is she *Englisch* or Amish now?" Grace Ann asked. "Will she want to come?"

"If what the letter in *The Budget* said has its facts right, she's been living with her Amish family for months," Joshua pointed out. "I'm pretty sure she'll know what to expect. I'll go up and collect them after bible study."

"You do that, Joshua," his mother said. "That poor lamb. She'll need a family away from home, and some feeding up. Yes, you do that."

So when he pushed open the back door of the shop and his father came out of the office, Dat took one look at him and said, "What's got you smiling like a barn cat under a cow?"

"I had the *Kinner* up to the park today to get their feet wet when we went in for supplies."

"And this has you so happy?"

"Partly. I'm going to use the phone." He grinned at Dat, which only made his father grin in return and shake his head. But he went out into the retail side, behind the cold cases and the cash register, leaving the office and its illusion of privacy to Joshua.

"Lost Creek Ranch," Teresa said when she picked up the house line. Used for local ranch business, it had a different number from the reservations line, and a different one again from the personal cell phones the Gundersons used.

"Joshua King here. Any chance Amanda Yoder or Hannah Riehl might be within shouting distance?"

"As a matter of fact, yes. My prep cook is right here. Hang on."

In a moment, a soft voice said in English, "Hello? This is Amanda Yoder."

What a sweet voice she had. It seemed to match the dimples in her cheeks, not the serious and modest way she conducted herself. Serious and modest, that is, until she smiled. He hoped he'd see that smile a lot.

"This is Joshua King."

"I don't know too many other Joshuas out here," she replied in *Deitsch*, "and the ones I know at home wouldn't be calling this number."

"Good points," he said, responding to the smile in her voice. "I called to ask if you might like to come to our house on Sunday, for lunch and a visit."

"This Sunday?"

Was that too soon? Was he rushing her, asking them to come when he'd just seen them not an hour ago? "If you'd like to. You said you wanted to meet some of the folks here, so I ..." Uncharacteristically, his voice faded in proportion to the rise of the dismayed conviction that he'd stepped out of line.

Been too forward.

He'd heard the Amish of Lancaster County called *blue bloods* because of their being the original community from which all the others had spread to establish church districts in other states. But it had never occurred to him until now that they might have customs different from the ones in Kansas or Ohio or Indiana, which was where most of the folks here had come from, bringing their buggies of all different makes and *Ordnungs* of all different levels of plainness.

Maybe calling up a woman on the telephone and asking her and her friends to lunch just wasn't done in Lancaster County.

"Joshua, it's very kind of you to think of us. As a matter of fact, I was just talking to—oh."

"What? Amanda, is something wrong?"

"I—"

He could practically hear the embarrassment burning in her face from here. "Amanda?"

"I'm sorry—I assume—I hope you didn't mean just me. You mean Hannah, too, *ja*? The boys are away on a pack trip."

He nearly smacked his forehead. He'd used *du*, the singular *you*, in his invitation, not the plural. Was that why she hoped he wasn't inviting only her? His insides seemed to sink six inches. Did she mean she would only come as long as she didn't have to come alone? Was she saying she didn't want to be alone with him, even for the ride from the ranch to his home?

"If she would enjoy it, I do mean her, too," he finally said. "My family already knows about ... her troubles in the past, so it won't be awkward for her. With questions, I mean."

"Oh. *The Budget* has quite the readership, doesn't it? I'll go find her and call you back at this number."

"This is our office at the shop. It's the only phone on the place, except the cell phone my sister has in case Mamm needs help." They probably didn't approve of cell phones in Lancaster County, either. Maybe he should have quit while he was ahead.

He said good-bye probably more abruptly than he normally would, because when she called back fifteen minutes later, she sounded more subdued.

But at least she said yes. At eleven o'clock Sunday morning, she would be riding beside him in the family buggy, and he would keep such a close watch on his mouth that even a blue blood would approve.

He hoped.

On Thursday and Friday morning, he was gratified to see her supervising the daily delivery, instead of merely waving from her vantage point up on the hill, where it seemed she liked to watch the sunrise. He'd never caught her in that unguarded moment of worship again, but perhaps that was just as well. Moments like that should be between a person and God, with no witnesses.

He enjoyed talking to her about more than where the sausage was supposed to go in the big fridge, though. Enjoyed hearing about where they'd placed the quilts in the big keeping room up above, and about the hawk she was watching, and about the foreman getting a call to take a four-wheeler up the mountain.

This last was on his mind on Saturday as he worked in the back while Dat manned the store. The bell over the door rang, and he pushed away from the desk. It sounded like the voices of more than one customer, so Dat would need help. Sure enough, two men had come in, both clean cut and wearing brown Carhardtt overalls that carried rusty stains of what appeared to be blood. His own looked like that during hunting season, after harvesting a deer.

With a friendly nod, Dat asked, "Can I help you?"

Joshua didn't recognize them, but that was nothing unusual. Not along one of the major north/south routes through the valley.

"You surely can," the taller and older of them said. His gaze took in the shop with appreciation. "Nice shop you've got here. Just what we're in need of."

The younger put in, "We were coming home the other night and wouldn't you know, a buck bounced out in front of us." He hooked a thumb over his shoulder. "Got him outside. Any chance you could process and package him for us?"

Joshua said, "The other day? You gutted and hung him?"

The older one nodded.

"And it's been less than forty-eight hours?"

Another nod. "Night before last. I tried to swerve, but we were doing highway speed. Nearly lost control of the truck as it was."

"We'll need to see your permit."

The older turned to look at the younger. "Bobby?"

The young man nodded, then patted his pockets. His expression turned to one of alarm. "Of course I have it." But he couldn't find it. "It has to be in the truck. It must have fallen out when I reached for my wallet at the gas station."

Joshua watched with some amusement as they turned out the cab of the truck, with no luck. The older one swore, then apologized to Joshua—as though a few curse words would bother him, considering the number of hunters he dealt with every year. He went outside as the older one got well and truly started on a lecture to the younger, who stood there with sagging shoulders and took it not like a man, but like the boy he'd probably been not all that long ago.

"Dang it, Bobby, you eejit, now we got an eighty-mile trip home and another eighty miles back! You just tell me what shape this animal is going to be in by then, lying in a hot truck all that way. This could have meant good eating, and do you think my disability is going to cover groceries for the family? Huh? Do you?"

"Dad, I said I was—"

"Sorry! Yeah, I know. But sorry isn't going to help put food on the table. Not unless you're about to get your behind into town and get a job."

Joshua judged this might be the moment to step in. "No need to be so hard on him. You can call us with the permit number—and you're right about the state of this animal. He's had a rough enough time. Better yet—how about you tell me which warden signed off on it, and I'll give him a call. Meanwhile, you bring him in to the big fridge and I'll write you up an order, all right?"

The younger one—Bobby—slumped even more, this time in relief. "That's good of you, mister."

"Name's Joshua King, and this is my father, Wilmer."

"Neil Phelps. My boy, Bobby." He shook hands with them, Bobby's as cold as a landed fish, probably because of his brush with his dad's temper.

"I can't remember the warden's name offhand," Bobby's father said, "but when we get home I'll call you. One way or another, you'll have the name or the permit number, whichever we find first."

Once the deer was put into cold storage and the order written up, the elder man asked the price and handed Joshua the cash. "Thank you. We'll have this ready for you on Tuesday."

The man's surprise made his square, all-American face lengthen. "So long? The place we went to in the Sierras had it ready the next day."

Joshua smiled. "It's late to get started this afternoon, and tomorrow is Sunday, when we don't do business. It'll take me most of Monday, since I do it by hand, which brings us to Tuesday morning, when you can pick it up."

The men looked at each other, and Bobby shrugged. "All right, then," Neil conceded. "I guess if we want it done, it gets done here. Westcliffe would probably be closed by the time we got there today, and the same Sunday rule would apply, right?"

"Right," Dat said. "I'll pitch in, and we can make it first thing Tuesday morning. We open at eight."

"Sounds good." Neil swung into the cab of the truck. "See you then."

The truck pulled out, and accelerated away down the road that led out to the highway. Joshua turned back to the shop. "Nice of them not to spray gravel."

"Seemed like nice folks," his father agreed. "I don't think I'll ever get used to the forty-eight hour road kill law here, though. Come on, let's close up. I'm hungry and Grace Ann said something about pie."

As he and his father crossed the scrubby stretch of grass and sagebrush that Mamm optimistically referred to as the lawn, he counted his blessings once again.

And when his father went in to wash up, Joshua leaned against the fence and gazed at the spectacular sight of the mountains to the west lifting their faces to heaven. Sometimes, when the wind blew, he thought he could hear them singing praises to their Creator.

Lieber Gott, I raise my thanks to You, too, for providing for me and my family so richly here in these mountains. In Kansas you gave us signs, and made Your still small voice so audible that we couldn't disregard it. In stepping out on Your promises, we've found ourselves richly blessed.

Be with us tomorrow, Lord. You've brought Amanda into my life, and I want to get to know her better. As a friend. Anything else is in Your hands. If it's Your will, bring her heart close to mine and bless our friendship.

In the name of your blessed Son, amen.

11

How strange it felt to leave the breakfast table and not plunge straight in to work afterward. To know, in fact, that she had hours of leisure time before Joshua King came to collect them.

"What are you going to do with yourself until eleven?" Hannah left the staff dining room with her, climbing the slope back up to the cabin and leaving Teresa to wrangle two of the cowboys into kitchen cleanup duty.

"I'm going to write a letter home. And I'm going to do it from the deck, looking out at our amazing view. I might even draw a picture of it."

"Seriously?" Hannah didn't look as though this sounded very appealing, picture or not. "I'm going for a walk along the creek."

"Take a fishing rod."

"Not me. Smelly, slithery critters are not my cup of java."

So, a few minutes later when Amanda settled at one of the outside tables with a piece of paper and a pen, she saw Hannah wander down into the meadow in the direction of the water. It looked like the livestock foreman, Jim Strever, was out there already, his wiry frame bending to and fro as he cast a fly into the riffle over a gravel bank.

Something about that calm, rhythmic movement reminded her of Dat. He loved to fish, and hardly ever got the opportunity. Englisch Henry had promised to take a lesson or two from him, giving them an excuse to go down to the creek together, but she wondered if he'd ever take time away from Sarah and his pottery studio to do it. And now with the blessing of a baby coming ...

She picked up the pen and thought for a moment, arranging words in her mind. *Deitsch* might be the language spoken on home and farm, but English was the language of letter writing, starting when she'd been a small scholar carefully forming her *a*'s and *b*'s.

Dear Mother and Dad,

We arrived safely on Wednesday nearly two weeks ago, and now it's off Sunday and the first moment I've had to write. I'm sitting on the big deck at the front of the ranch house, looking out over a meadow where Hannah is taking a walk by the creek. Beyond are the foothills, and above them, the mountains leap into the sky. I thought the hills in Whinburg Township were big, but Oak Hill is smaller than even one of these foothills.

Quickly, she sketched the scene she had just described. She wasn't much of an artist, and art lessons were not something the Amish indulged in, but the *gut Gott* had given her the ability to make a few lines here and there that told a story. She didn't do it a lot, only in letters to her family and her buddy bunch. Some things—like this view, and baby chicks, and the first roses of June—just begged for a little sketch.

It's wonderful country out here. There have been some trials (nothing to worry over, just our Englisch roommates) but there have been many more good moments.

Today Hannah and I have been invited to the home of Joshua King, who is the butcher who supplies Lost Creek Ranch with our breakfast sausage and many other things. He seems a very kind man. He will come in the buggy at eleven to pick us up, but since it's only eight now, I have a nice couple of hours to myself.

The boys are away on a pack trip with four fishermen. I hope they catch lots of fish! You can't buy fresh-caught trout from people outside a retail market (it's against the law) but they can give it to you. Some of the guests here catch their own breakfast and Teresa Rodriguez cooks it for them. Dad, I hope you can get down to Willow Creek with your rod and reel sometime—there is nothing like fresh trout.

Which reminds me—I've been promoted from housekeeping to the kitchen, as of a week ago. I think it has less to do with my skill with a skillet than it does with the prep cook forgetting to come to work and being fired. I'm looking forward to learning some of the dishes Teresa makes. They're pretty fancy—yesterday we wrapped a roast in pastry, baked it, and called it Beef Wellington. All that for only one couple! At least they enjoyed it, and the cowboys will get beef sandwiches with tomato, lettuce, and horseradish for their lunch today. The food the guests have is so fancy that some dishes are almost uneaten and if they aren't touched, the staff gets them for their next meal. I'm not sure why Mrs. Gunderson—she's the owner's wife—insists on food that just goes to waste, but it's not my place to ask questions like that.

I miss you, and Sarah and Henry and Caleb, too. When I get my first paycheck I'll send half of it along. I saw one bank in Amistad, so I guess that's the one I'll be using.

With much love,

Amanda

Teresa had told them all where the stamps and envelopes were during their tour on the first day. The Gundersons, the guests, and the staff all put their letters and bills in a bowl by the front door, and whoever was going past the mailbox at the highway junction took down whatever was in it every day.

Once her letter was addressed and stamped, Amanda had nothing to do with herself for two hours yet. She wandered back to the cabin. Farther up the slope, the cleaning cart stood outside the honeymooners' cabin, which meant Bonita and Jenny would be busy and not likely to intrude on her.

The cabin they shared was a mess—which was strange considering there were professionals in residence who could make a room look as welcoming as it was pristine in under fifteen minutes.

It was a sin to work on Sunday, but she made her own bed before church when she was at home, didn't she?

If you were were at home, you wouldn't be wandering around at loose ends like this.

There would be family bible study in the sitting room, with Dat's wonderful voice lifted up in a form of worship, and everyone taking turns reading the verses. There would be quiet time with Caleb, maybe, to read the *Martyrs' Mirror* together, or a visit with Mamm and Sarah while they prepared lunch. And after lunch, they would hitch up the horse and visit any one of their neighbors or the Yoder relatives in the district, and she would go to singing later and catch a ride home with the Whinburg *Youngie* who didn't happen to be courting.

Amanda swallowed a pang of homesickness, and got busy making her bed. When that was done, she made Hannah's, too, and then—in for a penny, in for a pound—made up the upper bunks as well. She didn't want to interfere with the *Englisch* girls' things by picking up their clothes and hanging them in the stuffed closets, but she did that for Hannah's few items. Better not clean the bathroom, though. That really did fall into the category of work, and could wait until a weekday. But she did go out along the path into the woods and collect a few stems of sagebrush and some anemones. These went into a Mason jar, which she put on the counter next to the coffee maker they never used. Flowers always made a place look nicer.

And now she had an hour and fifteen minutes left.

This was no way to spend a Sunday morning, and there were a whole procession of them marching down the pages of the calendar that hung over the counter. Next time, maybe she'd ask one of the Amish families here if she and Simon and maybe even Hannah could join them earlier. She missed the fellowship, the reading of the Bible, the quiet conversation. Even reading the familiar stories of the sacrifices of the faithful during the difficult times in the old country was better than this feeling of idleness. This void that she couldn't fill on her own.

Was there even a Bible in the big house? And would they mind if she read it?

There was a reading room, she remembered, though she hadn't been in it since the tour they'd been given the first day. Amanda slipped into the big house through the staff entrance, and ran up the stairs with the sound of pots and pans clattering behind her. Bathroom, bar, great room, dining room ... aha, here it was.

They might call it the reading room, but did people really come to a dude ranch to read? Magazines with titles like *Western Art* and *Ranching Life* and *Field and Stream* lay on the big low table between comfortable sofas upholstered in a fabric with a design of blowsy Victorian roses. The pattern softened the angular squares and triangles of the woven wool rugs like the ones they had in the guest rooms. Around the walls were big, dark bookcases holding a collection of books interspersed with pieces of art.

Amanda finally found a Bible in the drawer of the table, of all places. With a feeling of relief, she kicked off her shoes, curled up in the corner of the sofa, and opened it to the book of Psalms. She didn't dare take it over to the cabin without permission, but surely they wouldn't mind if she stayed quietly in the reading room doing what the room was meant for?

She turned to her favorite verses in Psalm 139 the way some folks nibble at dessert before the meal is served.

> If I take the wings of the morning, and dwell in
> the uttermost parts of the sea;
> Even there shall thy hand lead me, and thy right
> hand shall hold me.

What unutterable joy to know that! No matter how small she felt in the world, no matter how huge and unfamiliar the landscape, here was God's promise—his mighty hand would still be around her. She would never be alone. And what beautiful words those were: *the wings of the morning*. They always made her think of the wings of the doves at home, on the occasions she came out of the house suddenly and startled them. They would fly up into the treetops, the light gilding their feathers, and they would coo at her, even their scolding gentle and soothing.

"Well, look what I found."

The man's voice startled her so much that if she had been a dove, she would have been startled right up onto one of the open cross-beams in the ceiling. Amanda gaped at big, bluff, cowboy-booted Mr. Gunderson as she tried to disentangle her stocking feet from her skirts so she could stand.

"Relax, young lady. No need. It's just me."

Awkwardly, Amanda straightened up and put her feet on the floor, her knees together modestly, the Bible in her lap.

"What's that you're reading?" Mr. Gunderson flung himself on the opposite sofa, picked up a magazine, and tossed it back on the low table again. "Is that my mother's Bible?"

Oh dear. She was in trouble now. "Yes," she whispered.

"Haven't seen anyone reading that since she died. Where'd you find it?"

"In the drawer." She nodded toward the table and gathered her courage. "Would it be all right if I took it with me? I'm in staff cabin number four. Not for good—just for—while I'm here."

"Sure." He waved at it as though it were insubstantial and would waft away on the breeze at his command. "You can take anything you want out of this room. That's what it's for. It all comes back eventually."

Probably when housekeeping turned out the rooms after every departure.

"Thank you."

"How are you liking Lost Creek so far?"

"I do like it," she said shyly, her heart rate finally slowing to a normal pace. "I wrote to my parents out on the deck earlier, so I could describe the view for them."

He smiled with satisfaction. "That's a million-dollar view, all right. Literally. When I saw it, I knew just where I was going to build the house. Everything else falls into place once you get the house oriented right, you know what I mean?"

"Was there a farm here before?" Down in the meadow

there were a couple of outbuildings of a different era from the main barn and stables.

He nodded, one up-and-down movement of his chin. "The couple left it to their grandkids, who had never been here. The boy was my business development manager in California. He mentioned it one day, and I came out to have a look. The rest is history."

"And you live here?"

"Here and California. Depends on the season and my wife and what's on sale at Saks." He laughed, and Amanda smiled, too, to be polite. "I like spring and fall. When the grass greens up and the deer start dropping their fawns, it's God's country."

Amanda resisted the urge to remind him that the whole world belonged to God. But that wasn't her place to say.

His gaze moved from her prayer covering to her black cape and apron, which she had neatly pinned for Sunday, her black Sunday dress, and down to the black Oxfords that lay where she'd toed them off on the rug. "So, Amish, are you?"

"Yes. From Whinburg Township in Lancaster County."

"Good folks, the Amish around here. Good for tourism."

So she was all too aware. "We're used to it in Lancaster County. After that movie came out, my father says, the tourists came like grasshoppers." She stopped. It had been what Dat had said, but that might not be the most complimentary thing to pass on to an *Englisch* person.

"What movie? You mean *Witness*?"

She nodded. "It was filmed near where we live. I don't know. That was before I was born."

He made a face. "I went to see it in the theater with my second wife. It doesn't seem very long ago." Thick fingers scrubbed at his face, making a scratching sound. "Good gravy, that makes me feel old."

Maybe she should just stop talking. Or change the subject.

"Has the sheriff had any news about the poaching?" she asked, and then wished she hadn't. He would think she was insufferably nosy about something that wasn't even her business.

But somehow it was the right thing to say. He brightened and leaned forward, clasping his hands between his knees. "In fact, there have been some developments. Another deer was shot a few days ago, close to the trail where the pack trips go up to the lake, and they were close enough to find it and put it out of its misery."

This didn't seem like good news to Amanda. In fact, it was awful.

"One of your friends tracked it back to the shooting site, hoping that from there he'd be able to see where the shot might have come from."

"One of my friends? You mean Ben? Or Samuel?"

"Samuel, that was it."

"I didn't know Samuel knew how to track animals."

"You Amish, you live close to the land, don't you? Isn't that what it's all about?"

"We farm, yes, but there's not a lot of wild animals in Whinburg Township. Maybe a few deer, mostly on deer farms."

"Deer farms, hey? I guess that's like our friends over across the highway with the buffalo ranch."

Amanda had never seen a buffalo, and never planned to. Her interest right now was in what was going on up in the mountains. "They're not in any danger, are they? From the poachers?"

"That's up for debate."

"What do you mean?" A cold feeling hovered near her stomach, waiting for a chance to settle.

His blue eyes, that had been so genial a moment before, seemed to harden. He certainly shared that in common with his third wife. "I hate to say this, but a couple of your boys were unaccounted for during the time of the shooting."

"I don't understand." She found herself hugging her elbows as though she were cold, something she hadn't done since she'd been Jesse Riehl's special friend and hadn't told her parents.

"I don't either, though I mean to when they all come back tomorrow. All I know is the facts. The other two boys weren't in the tent—a deer was shot—they turned up after all the excitement was over."

"Mr. Gunderson, I don't believe that Simon and Ben would have anything to do with—"

"Maybe, maybe not. Probably coincidence that all this started around the time you all arrived—lot of people coming through the valley at this time of year. I'd hate to think that any employee of Lost Creek Ranch would even think about harming an animal out of season—to say nothing of the damage it could do to our reputation. One of those boys is a relative of yours, isn't he?"

She swallowed. "Simon. He's my oldest brother's son."

The eyes turned positively arctic. "Simon. I remember him. Back again." Then he blinked, and seemed to return from some faraway, cold place. A smile restored the warmth to his face, as though he'd remembered she worked for him. "You'll keep this between us, won't you, ah—"

"Amanda. Amanda Yoder."

"Right. No running and telling all this to your friends before I've had a chance to get to the bottom of it, you hear?"

"No, Mr. Gunderson."

"Good. All right, then." He slapped his knees and got up. "Have a nice day."

His big body seemed to push the air ahead of it—she could feel it move as he left. It felt cold on her cheeks. Or maybe it was she who was chilled, the blood drained out of her face.

She shoved her feet into her shoes and fled the big house, carrying the old-fashioned, heavy Bible in her crossed arms as though it could warm her up ... or shield her from something.

But what that was, she couldn't have said.

12

By the time Amanda heard Joshua King's horse clip-clopping up the hill and the grinding sound of the wheels on the gravel, she was such a bundle of nerves she could hardly speak. Thank goodness Hannah was with her —if she had to sit all alone next to a man she didn't know well for the three miles into town and try to think of ways to make conversation, she'd probably just burst into tears. Sitting on a park bench surrounded by children was one thing. But the buggy was much more intimate. People couldn't see you, though you could see them. That was why some churches didn't allow their young couples to go courting in closed buggies.

Jesse Riehl hadn't been much of a talker, either, which meant she hadn't had much practice in the art of conversing with a man who wasn't family. And the one buggy ride she'd had with Sarah's suitor last summer ... well, mostly she had blocked that out of her mind. With Jesse, the outings in his car during their brief few weeks together had been silent, more about sharing the rebellion than sharing each other's thoughts.

And for most of it, no one had even known they were seeing each other.

"Guder mariye." Joshua waved as he rounded the corner into the courtyard behind the big house. "I'm not late, am I?" He checked his watch on its leather strap—the *Ordnung* at home didn't allow metal watch straps either, for men or women. Too much like jewelry.

"Not at all," Amanda managed. "We brought a jar of jam for your mother."

"Teresa's strawberry?" Joshua looked so hopeful that Amanda could tell it must be one of his favorites, too. "You'd better give it straight to her when we get home, then." He indicated they should climb into the family buggy. "If I get my hands on it, she might never see it."

Hannah, that rascal, beat Amanda through the sliding door of the buggy and claimed the second bench, which left Amanda sliding onto the front seat next to Joshua. Ooh, wouldn't she have words with her as soon as they were alone! She clutched her canvas carry bag with the Lost Creek logo on it. It only held her purse and the jam, but at least hanging onto it gave her something to do with her right hand while the left gripped the bench. She kept a good three inches between herself and Joshua, though it meant she was a bit crowded against the door. That was all right. The last thing she wanted was for him to think she was forward—or worse, inconsiderate. A man needed room to manage the reins, the brake, and the signals.

He backed the buggy around and in a moment they were off down the hill. "I hope you don't mind my saying that I'm glad the two of you could come today. Mamm loves company, though she isn't able to cook and serve as much as she used to."

"What happened to her?" Hannah leaned between them. "Is she an invalid?"

"*Neh,* she slipped two discs in her back several years ago, and finds it hard to move about without pain. But she's as cheerful as anyone can be in that situation, and Grace Ann is good in the kitchen. You'll see." He glanced over his shoulder. "Not to be nosy, but you won't find anyone asking questions about your family or your experiences in the past, Hannah. I hope you'll feel comfortable with us."

"I—my—" Hannah stopped herself. "How would anyone know that my life is any more or less weird than anybody else's?"

"There was a letter in *The Budget*, the Amish newspaper," Amanda said quietly. "It was a good letter, saying how thankful the writer was that you had been returned to your family. But it—the paper—goes to nearly every Amish community there is. If Joshua recognized your name, others will, too."

"Seriously." Hannah sat back. "Must have been someone in Willow Creek, huh? My fifteen minutes of fame in an Amish newspaper. Who knew?"

"I'm glad you can laugh about it," Joshua said.

"What else can I do? Cry?"

"I hope not. None of the adults will press you, but I can't speak for my little sisters. Anything they hear flows right through them like water through a sieve."

"I don't mind little kids. With twin brothers—seven-year-olds—I know all about sieves."

Joshua pulled on the brake as they rounded the curve past the horse barn to descend the steeper part of the hill. Amanda supposed that except in the flattest country, buggy brakes were the norm. You wouldn't want the buggy pushing on the backside of the horse and even knocking it off its feet on the way down. Joshua had to concentrate, gauging speed versus drag, until the road leveled out and took them across the end of the meadow where Lost Creek ran.

"Will you have other company today, Joshua?" Amanda ventured when he straightened and flapped the reins across the horse's back.

"Just you." He smiled at the beautiful view through the storm front. "We're quite the crowd all by ourselves, *ja?* Wouldn't want to scare you with any more names to remember. Along with our family, my uncles are coming—Dat's brothers. His father married twice, so his half brothers are quite a lot younger than he is. More my age."

"A little like Simon and me," she said. "People laugh at my becoming his *Aendi* at three years old, but his father and my next oldest brother were a lot older than me. Joshua, did Simon—" She stopped.

Oh, why had she said that? The question just seemed to bubble up out of nowhere and now she had to squash it back down again.

"Ja? Was ischt?"

"It's nothing. Never mind. Oh look, is that an antelope?"

She pointed, and he dutifully looked. "That's a rock. Antelopes move a lot faster. Come. You can ask me anything. What were you about to say?"

She released her grip on the bench and knotted her fingers together on her bag. "It's disloyal. I shouldn't have said anything."

"Did Simon what?" he persisted, so gently and kindly that she sighed and resigned herself to coming out with it.

"Did Simon—did he behave all right when he was here last year?"

Behind her, Hannah made a sound somewhere between a snort and a cough.

"I hardly know." Joshua had to have heard her, but he politely ignored it and concentrated instead on giving Amanda an answer. "We didn't see much of him, but it wasn't for lack of invitations. But as you know, there were a lot of pack trips and only four wranglers then, so he and Joe were gone a lot. I think I only saw them in church once all summer, and that was before Simon got hurt. Why do you ask?"

"It's odd, that's all. People here seem to ... change ... when they talk about him. And this morning, Mr. Gunderson—when he found out I was Simon's aunt, he said something like, 'Oh, he's back again.' And it didn't sound like he thought it was very good news."

"Maybe we should ask Simon when the fishermen come back," Hannah suggested. "Sounds like he might have been doing a little *Rumspringing* after his baptism as well as before."

"Some of the young men do," Amanda said a little stiffly. "It doesn't mean they're bad. And Simon is a character."

At home, a *character* was someone who didn't quite fit the mold—someone like Ruth Lehman, the *Dokterfraa* in Whinburg who was so blunt and outspoken, or like Englisch Henry next door, who had been a fence jumper and then had repented and come back to God twenty years later.

"You mean he's a flirt, and self-absorbed, and too good-looking for his own good," Hannah said. "Not that I don't like him—who can help it? But I feel sorry for his future wife. She's going to have her hands full."

Since Amanda had thought this more than once, she couldn't very well be irritated with Hannah for saying it out loud. But did it have to be in front of Joshua King? What would he think of her family and how they brought up their children?

When he glanced at her, she forced herself to release her lower lip from between her teeth. "How far is it to your house?"

"Not far—just a couple of miles." He fell right in with the change of subject. "We're just within sight of the main highway, or the shop is, at least. We wanted to make it as easy as possible for hunters and our regular customers to find it, so we planted a hedge of pines along the road, both for a windbreak and to give people a landmark when they ask for directions."

That was good thinking. "My neighbor Englisch Henry is a potter. He built his shop close to the road, too, though my sister-in-law—Simon's mother—says it's so she won't be tempted to plant a bigger garden. She's a *Dokterfraa*, you see, and plants and herbs are her business."

"I remember the boys talking about the box she sent to Simon so that Joe could doctor him."

So much for changing the subject.

"I wouldn't spend too much time worrying about your nephew," Joshua went on. "He's of age, and responsible for himself."

Amanda thought of Sarah's eyes when she'd asked her to come along on this trip and look out for him. What had she expected her to do? Behave like his mother? Or go around afterward cleaning up his messes and soothing people's feelings? What kind of man would cause a woman to do that without being convicted about his own behavior?

Not that Simon was causing anything. He was simply being himself. Though one's self was enough of a problem for any mere human to handle. A person needed God's help.

"You're right," was all she said, and the talk—thankfully—turned to other things for the last mile.

The first thing Amanda noticed about the King place was how spacious and well kept it was. The shop had wood siding and a corrugated red roof, which made it look both rustic and cheerful. The sign out front read KING CUTS AND MEATS, and in the window a smaller sign said NO SUNDAY SALES. Some distance behind it, the house was spreading and generous, with two storeys and big windows so people could appreciate the mountains. The garden had been staked and mulched for planting, but was otherwise bare. At home Mamm would have lettuce already, and radishes and green onions, while she planted the corn and tomatoes and potato sets. But Mariah Gingerich had said it could snow here in May, so clearly the growing season was a lot shorter.

The little girls spilled out of the kitchen door closest to the garden and the yard that lay in the L between the house and the barn, which also had wood siding and a corrugated roof.

"Amanda! Hannah! Come see the kittens!"

Hannah laughed in delight. "It's things like this that make me miss the twins." Then, in halting *Deitsch*, she said, "Wait, *Maedeln*, we have to say hello to your Mamm and Dat first." Before the little ones became scholars at the age of six, they didn't learn much English. Hannah was learning *Deitsch* from her little brothers. That would make them no end of happy—to be able to teach someone older what they knew, instead of the other way around.

"There is that smile I've been waiting for," Joshua said as he led the horse away.

Which only made her blush scarlet and turn so that he couldn't see it.

Wisely, he said no more, and when he came out of the

barn, his brothers had joined them. "Come and meet the rest of the family."

The inside of the house was just as spacious and welcoming as the outside. A young woman about Amanda's age came forward, smiling, to greet them. "I'm Grace Ann. I'm so happy you could come." She ignored the color still in Amanda's face, but then again, her skin was so fair and delicate looking that she probably had the same problem—blushing every time she spoke up. Her nut-brown hair under her pleated, bucket-shaped *Kapp* had the same lift and curl in the front that Joshua's did.

"I am happy to be here," Amanda said shyly. "Thank you so much for including us in your Sunday." She turned to the older woman struggling out of the recliner, and since she was closest, bent to help her up.

"*Denki*, Amanda. I'm Savilla, and this is Joshua's father, Wilmer." The uncles came in from the barn, then, and Amanda felt a little overwhelmed at so many genial young men in one room. She could hardly keep them straight—their names were Simeon, Noah, and Andrew, but already she'd lost track of which was which. One fact she did retain, though ... they'd come to work in the valley last summer and had returned just this month with the intention of staying for good.

"Amanda, Hannah, if you wouldn't mind helping me, lunch is ready to go on the table," Grace Ann said.

Which was a perfect opportunity to present the little jar of jam to Savilla, who took it with delight. "How very kind you are! You just go ahead and put this on the table and we'll see how long it lasts once Joshua and the boys get hold of it."

The two women had prepared a big meal—one that Amanda could only hope was their usual Sunday dinner and hadn't been made in her and Hannah's honor. The beef roast was so big it was all Grace Ann could do to carry it in for her father to carve. To go with it were mashed potatoes and gravy, fresh bread, creamed corn, and three kinds of salad—one with dressing so good it had to be homemade.

When all the food had been brought out and Grace Ann and Savilla had taken their seats, heads bowed all around the table. Little Mary Liza pressed her hands to her face as everyone said a silent grace. A long breath and an Amen from Wilmer was the signal for each one to dish up what lay in front of them and pass it along.

"Amanda, you can't keep that jam from me forever," Joshua teased. "I'll have it now, *bidde*."

Smiling, she handed it across the table. "I'll have to tell Teresa how much you like it. She'll be pleased."

"I don't think it's the hand that made it he likes," one of the uncles said to no one in particular, farther down.

"I think it's the hand that gave it," the one beside him agreed.

"Now, you boys just be quiet," Savilla chided from her place at her husband's right hand. "You don't want to frighten her off the moment she gets here, do you? Grace Ann and I appreciate other women around the place once in a while, and we want them to come back." Her kind gaze took in Hannah, too. "We understand you've only been at the ranch a few weeks. Do you like it so far?"

"Almost two weeks. And it's one of the most beautiful places I've ever seen," Hannah said with sincerity. "For the most part, the people are nice. I haven't talked to more than a few, though."

"Hannah is in housekeeping," Amanda said. "I was, too, but now I'm in the kitchen."

"You like it?" Grace Ann asked, passing her the three-bean salad.

"I do. I've learned a lot that I'll probably never use again when I go home—the food they serve there isn't like anything I've ever had before." She smiled at the thought of it. "I can't really see Mamm wrapping store-bought pastry around a Beef Wellington, or me making strawberry and ricotta crepes while Dat does the milking."

"Sounds like a dessert, not breakfast," Joshua agreed. "But they do like their meat up there, for which we're thankful."

"The staff breakfasts are hearty, at least," she said. "And your sausage is delicious. One day I would love the recipe."

"It's the herbs and spices that go into the mix," Wilmer said, nodding. "We've learned a thing or two about chile in the last couple of years, and now Grace Ann and her sisters have a chile garden. The plants really seem to like the soil here, though the season is pretty short."

"What about you, Hannah?" Savilla asked. "Do you like your work?"

"It's just like being at home—making beds, cleaning bathrooms, sweeping. Except the people at home are easier to get along with."

"What do you mean?" Grace Ann said. "I've never been up to the ranch, but Joshua says the folks he's met are nice."

"Joshua isn't cleaning rooms with the Queen Bee and her princess." She glanced at Amanda. "I miss you. When the real busy season gets here, I'm not sure how I'm going to handle it."

"They'll probably hire more staff," Amanda said. "At least, I hope so. You three will have a hard time when all the rooms are filled. I'm sorry. I know it's difficult."

Hannah snorted. "Don't be sorry. It's not your fault. I'm

just whining." She helped herself to another slice of bread. "So, Noah—you and your brothers have moved up here for good? What are you going to do?"

Noah swallowed a huge bite of roast and horseradish with a gulp, making his eyes water. His brother—Simeon? the oldest, anyway—stepped in to reply while he recovered. "Since the butcher trade seems to be pretty much monopolized by a certain branch of the family—" He grinned at his relatives. "—and the house and barn on our place are finished, we figured we'd hire ourselves out as carpenters and see if it turns into something permanent."

"I'd think you could make carpentry permanent," Amanda said. "If more people move into the valley, they're going to need homes, *ja*?"

"True, but that still leaves us with idle hands and appetites no smaller in the winter months." Noah wiped his eyes. "Good horseradish, Savilla. Since renovations of *Englisch* houses for our folk often involve mechanical conversions, we were thinking that might be worth getting into. It's work that can be done by one or more of us all year round."

Wilmer nodded. "Sounds wise. Though many will have come with their washing machines and corn augurs already converted."

"Those break down eventually, and it seems to me it would be a lot cheaper to get a washing machine in Monte Vista and convert it than to bring it or even order it all the way from the nearest big city."

"There's going to be a need for a buggy maker soon," Savilla put in, passing the gravy down to Andrew. "People bring their buggies from their home districts, and they last a long time, but eventually the bishops here will settle on a style that's right for these parts, and someone will need to build them."

"Let's hope they don't settle on yellow," Noah said into his food.

"Not too much danger of that," Andrew told him as they chuckled. "Folks hereabouts have all pretty much brought in black—whoever makes that decision will just have to figure out what kind of body and interior is best."

"And steel versus wood wheels, and how many reflectors go on the back," Simeon added. "There are lots of decisions that go into making a buggy, but it's not likely we'll be called upon to make them."

"Best stick to butchering and carpentry," Wilmer agreed, "and machinery conversions if you decide to go that way."

"I hope you're going to put in that garden, Noah," Grace Ann said. "We could use some more varieties of chiles for our sauce, and I'd like to try my hand at drying them, crushing them, and putting them in sprinkle jars. Bill Wyland at the Plow and Pitcher has already told me he'd stock it for the tables instead of the commercial stuff, for people to sprinkle on their pizza. But our garden doesn't grow enough for the amount he'd want."

"Our Noah might be young," Savilla said to Amanda, "but he has the kind of mind that's always casting about for work."

Amanda nodded. "My nephew Caleb is like that, too—just turned fifteen and already quite the businessman."

"That would be Simon's brother?" Joshua asked.

"Six years younger. And now I have a little niece or nephew on the way with an even bigger gap between. Still, Caleb can't wait to be the big brother. He's already pushing Simon to get married and find a home of his own so that he can have nieces and nephews."

"I'll buy a ticket to see that," Hannah muttered, but Joshua heard it and laughed.

"Here we are, talking about Simon again, and him not around to defend himself. Say, Grace Ann, did I hear a rumor of apple and rhubarb pie?"

"You did, and I'll dish it up just as soon as we get this table cleared."

"That was a wonderful meal," Amanda said to Savilla. "We don't know if we'll be able to return the favor, but I hope you'll have us again."

Savilla's glance at Joshua was so quick that Amanda might have missed it if she hadn't been looking right at her. "Oh, I'm sure we will."

Which made the color burn into Amanda's face. She pushed back her chair and picked up the nearest plates. "We'll get these washed in a jiffy, won't we, Hannah?"

"You don't need to—" But Amanda was already at the sink, running water and soap into it. Anyone could wash dishes, and she wasn't about to sit there like a queen and expect Grace Ann to wait on her after all the work she'd done.

But it wasn't Hannah who joined her with the dishtowel. It was Joshua. Surprise made her jaw sag for a moment, and the ability to speak completely deserted her.

"Hannah doesn't know where the dishes go, and Grace Ann has her hands full. I'll pitch in." He smiled, and she was disarmed again by the kindness in his brown eyes. "You don't mind a man in the kitchen, do you?"

Not if it's this one. "It's yours," she managed. "Or your mother's."

"And I don't mind a bit," Savilla called from the table, where she was stacking plates from her chair. "We'll have coffee and dessert in the sitting room once you two have finished."

Embarrassed all over again at the *you two*, Amanda got busy with the dishcloth and scrubber.

Joshua was no stranger to the dishes, she soon discovered. "When I was younger, Mamm made Grace Ann and me do them. I always liked making cleanliness out of chaos. No matter how topsy-turvy the kitchen was when we started, by the time we were done, it was spotless and neat."

"I like that, too," she told the suds in the sink. "Cleanliness out of chaos. It's a little like what the *gut Gott* does for us when he takes us in hand, isn't it?"

He laughed again, that musical, unforced laugh that she was coming to like more and more. "For sure he does. Though some start out a little more chaotic than others. My sister, now." He bumped shoulders with her as she deposited a stack of dirty plates next to him. "She's as smooth and orderly as a spool of thread."

Grace Ann rolled her eyes. "A lot you know. *Der Herr* has as much work to do in my little garden as he does in anyone's."

"A little too much chile growing there?" Noah teased from the doorway as he followed his brothers into the sitting room.

Grace Ann had to laugh. "Maybe there is, at that. It didn't stop me from starting baptism classes this spring, though."

"You're going to join church in the fall?" Amanda asked her.

"The time seems right. My buddy bunch back in Kansas have all made the decision, and I want to as well."

"You're still in contact with them? That's wonderful."

Grace Ann pushed a strand of hair out of her face with the back of her wet hand. "We came here when I was sixteen. I'm twenty-one now. It was hard, at first, to leave everyone when we were just all able to go to singing together, and we had so many plans. Then to have to make new friends ..."

"You have friends here," Joshua said, sounding puzzled. "You girls always have your heads together."

"We do now, but it's not the same as growing up with people, and knowing their pasts as well as your own, and being buddies together."

"I suppose it's different for men," Amanda said thoughtfully. "Though in Whinburg Township many of them join the gang they like, usually if all their friends do. Are there many young men here?"

"Oh, that there were." Grace Ann brought the serving bowls to the counter and scooped the leftovers into plastic containers. "I can't tell you the joy there was in Amistad when my uncles came to town."

"Surely there must be more single men than just you four." Amanda scrubbed the bowls as Grace Ann handed them to her. "In a district this size? Joshua, didn't you tell me there were a couple dozen *Youngie*?"

"There are—but a lot of them are teenagers yet," Joshua said. "Not so many in their twenties or ancient like me. I suppose most men find a woman who doesn't mind starting off her marriage with an adventure, and they bring her to Colorado with that understanding. Land is easier to get here, that's for sure, if you're a newlywed just starting out."

"There are lots of girls who are older," his sister reminded him. "You're just determined to be a ancient bachelor. Either that, or you like them chasing you."

Joshua made a face. "What man wants a woman who chases him?"

"I'd be happy with one," Noah called from the sitting room.

"You would not," came Savilla's voice. "Besides, everyone knows that a man chases a woman until she catches him."

"Not if you're Sim," Andrew said dryly. "He just works all the time and they give up and go away."

"Somebody has to work," Simeon protested. "Otherwise, you'd starve."

By this time Amanda was laughing and Grace Ann was rolling her eyes. "The problem with a girl marrying one is that she'd get all three," she murmured to Amanda as she passed on the way to the fridge.

All the same, it would be fun to have this kind of humor in the house, this teasing and back-and-forth among people her own age. Well, Simeon and Joshua were older than she was. Noah and Andrew were closer, somewhere between her twenty-four and Grace Ann's age.

Time flew when you were having fun—or a good conversation. Amanda finished up the dishes and wiped down the counters, and then while Grace Ann cut the pie, she scooped the ice cream on top. By some mysterious call of sweets, Hannah and the girls came down from upstairs just in time to carry the plates in to Savilla and the men in the sitting room. Amanda brought Grace Ann's plate of pie with her own while the latter carried the tray of coffee mugs, cream, and sugar.

She couldn't remember when she'd enjoyed a piece of pie so much. Or maybe it was less the pie than the people. She loved being at home, and her parents were good company, but it wasn't like this, with jokes flying back and forth and Hannah teasing Noah as though she'd known him half her life. Amanda even coaxed a smile out of serious Simeon, who seemed to bear the burden of responsibility not only for his brothers, but also for the family in general, though goodness knew Wilmer and Joshua were perfectly good providers who knew their own capabilities and filled a respectable place in the community.

When Grace Ann brought up the chile garden to Noah again, more seriously this time, Amanda had to admit she'd never seen such a thing.

Joshua got up and held out his hand for her empty plate, scraped clean of every tasty morsel. "Come on. Let's talk a walk and I'll show you."

Instead of letting him have her plate, she swiped his. "I think I should go with Grace Ann, don't you? She planted them."

"No, you two go," Grace Ann said with airy unconcern, shushing Rachel, who had squeaked with the sudden realization of what *going for a walk* might mean.

Amanda felt like squeaking out a protest, too, with *you two* coming up twice in one afternoon. "But the dessert dishes—"

"Rachel and I will do them. Go on." Grace Ann shooed her toward the door. "It's Sunday. We didn't invite you here just to make you work for your dinner."

And with a rising babble of voices and laughter that sounded all too knowing for Amanda's peace of mind, she found herself outside on the wide, breezy deck with Joshua. She hardly knew where to look. Had he really risked the teasing of his family to take a walk with her? What did that mean? Especially when she now knew that more than one young woman had set her cap at him without success. Was he just trying to see if she'd do the same?

When it came to talking to and being alone with a man, Amanda didn't even possess that kind of cap, much less know how to set it.

She'd always been so shy that talking to someone she didn't know was difficult. And with her skin and plump figure, she didn't have boys offering her rides home from singing the way some of the other girls did. Girls like Rosanne Kanagy and Priscilla Mast seemed to have young men around them constantly, and Amanda had never been able to figure out how they did it. It had always seemed insurmountably difficult to her.

But there was no getting out of it now. Joshua was already leading the way along the verandah and down its three stairs to the sunny backyard.

"Mamm and Grace Ann have the kitchen garden, of course," Joshua said, indicating a stretch of earth about thirty by forty feet that already had strings set out in rows, and teepees for the peas and beans that would soon have curling tendrils climbing along their strings toward the sun. "The chile garden is over here. It's already up."

Both gardens were neatly fenced off. "The fence is quite high," she said hesitantly. "Do you have a problem with animals getting in?"

"*Ja.* A deer can jump a five-foot fence without even thinking. Dat and I considered a double fence, but we figured getting the culprit out from between them would be more trouble than simply building it three feet higher."

Amanda pictured it and had to admit they were probably right.

"There's an awful deer problem in Westcliffe," he went on. "When I first drove down there, I thought there must have been a big sale on lawn ornaments, since everyone had them. Until they moved."

"So many!"

"They do special hunts now. And a lot of animals are brought to Dat and me that people have hit with their cars. I have a job like that to do tomorrow, in fact."

"Do the deer like the chile plants?"

"They sure do, if they can get to them. See all those nice, tender leaves? Even Mamm's chickens will eat them if the girls forget to close the gate when they're weeding."

"The leaves aren't hot, then."

"No, but they must be pretty tasty." He grinned. "I like a bit of heat, myself. This idea of Grace Ann's to dry the chiles for sprinkle is a good one. I just hope no one in the district beats her to it. There is already one other lady who makes cooked salsa."

An idea of her own whisked across Amanda's brain. "I'm going to be here all summer. I wonder if the Gundersons would mind if I planted chiles somewhere on the ranch? I could add those to the number she would need."

"At that kind of scale, we're talking bushels of them, so you'd need a pretty big fenced garden up there. I doubt that would fly. Grace Ann will appreciate the kind thought, though." He smiled down at her, which warmed the edges of her disappointment and made it twist away into vapor. "My uncles' place would be just the thing—they have a nice south-facing hill, and of course putting up a drying shed would be nothing for those three. Grace Ann will get her way, just you wait."

"I hope it's soon. It would be a shame to waste these sunny days."

"When she was little, she could wrap Sim around her finger. I think you'll find a garden going in pretty shortly."

Amanda smiled, a little wistfully. What was that like—being able to wrap a man around your finger? "Does your sister have a special friend here?"

"Well, we're not supposed to know about any of that, but she has had a ride home a time or two with one and then another. But if she has a preference, she hasn't shared it with her big brother. Mamm might know. They're pretty close." He paused. "Do you miss your family? I know you haven't been out here long, but homesickness doesn't have an incubation period."

Now her smile held nothing but appreciation for a good observation. "I did feel it for a little while when I wrote home this morning. I want to share all this with my family, but words and pictures just don't do it justice." She indicated the wide valley with a sweep of her arm, rising to include the mountains beyond, their blue and snowy heights a deeper shade than the sky and clouds.

"Pictures? Do you have a camera?"

"No, no. Just little drawings."

One eyebrow rose. "An artist?"

This time she laughed. "Far from it. A bit of earth and sky, or a flower, or a silly face is about all I can manage."

"I'd like to see a drawing sometime."

"If I ever write you a letter, I'll put one in," she said. And then wished she could drag the words back and stuff them where they'd never be heard. But it was too late. They were already free, and sinking into his mind like a flock of starlings landing in a cherry tree.

Because only a couple who were serious and living at a distance from one another would write letters. In fact, at home, saying of a girl that she was writing to someone was the last stop before an engagement was announced.

Oh, how forward he would think her! She'd just practically asked him to be her own special friend. Could the earth just open up and swallow her now?

"I'd count that a rare kind of privilege," he said as casually as though he didn't know the implications. "Maybe now that you're working in the kitchen and giving me the weekly list, you could draw something on the back of it."

She didn't know where to look. Finally she settled for stepping away, where she could look at anything but him. Then she realized what she was looking at. "Is—is that a borage plant?"

"What, that fuzzy one? Grace Ann is the expert. Is it something special?"

A borage plant, growing in this high, dry climate. And looking healthy, too! "Borage for courage, my sister-in-law says." She touched a fuzzy leaf, where new buds were already coming. "The flowers are edible—they taste like cucumber. Sarah puts them in sparkling water in the summer, and it's delicious as well as pretty. Sometimes, for a wedding or an anniversary, she'll freeze them in ice cubes so it looks like flowers are floating in the punch."

"She sounds like a special woman," he said.

Amanda nodded, affection tilting the corners of her lips up. "She is."

"That makes two of you."

She glanced up, and here came the hot color into her cheeks for the twentieth time today. Would she ever get comfortable enough to speak to him without blushing? Without saying something stupid and misleading?

But before she could get even one word out, he said, "Amanda ... would you ride with me to the singing this evening?"

13

Hannah wasn't sure what she was supposed to be doing here in this big, happy family, but joking and flirting with Noah King probably wasn't it. If Ben were here, would she be trying to make the young Amish man laugh?

I mean, they know who I am. That I didn't grow up Amish, that I'm not baptized, despite the Kapp and the cape and apron. Right?

Grace Ann and Rachel were out in the kitchen doing up the dessert dishes, flushed with the success of getting Amanda out in the garden alone with Joshua. Hannah felt a little weird sitting here not doing anything. While the Amish said thank you as often as anybody, she'd learned that with them, the best way to really mean it was not with words, but with actions. So she got to her feet.

Savilla might have been laid up, but she didn't miss a thing. "No need for you to help, Hannah. Grace Ann and Rachel will take care of the dishes."

"That was a wonderful meal," she said. "I wanted to show my thanks as well as say it."

"Consider it shown." Savilla smiled. "Maybe you'd like a game of Snakes and Ladders with Mary Liza? Or a drive? Simeon, you ought to take Hannah with you to singing. There isn't going to be enough room in our buggy for all of you."

"Oh, no, that's okay," Hannah said hastily. "I hope Joshua won't mind if I ask him to take me back to the ranch. It's been quite a week, and I could use the downtime."

Which was all true, and had nothing to do with being closed into a buggy with three young men who weren't Ben.

"What's downtime?" Little Mary Liza curled up against her on the floor.

When a computer network isn't running and you can't play RPGs with your friends. But that was a joke from a past life—and it had been nearly six weeks since she'd been able to get online at the library in Whinburg and check in with the people she used to game with. "That's when you lie down and rest for a time."

"Like Mamm is going to do." Savilla wobbled as she got up, and Wilmer stepped in to steady her. She straightened slowly, her lips pinching back what had to be an exclamation of pain. "You all enjoy your time together."

"Thank you again for lunch," Hannah said.

"Thank you for coming. It's not your own family, but we're glad we can welcome you to ours." Savilla moved slowly down the hallway on her husband's arm, and at length the bedroom door closed.

"I don't want any downtime," Mary Liza confided. "I'm wide awake."

"Do you kids usually nap on a Sunday afternoon?"

"I'm not a kid," she said. "Kids are baby goats. Does *kidnapped* mean baby goats take naps?"

The room went silent. Even the clink and swish of dishes in the other room seemed to stop. Then Grace Ann appeared in the wide opening between the rooms, drying her hands on a towel. *"Mary Liza, kummst du hier und hilfen mir."*

"It's okay," Hannah said, rubbing the little girl's shoulder to show her there was nothing to be upset about. "She probably heard the word after that letter came out in *The Budget*."

"Ja, but there's no reason to bring it up and upset you."

"I'm not upset." Really? Then what was this tight feeling in her stomach, the feeling that had been there all day, that not even her own laughter and jokes could chase away?

She was waiting for someone to bring it up.

"I appreciate that you've all been speaking English for my benefit. But it's kind of like the elephant in the room, isn't it? That no one wants to talk about. It's okay if you do."

"Talk about what?" Mary Liza fidgeted. "What do you mean, Hannah? There aren't any elephants, or any goats either."

"Maybe not, but it's true baby goats do nap," she told the little girl gently. "Just like baby chickens do. But that's not what *kidnap* means—it means to steal somebody's child. That's what happened to me and my sister when we were little."

Such things clearly didn't exist in Mary Liza's world, and in her wide brown eyes, Hannah saw the first kindling of fear. "Somebody stole you?"

She should never have opened her mouth. Amanda was going to kill her if Wilmer and Savilla didn't first. "It turned out okay. They gave us back again, and now I live with my Mamm and Dat just like you and Rachel and Grace Ann live with yours."

Her gaze searched Hannah's face—the kind of gaze that demanded truth. "They gave you back?"

Sort of. "*Ja.* And I was so happy, because I had my big brother again, and my twin little brothers, and my sisters Leah,

Barbie, and Katie. The twins are the same age as you. They've just finished their first year of school."

A glance over the little girl's head showed her a tableau of tense faces. But whether Grace Ann and her uncles were worried about bringing up bad memories for Hannah, or about shattering a child's innocence with knowledge of the ugly side of the world, she didn't know. Maybe a little of both.

"I like school," Mary Liza said eagerly, abandoning Hannah's life for one that interested her much more—her own. "I already know all my letters. Grace Ann is helping me."

"Can you show me?"

Rachel went to a desk and produced a piece of paper and a set of crayons, and soon Mary Liza was absorbed in writing out the alphabet in slow, tipsy capitals, her sister watching over her shoulder.

"She will be busy for a long time now," Noah said. Then he let out a long breath. "Out of the mouths of babes."

"That's one of the reasons I'm not sure I can handle going to the singing tonight," Hannah admitted. "An even bigger crowd of people, all wondering the same thing as Mary Liza. I thought I could when I left this morning, but now I'm not so sure."

"No one would say anything to upset you," Simeon told her, his brows furrowed in concern. He reminded her of a teddy bear. A big, protective teddy bear with a bowl cut and suspenders. "No one would want to cause you pain, especially when—" He stopped.

"When?" She tilted her head in its heart-shaped Lancaster County *Kapp*, curiously.

"When you have already been through so much. Not that any of us know the details. Only what we have read."

"Nor do we want to know," Grace Ann said, coming in and

sitting on the hassock next to Hannah's chair. "We can't dwell in the past, because we can't change it. And God holds the future in His hand. All we have is the present, and each other, and good company." She smiled at Hannah, and it was impossible not to smile back.

She was sweet, but she really had no clue.

Not dwell in the past? That was pretty hard to do on the nights when she woke, gasping, from a nightmare. When over and over again she saw the woman she had believed to be her mother taken away by the police, crying out the name of a dead girl. Or the expression she caught in her Amish father's eyes sometimes, where she knew down to her bones that he was comparing the girl she could have been with the girl she was, and grieving that other girl's loss.

Well, Grace Ann was right about one thing. She had the present. It included Ben, and nothing could make her happier than that.

AMANDA HARDLY KNEW WHICH WAY TO LOOK, AND JOSHUA was waiting for an answer. "I—we—aren't we all going together in the family buggy? It will take six, won't it?"

"Six, if four of them are *Kinner*. If Grace Ann goes with the uncles, that leaves you and Hannah and me in ours."

"Oh, Hannah." Of course Hannah was coming. How could she have been so proud as to think he was suggesting that *Will you go with me* meant they should go alone? What would poor Hannah do then—be squashed into the back of Simeon's buggy? Her whole body seemed to flood with shame. "Then y-yes," she stammered. "We'd be happy to go with you."

He stood beside her, gazing above the garden fences and

beyond, to the high, distant mountains. "Amanda, is there something about me that distresses you?"

Startled, she glanced up at his profile, her fingers knotting together as though she had no control over them. "I don't know you very well." Oh dear. That sounded as though he had all kinds of sins hidden in his heart, and it was only a matter of time before they came out. "I mean—"

"No, you're right. We've only known each other a short time. But I don't think I've ever made anyone this uncomfortable. Is it—is it because of your church district?"

She stared at him wordlessly, utterly at a loss. No matter how her mind turned this about, she couldn't make sense of it. "I don't understand."

"Well, we're a new community here, built out of folk from half a dozen different districts in as many states. Some might see the Amistad *Gmee* as a house made from scrap and recycled materials—strong and weatherproof, but still mixed-up-looking on the outside."

She appreciated the metaphor, but—"What does this have to do with—with what you said? My being uncomfortable?"

"They call the Lancaster County Amish the bluebloods," he finally said in a rush, as though he'd been holding his breath and let it all out at once.

"They do?" Who were *they?* "Why, that's just silly."

"Is it? Your traditions and your families go right back to the martyrs. Men and women from your churches went to court over school attendance and tractors and buggy wheels and changed history—or at the very least, changed the lives the rest of us live. Protected our traditions and allowed them to live on."

"That doesn't make us any better or worse than any other church body, and anyway, it was God's hand that did all those things. It doesn't make us special, just maybe a little less willing to adapt to new things as the world changes. Like cell phones. Here they're necessary, whereas at home they're forbidden." She faced him now, anxious to clear up what had to be an enormous misconception. "And don't forget, every Amish man or woman in the country who ever left Lancaster County to find land or to follow God's will has the same blood running in their veins, no more red or blue than anyone else's. We are all the family of God, Joshua. Anything else is simply pasting an *Englisch* label on to Amish people—and you know that never works."

The corners of his lips tipped up. "You're an eloquent speaker when you feel strongly about something."

Compliments were so rare in her experience that she hardly knew how to accept one. "I'm sorry. I didn't mean to speak out of turn."

"I think you should do it more often."

This surprised a laugh out of her, like a bird startled out of a hedge. "I don't think so. But truly—I hope you don't think that about us any longer. The folks in our district would be horrified that God's people in other states thought we were proud or somehow better than anyone else. That would be directly against Scripture."

"I think you've convinced me." He smiled, that easy smile that made her want to smile back. Or would, if she hadn't been so rattled that he had actually thought she was a—a *blueblood*. "Speaking of Lancaster County, is there a butcher like me in Whinburg Township, or do you get your meat at an *Englisch* store?"

There's no one like you at home, and if there were, he'd have been married off long ago. "This winter Sarah and Henry went in together with Mamm and Dat to buy a side of beef from a man who was reducing his herd. We have our own pigs and chickens, of course, but I don't like the butchering. I know I should be practical about it, but I just can't bear it. I find something else to do that morning, and come back to help later."

"Soft-hearted, are you?"

"Ja," she admitted. "There's a woman in Whinburg—Carrie Miller—who doesn't harvest her chickens at all. She keeps them for their eggs, and they sit in her lap like cats."

He looked as though he couldn't quite believe it. "Chickens will do that? I've never seen such a thing."

"Hers do. I've made Dat promise not to even show the killing cone to a couple of hens I've made pets of, but the closest they'll get to me is to eat sunflower seeds out of my hand when I cut the plants down in the autumn."

"We have a couple of barn cats, but they won't sit in anyone's lap. Sim has a dog, but no chickens yet. They get their eggs from Mamm. I suppose when Sim looks about him for a wife, whoever it is will keep chickens."

"Is he taking his time?"

"I'd say he was an old maid, except he's a year younger than me."

Amanda laughed, this time less like a startled bird and more like a robin in its natural element. "I'll be interested in seeing who is who at the singing, then. Maybe I can help the two of you choose."

She thought he said, "You can help me choose," but Hannah called to them as she walked across the lawn, and he had already turned away to see what she wanted.

"Joshua, I'd like to go back to the ranch, if that's okay," Hannah said as she reached them. "I'm not going to go to the singing."

"You're not?" Amanda exclaimed. "Aren't you feeling well?"

"I'm fine. But the *subject* came up just now, and I handled it, but I don't think I can in front of a room full of strangers."

"How did it come up?" Joshua asked gently. "I hope you know no one here would deliberately say anything hurtful, or bring up bad memories."

"I know. And they didn't. It was Mary Liza, asking if *kidnap* meant that baby goats took naps." She smiled a little ruefully. "I wish it did. I'm sure no one at the singing would come right out and ask for the lurid details, but I don't think I can handle everyone looking at me and being as careful not to say anything as they would to just say it."

"Then of course you don't have to go," Amanda told her. "I'll come back with you, too."

"Not a chance," Hannah said, already shaking her head. "It's different for you. You need to get out and have fun."

"You sound like an old *grossmammi*—though mine never told me to have fun. Kind of the opposite."

"I mean it. You don't need to babysit me."

"Would you like to go now?" Joshua asked. "I can have the horse hitched up in no time—and normally we would leave in about an hour anyway. We'll just be a little early and play some volleyball with the Gingeriches."

"Are they related to that lady in the quilt shop?" Hannah asked. Amanda knew that after living with her real family for all this time, she knew the custom—that the *Youngie* would go to the singing in a different home each week. So the Gingerich family clearly had *Kinner* who were old enough to host a singing and some volleyball.

"*Ja,* it's John and Mariah Gingerich's place. Sure you don't want to come? You met her in town, didn't you?"

Hannah nodded. "Still, I'd rather go back to the ranch. Get an early night. Or as early as a person can with Bonita and

Jenny yakking constantly. At least now they've taken over the staff lounge and the TV remote, so that means they won't be keeping me company. The cowboys have been driven back into the bunkhouse to watch TV on the little one they have up there."

"You don't watch TV?" Joshua asked. "If you have the chance?"

Hannah shrugged, and they turned in the direction of the house. "I've kinda gotten out of the habit of it. And when I try to watch the shows I used to like, Bonita kicks up a fuss and we have to watch *The Bachelor* or some other stupid thing."

"You can watch four bachelors right here," Amanda pointed out, to Joshua's amusement.

"Maybe next week she will," he said. "For now, let us get you home."

And then, just as she'd imagined—feared?—earlier this afternoon, Amanda would be alone in the buggy with Joshua for miles—all the way to the Gingerich place.

Maybe she'd better pray that the hand of the *gut Gott* would gently push Grace Ann to join them.

14

Joshua had never been so thankful that his sister was not the type to tease. She had a good sense of humor, sure enough, but never at anyone else's expense. His uncles, though, were a different matter. Their good-natured teasing and ribbing were a lot of fun—until they weren't. Until there was a young woman so sensitive and shy that even speaking aloud was an effort for her. Until for him, it became more important to protect her feelings than his own.

All in good fun or not.

By some mysterious method, he managed to get out of the yard with their two visitors before anyone realized that it would mean he and Amanda would be driving alone to the Gingerich place. He had no doubt at all that he'd hear about it once everyone got there, but if he was lucky, they'd have the grace to do their teasing when Amanda was out of earshot.

He had broad shoulders. He could take it.

At the Lost Creek Ranch, Hannah jumped down and thanked him for the ride. "Have a good time," she said over her shoulder, and hiked on up the slope to the staff cabins before Amanda could get in another word. She'd already asked twice if Hannah was sure she didn't want her to stay, and had twice been told no.

Now, as Joshua leaned on the brake and Rusty took them confidently back down the long, familiar road, she sat up straight beside him, her hands knotted together over the bag in her lap. Her throat moved convulsively, and finally she got out, "T-tell me a little about the *Youngie* here. Who will I meet?"

It was a relief to speak *Deitsch* again. Out of respect for Hannah's slim vocabulary, they'd been speaking English for most of the day, though Mary Liza in particular had fun teaching her new *Deitsch* words. Like most Amish folk, he was fluent in both, but there was something about speaking to a woman in the language of home that was comforting somehow. Right. He hoped that would help to put her at ease.

"You want me to tell you about all two dozen? I'm going to have to slow the horse to a walk."

Ah, a glimmer of a smile. "Maybe just the ones you are friends with, to start. And one or two you think I might become friends with."

That he would be more than happy to do.

Luckily—or not so luckily—the list wasn't long. "There aren't too many girls your age—Grace Ann, and maybe three or four others. Lydia Hertzler and Cora Swarey are Grace Ann's friends. Both of them have younger siblings who come as well."

"And your friends?" She watched the road ahead as intently as a hunter looking for signs of game.

"Besides my uncles and me, there aren't a lot of men my age who aren't married already. We're hoping more come, especially from back home. Once they hear the construction business is doing well, we might get more coming for steady work. Farming in most districts, as you probably know, is getting tighter as families grow but the land doesn't."

"I know." She nodded. "My family doesn't farm on a large scale. Dat has a few cows and Mamm has her garden and the orchard. My second brother is the farmer, and he bought a place a few miles away. Dat helps him at harvest and planting, and has a share in the yield. My sister-in-law next door—the *Dokterfraa*—she does well with that. Her husband is a potter, but he makes sensible things like plates and bowls and mugs. He's taking students now, too, among them my nephew Caleb."

"You don't often hear of an Amish man being a potter."

"He lived *Englisch* for twenty years, before he inherited his aunt's place. He moved back and met Sarah ... and realized he needed her and God more than he needed his own way."

"I like a happy ending." Joshua was delighted to see her smile.

"I do, too. His sister lives on their *Aendi's* place now, and he lives in Sarah's house—the one my brother Michael built for them when they were first married. He passed away when Caleb was just a toddler." After a moment, she steered the conversation back on course. "So with three women of an age to be married, and four men, my arithmetic tells me that someone is going to be left out of the equation, unless more come from other places."

"You're assuming that God has perfect matches made with the numbers as they are." They left the ranch property and he turned Rusty onto the main road in the direction of Amistad. "But for me, at least, there hasn't been any leading in one direction over another."

"But maybe a young woman feels God prompting her toward you, and you just haven't noticed."

He gave her a sidelong glance before returning his attention to the county road, where there was much more traffic. "I'm twenty-eight. Long past the age where I wouldn't notice. And don't think Mamm and Dat haven't had bucketloads to say on the subject. If Cora so much as turns her head in my direction while she swats a fly, Mamm is there to make sure I've taken notice."

"Is Cora nice?"

"Very nice. Good with *die Kinner*, and a good cook. A nice laugh, too. But—"

The eternal *but*. A person could have all the qualifications of a wonderful life partner that any parents could wish for, but without that little voice whispering, *This one,* a man was literally taking his life in his hands. And Joshua's faith was such that he knew very well the results of self-will, of not waiting in prayer for guidance, of taking someone at face value and then finding out they didn't have the qualities that lasted.

That hard lesson was part of the reason he was here in Colorado and not staying in Kansas to save the home place instead of letting the bank foreclose. Jacinda Lapp and he had gone to baptism classes together, made plans together, been the perfect couple together—so much so that he would go to bed at night unable to believe he could be so lucky. Until just before the Communion Sunday of that final autumn, the season of asking forgiveness and clearing the slate, when she had come to him to confess. To say she couldn't go through with the wedding the next month. That in fact she had been seeing someone else—a Beachy Amish man from a much more liberal community that appealed to her love of bright colors and electricity, with an *Ordnung* that was hardly an *Ordnung* at all, compared to the one in their Old Order community.

He had thought her the perfect woman. And all the time, she had just been showing him a shell, a picture every bit as false as a graven image, while the Beachy Amish man got to see the real woman.

One good thing had come out of that heartbreak and humiliation, that dark winter of self-doubt and mistrust of his own judgment. He had become prayerful. Cautious. Maybe too cautious, much to Mamm's exasperated dismay every time she saw one of Dat's young half-brothers talking to Cora Swarey.

But now, he couldn't erase the vision of the first time he'd seen Amanda up on that hill, framed by trees, her face tilted toward heaven with an expression of such joy in the Creator's handiwork ... She hadn't known anyone was watching her. That had to be a glimpse of the real woman. It had to be.

Is it Amanda, Father?

But the wind coming down the valley from the highest mountains to the east held no message. No still small voice. No word of advice, or caution, or prompting.

Not yet.

He was more than happy to bring her to the singing, and to have this time to get to know each other better. But he would walk circumspectly once they arrived. The last thing he wanted was for her to have to face any teasing or whispers. And besides, clearly she wanted to make friends. If he were hanging around when she was trying to talk with the other girls, it would make things awkward. Awkwardness led to questions, and speculation, and he didn't want that.

He would do what was right. But he didn't have to like it much.

THERE WERE ONLY TWO DOZEN YOUNG FOLKS LINING BOTH sides of the collapsible tables in the dining room of the Gingerich home, but to Amanda it seemed like a big crowd. When they'd arrived a little early, it had been easy—she had met Mariah Gingerich already, and it was natural to greet the *Kinner* and then offer to help in the kitchen. The eldest daughter of the house, Lizzy, who was sixteen, was trying to contain her excitement at acting as hostess for the very first time, reciting her list of things to do like a prayer that everything would go right.

Finally her mother shooed her outside, where volleyball teams were forming up as buggies rolled in. "I'll look after the food, and Amanda here will help me. Greet your guests, and Lizzy, try to stay calm. It's not like the bishop is coming."

With a sigh that was half exasperation and half memory, Mariah turned back inside. "You don't want to stay in here the whole time," she told Amanda. "I can manage—everyone will bring something, so it's just a matter of telling them where to set it out."

But Amanda had assured her that she didn't mind helping at all. At home, sometimes the crowd for singing was nearly as large as the one for church—forty or more—because the *Youngie* came from other districts to see their friends and spend the weekend. Some of the gatherings in Lancaster County were much bigger than that.

But she knew people at home, and could sit with her buddy bunch and laugh at in-jokes that had been formed when they were all little scholars walking to the one-room schoolhouse in Willow Creek together. Here, she knew no one.

But wait—that wasn't true. She knew Joshua, and his uncles. And Grace Ann.

Grace Ann had greeted her warmly when she arrived in their buggy, but instead of Joshua acting as a friend might and staying by her side to introduce her to people, Grace Ann took that place by her side. Not that Amanda wasn't grateful, but still. After she'd climbed down, Joshua had unhitched the horse and gone into the barn with his uncles as though their conversation in the buggy had never happened, as though he didn't want anyone to know that they had arrived together.

Amanda's heart had begun to sink then. Had she been so mistaken in his character? Was this nonsense about bluebloods real?

After the volleyball game had ended and the meal devoured, he sat with his relatives at the men's table, where she was certainly not going to approach him to ask if she'd managed to offend him somehow with the few sentences she'd spoken.

So hesitantly, she slid into a spot next to Grace Ann and across from Cora Swarey, whose ripply auburn hair was rolled on either side and tucked under her Kapp. She had blue eyes and long lashes, and a trim figure under her modest cape and apron. Could she have been one of the reasons that one of Joshua's uncles might have wanted to settle here? Two places down was Lydia Hertzler, laughing with two teenagers who had been introduced as her twin sisters. The similarity would have told Amanda that, if nothing else, to say nothing of hair so blond it was almost white, and eyes that ranged from gray to blue.

After the first hymn from the Ausbund—*"Obgleich die Harf"*—a common choice in any district Amanda had ever visited, and the *"Lob Lied,"* Joshua spoke into the lull after the last long note died away.

"Maybe the newcomer would like to choose the next song?"

This was how he chose to speak to her, after two hours of talking to everyone on the place but her? To shine a bright light on the person he had to know was least comfortable in it, and force her to speak up in front of the whole room? Not only to speak up, but because it was the tradition, the one who chose the song had to start the singing.

From somewhere deep inside—probably the same place that had prompted her to say yes when Jesse Riehl had invited her to go riding in his car—an urge billowed up. An urge for something that would be completely unremarkable in Lancaster County. How would it be received here?

She moistened her lips. "How about 'Take Me Home, Country Roads'? We can start with the chorus, if you like."

Silence fell in the room.

At which point she understood how large the gap could be between the traditions of home and those in other places far from it.

"That—that's not in *Heartland Hymns,*" Cora Swarey objected. "Or the green book."

"That's a *worldly* song," breathed Lizzy Gingerich, looking as though Amanda was about to singlehandedly ruin her very first singing.

"Maybe it is, but don't you sing some of the faster ones here? What about songs like 'The Old Rugged Cross' and 'Amazing Grace'? Those are in *Heartland.*"

"We sang 'Amazing Grace' last summer," said one of the girls. "I put it in my songbook, but we haven't sung it again."

"Do you know 'Country Roads' at all?"

"No, and I don't think we want to," Lydia Hertzler said a little primly.

"It isn't worldly," Amanda protested. "It's about coming home. We don't sing the verse about the woman, of course, but the first verse and the chorus are fun."

"Why don't you teach it to us?" Noah suggested.

Grace Ann rounded on him. "She's not going to sing a solo in front of all of you, for goodness sake." She turned back to Amanda. "I'm sorry we don't know it. We don't do things here the way they do in Lancaster County."

"Bluebloods," someone murmured.

"A little higher than we are, maybe," someone else said.

She had two choices—sink into her seat and spend the evening in silence, or speak up one more time. Amanda chose the second option. "All right, then, let's sing 'Amazing Grace'." And without a second's hesitation, she began the first verse.

Maybe it was shock, or maybe they'd had a moment to think about how unwelcoming and judgmental they'd just sounded, but by the third word, Cora Swarey's beautiful voice had risen in support of her own much less beautiful one, and half the girls at the table joined in. By the sixth word, everyone else had, too. She still couldn't hear Joshua's gentle bass behind her the way she had during the opening hymn.

He had opened this door, so he could step through it, or not, as he chose.

As the second line began, she heard him join in, as confidently as if it had been his choice all along. And then for the next hymn, he chose 'What a Friend We Have in Jesus,' which led naturally to *"Wo ist Jesus mein Verlangen,"* sung to the same tune.

At which point the voices broke into four-part harmony. Well, goodness gracious! They had been so vehemently against a song they considered worldly, and here they were singing parts, which was strictly forbidden back home! Did they sing this way on Sunday, too? Surely not—for the reason no one sang parts in any district she'd ever been in was that it was all too easy for the finer singers to stand out and be noticed, all too easy to become proud of a gift God had given them.

"*Der Herr* created the crow as well as the lark," Dat used to say. "The songs of all the birds are beautiful to Him."

Cora was clearly the lark here, but she was singing the main melody, as was Amanda. Was she trying not to stand out?

By the time they ran out of choices—or at least, people who were willing to make them—it was time for a snack in case anyone was hungry before the trip home. She and Grace Ann were helping Lizzy and two of her buddy bunch clean up afterward, doing the dishes and putting plastic wrap over desserts in preparation for the ride under a seat in someone's buggy, when Grace Ann said quietly, "That was brave of you, to stand up to my brother and choose that song."

Amanda managed a shrug, though she felt far from casual about it. "We sing it at home, and the parents and elders don't consider it so very worldly."

"I hope you don't think we were rude. We didn't mean to be. It was just—a shock."

"As much a shock as singing parts—or being called a *blueblood* in public?" she said before she could control that unruly member, her tongue.

"We only sing parts among ourselves," Grace Ann protested. "Never on Sunday. Imagine what the bishop would say."

"Who called you a blueblood?" Lizzy asked, quelling the girl next to her who looked as though she might break out in a giggle. "I didn't see who it was."

"I don't remember. One of the boys. But Joshua said it was a common opinion about people from Lancaster County. That lots of people think that way, just because the church has been there a long time."

"I'm sure they don't mean to be unkind," Grace Ann said, her voice soft with distress.

"I'm sure they don't." She turned away to put a gallon jug of juice in the fridge. But they had been, all the same. Or was she simply thinking too highly of herself? Shouldn't she instead be considering her own behavior, the way the gospel said?

It were better for him that a millstone were hanged about his neck, and he cast into the sea, than that he should offend one of these little ones.

It was better not to offend anyone else, than worry so much about being offended. Offense was simply wounded pride, and with the *gut Gott's* help, that had to be rooted out of her soul's garden wherever she found it, before its hidden roots hindered someone else.

She closed the door of the fridge and turned to Grace Ann and the younger girls with a rueful smile. "I guess I was too quick to take offense. Next time I'll remember I'm not at home, and choose differently."

"I hope we will see you next time," Lizzy said in a rush that seemed to combine compunction and relief. "Church is at Cora's next week, on the west side of the highway. It's pretty far out, so we usually stay for lunch and the afternoon, and have singing there instead of moving somewhere else."

"We'll make sure she is there," Grace Ann said to Lizzy, giving her a hug. "And Simon and her other friends, too."

"Simon? Simon Yoder is back?" Lizzy's eyes grew wide, and her two buddies exchanged a speaking glance. "Oh my—does Cora know?"

What does Simon have to do with Cora? But Amanda bit back the words—she already knew. "Simon is my nephew," she said mildly. "Are he and Cora friends?"

All three younger girls, as though they'd had the same thought simultaneously, turned and fled the kitchen in a welter of skirts and aprons.

Grace Ann sighed and picked up the dishcloth. "Going to tell Cora. She's Lizzy's cousin. Her mother and Mariah are sisters."

"But I thought Simon only got to church once or twice when he was here." Amanda gazed after them, feeling a little bemused. "Surely that wasn't enough time to cause a news headline like this."

"Who said they only saw each other in church?" And Grace Ann plunged her hands into the sink as though that were the end of the matter.

To Amanda's immense relief, when it came time to leave, Grace Ann was firm that she would not be going home with her uncles, and further, indicated Amanda should get into the buggy first, while she rode next to her brother. As they clip-clopped out of the yard to a chorus of good-byes, it was clear that Grace Ann wasn't going to allow the *Youngie* any more talk about Amanda. What a relief it was to have a new friend who would stand in the breach for her. Had she left Amanda and Joshua alone for the trip up the mountain, the church might have had him engaged to Amanda by the following Sunday.

Joshua seemed to come back to his normal self, to the point that Amanda began to think she'd misunderstood his behavior the whole evening. The three of them had such freedom of spirit together that she actually had more fun on the drive, as they laughed and joked and told stories, than she had at the singing.

When a coyote ran across the road and Amanda gasped, having never seen one before, Joshua stopped the buggy just long enough for the lamps to illuminate it, alert on the hillside for a moment, so that she could get a good look before its legs bunched beneath it and it loped off into the trees.

"We might see a mountain lion, too," Grace Ann said, gripping the bench for balance as Joshua flapped the reins over Rusty's back.

"I hope not," Amanda said fervently. "Deer are one thing, but creatures who can eat a horse—or me—are quite another. Do you think the boys are all right, up there on the pack trip?" She'd known there were wild animals out here, of course, but it was quite another thing to see them in the flesh.

"Sure they will," Joshua said comfortably. "Dat and the uncles and me, we got permission to do that trip last autumn, for deer, not fish. The Gundersons even gave us horses at a discount. The wild animals stayed out of our way, and we stayed out of theirs. The news that we had rifles probably went out all over the mountains."

"Simon has been on many pack trips and survived every one," Grace Ann said over her shoulders. "I'm sure you don't have to worry."

Simon.

"Grace Ann, was there something between Simon and Cora Swarey? I know you didn't want to say anything before, but if there was, you must tell me."

Joshua shifted on the bench, and not because a wheel had hit a pothole, either. Grace Ann glanced at him and then out the storm front. "I don't feel right, talking about him behind his back."

"It's not right if he did something that would *cause* talk."

"In either case, it's in the past," Joshua said. "Hopefully he'll have learned something, and he'll be different this time. After all, she invited you all to come, didn't she?"

It took Amanda a moment to figure out who *she* was. Not Cora, certainly. "Mrs. Gunderson? What does she have to do with anything?"

"Joshua," Grace Ann said on a sigh. "If you didn't tell her before, you'd best do it now. And quickly, before we get up to the house."

They were already halfway up the hill, the lights of the outermost ranch buildings winking between the pines.

"Tell me," he said to Amanda, "have you been given Sundays off?"

"*Ja*, both me and Hannah, and Simon, too." What did that have to do with him? "I had to be ... firm about it, though. I had to tell Mrs. Gunderson that if she wanted Amish staff, a few requirements came along with us. Like not working on Sundays. She wouldn't listen to Simon when he asked, but she couldn't argue with what she wanted herself."

"Good for you," Grace Ann put in.

"Well, last summer it appears Simon and Joe weren't so firm about their standards," Joshua said. "Their days off could be Sunday, or they might not. But now and again you'd see Simon in town, and at some of the homes of the *Youngie*, and not on a Sunday or a Friday, either."

"How did he get there? It's at least three miles to town from the ranch. I suppose he could have walked." A chill darted through her stomach. "He didn't learn to drive a car like the *Englisch*, did he? He's been baptized!"

Joshua huffed a laugh. "No, at least he didn't do that. He rode."

"A bicycle?"

"A horse. Like a cowboy. Like we did, on that hunting trip."

"Holy smokes." The expression blurted itself out before she could keep it back. "It's not specifically part of the *Ordnung* at home, but for us, horses are for work and travel, not for riding. Where would he have learned?"

"Any one of the hands, I expect," Joshua said dryly. "Doesn't take near as long to learn as driving a car, and you don't need a license. Anyway, he'd ride into town, and pretty soon we all realized why. He'd wind up out there at the Swarey place sooner or later, or Cora would take an open buggy into town to meet him for an ice cream."

"I still don't see what this has to do with Mrs. Gunderson hiring us." Granted, it was disappointing of Simon not to stand up for his own time with God on a Sunday. But maybe the Gundersons hadn't been quite so accommodating then. Maybe Simon and Joe had paved the way for their Amish staff the following year, and it had given Mrs. Gunderson the idea to make her Amish staff into living advertisements.

"Everyone was talking about them, and Cora started to call him her special friend, mostly when she was with me and Lydia." Grace Ann took up the story, speaking a little faster as they rounded the big curve and the glowing angles of the big house's front windows could be seen up on the hillside. "She only would have said that if he'd asked her to be. She's twenty-two, and ready to be married, and it seemed that God had brought them together here in the valley for that purpose."

"But Simon—much as I love him—he's not ready to be married. He doesn't have a home of his own, or much in the way of savings. He doesn't even have a trade, outside of one year's apprenticeship to a buggy maker."

"That would be between him and Cora's parents," Grace Ann said. "All I know is that one day it was off. Finished. And we never saw Simon in town again until the day he left, when someone saw him and Joe getting on the bus in Westcliffe."

"But why? What happened?"

Joshua looked over his shoulder, but Amanda was sure he couldn't see her face in the dark interior of the buggy, even with the battery-powered dashboard lights. "It pains me to say this, but you asked for what we know. Seems there was some kind of flirtation with Mrs. Gunderson at the same time as he was courting Cora, and Mr. Gunderson didn't like it. Neither did Cora."

"Atten—what? *Simon?* Are we talking about the same Simon? He would no more take up with a worldly woman than fly to the moon!"

"I'm not saying he did. Maybe he'll tell you. All we know is that it was off with Cora, and Simon and Joe went home earlier than they'd been hired for—as though they'd been let go."

"I remember that," Amanda said reluctantly. "They came home without warning, not even a phone call. We just thought they were homesick."

No wonder Mr. Gunderson had looked grim when she'd told him in the reading room that she was here with her nephew. No wonder Simon had been so familiar with Mrs. Gunderson that he could telephone her and ask for a job, not only for himself but for his friends and relations as well, and come up with good offers for all of them. This would explain the behavior of people when she met them for the first time and explained her connection to him—that tone as they said, *Oh. Simon.*

She let out a long sigh. His poor mother. Had he told her what he'd been up to when he was far from home?

Betting was a sin, but she'd bet he hadn't.

"I'm sorry." Grace Ann turned on the bench and touched Amanda's knee. "We didn't want to distress you, or hurt you."

"I'm not hurt," Amanda assured her, squeezing her hand and releasing it. "But it certainly explains a lot."

"Are you going to talk to him?"

"I don't see what good it will do ... unless he plans to take up with Cora again." *Or Mrs. Gunderson*. But that was so ugly, so disloyal, that she sent up a swift prayer to *der Herr* asking forgiveness. "His mother asked me to keep an eye on him, but I don't think she had any idea what that would mean. Certainly not this."

"As long as all is well at the big house, that's all that matters." Joshua guided the horse around the house and into the main courtyard where he made his deliveries. "Cora can take care of herself, and if she can't, she has two married older brothers who can."

"And you'll help." Grace Ann bumped his shoulder with hers in gentle teasing.

"All her friends will, I expect," he said a little stiffly. "He won't find as many opportunities to be alone with her as he once did. No one wants to see her hurt ... again."

Grace Ann got out, and when Amanda jumped down, she said quietly, "Are you all right?"

Was she? Amanda hardly knew. But that was no burden to lay on a young woman who had been such a friend to her and truthfully answered the questions she'd been asked. The fact that Amanda was appalled by the answers didn't take away from that.

"I am," she assured her, just as quietly. Then she leaned in the door of the buggy. "Thank you, Joshua, for driving all these miles for my sake. The day has been *wunderbar*."

"Even if the ending wasn't so *wunderbar*?"

His strange behavior earlier seemed to fade with his honesty now. "Even so. I'm with friends, so from my point of view, it's a good ending. Good night."

As the buggy clattered away across the gravel, Amanda looked up toward the staff cabins. The lights were all on in the one she shared with the girls.

She couldn't face any more people just now. Couldn't bear the thought of Bonita talking to her. Couldn't face Hannah's questions, if she was even awake—though sleep looked pretty impossible.

So Amanda walked up the path and under the trees, standing in their shelter while she took in the panorama of the mountains, lit now by starlight before moonrise and shining there on the horizon.

I will lift up mine eyes unto the hills, from whence cometh my help.

And like the psalmist, she focused on those gleaming heights and began to pray.

15

At their last breakfast on Monday morning, Jose settled into his camp chair in the circle by the crackling fire and said to them all, "Seems we can't take our time on this last stretch of trail today." He glanced at Samuel and Ben, who were shoveling in their food so that they could get on with tacking up the horses. Simon, who would oversee packing up the tents, was eating more slowly. "You boys are needed for a talk with the Colorado Wildlife Department."

Samuel nodded. "I knew I would be." He indicated Jose's jacket, where the bullet casing, both his and Jose's hair samples, and the cigarette butt he'd found had been reposing in a zippered pocket since Jose had returned to the lake and he'd handed them over. "There's no need for him to talk to Simon and Ben, surely? They didn't come tracking with me."

But they hadn't been in the tent when he and Jose had been awakened by the shot. Simon's explanation had been as careless as always, and a little puzzled about why Samuel was so concerned. They'd been ranging ahead, taking a hike.

They'd smelled something and wanted to make sure it wasn't a lightning strike or a greenhorn hiker starting a fire.

Except the night before had been clear and cold, and lit by the waning moon, besides. No clouds. No lightning.

Jose shrugged. "I only know what I've been told, and I've been told to bring everybody down pronto." He glanced apologetically at the fishermen. "The boss says he'll give you folks a discount on the next excursion if you want it."

The oldest one shook his head. "No need. The fishing is pretty good on Lost Creek, and my elk hair caddises aren't doing as well up here as I'd hoped."

"A dragonfly nymph might work," one of the others suggested. "I've got plenty, and caught an eighteen-inch fatty yesterday on it."

"Nah." The first one smiled at Samuel and the others. "If the warden wants a word, we'd be poor sportsmen if we held him up. There's plenty of fish down below. Besides, I'm looking forward to a real shower."

So Simon and Jose broke camp while Samuel and Ben got the horses ready. It didn't take long to get down the trail, and soon the roofs of the barns came into sight. As the sun sank behind the western mountains, they were taking the saddles off the tired animals and currying them down in their own familiar stalls.

Samuel had recovered to some degree from the ride up into the mountains. The ride down made him hurt all over again, so he turned in early while Ben went bounding like a jackrabbit up to the girls' cabin to see Hannah.

"Aren't you going, too?" Samuel said to Simon, who was peeling out of his dirty clothes and tossing them in the laundry bin.

"What, to see my aunt? I'll see her and Hannah at breakfast."

They heard boots on the stairs and in a moment Jose Rodriguez joined them. He took in Samuel, who was already showered and tucked up in bed like a little kid.

"Talk to you boys for a second?"

Simon pulled on a clean pair of jeans and sat on his bunk bare-chested. "Sure. What's up?"

They had the bunkhouse to themselves for the moment, but it wouldn't be long before the cowboys downstairs got tired of TV and turned in for the night.

"Warden'll be here at nine sharp tomorrow. Just wanted to let you know. Where's Ben?" When Simon told him, he nodded. "Tell him, too."

"Ja," Samuel said. "I still don't know what Simon and Ben can say that they haven't already."

Jose leaned on the post of the bunk opposite and crossed his arms. They were brown and ropy with muscle—the arms of a man who worked hard and got respect. "I know what you can tell me," he said to Simon. "Where were you, really, that morning the deer was shot?"

"I told you already. We were up the trail, trying to figure out where that smoke smell was coming from."

"The smell nobody else could smell?"

"Winds change. It faded after the pack train got moving." Samuel hadn't known Simon for long because they lived in different towns back home, but this was the first time he'd ever heard him sound defensive. Usually his confidence carried him through any conversation, whether he turned out to be wrong or not.

"What was it like?" Jose persisted. "The smell."

Simon's face pinched up, as though someone had waved a

bottle of vinegar under his nose. “I don’t know. Smoke. What else could it be? Maybe tires burning? Or rubber?”

“No tires up there other than the ranch four-wheeler,” Jose pointed out. “And while it’s possible folks would be burning cars on BLM land, it’s not likely. No roads in from that direction.”

Simon shrugged. “Can’t help you there.”

Jose pushed off the post and walked to the top of the stairs, his boots sounding hollow on the plank floor. “If it wasn’t a lightning strike and you couldn’t see a plume, I suggest you think pretty hard about what you’re going to tell the warden. Because boys, it doesn’t look good that you went missing when that animal was shot.”

“It wasn’t us!” Simon exclaimed. “We didn’t carry rifles.”

“I should have counted them, at the time,” Jose admitted. “But I didn’t, and I’ll tell the warden so. Now, I’m not accusing you of anything, son. I just wanted you to be aware that there’s going to be questions. And having no answer is just as bad sometimes as an out-and-out lie.”

“We wouldn’t lie,” Samuel told him. “None of us.”

“I’d like very much to believe that.” With a nod good night, Jose went down the stairs.

Someone passed him coming up, and they heard him murmur a greeting. And then there was nothing Samuel or Simon could do but stare wordlessly at each other.

So much for getting to sleep.

Samuel’s body might have been exhausted, but his mind sure wasn’t. It pushed and pulled at the facts until they did what facts always do at three in the morning, and became something frightening and hopeless. When he finally rolled out at five, having got maybe two hours total, he saw Simon looking—as one of the cowboys subsequently said at breakfast—"like you been drug through a hedge backward."

By then all the hands knew that the Wildlife warden was coming down from Salida, and why. So while there wasn't much point in trying to keep the meeting confidential, Jose didn't let just anyone into the bunkhouse—including Hannah, who got sent away protesting with firm instructions to go back to work. The fishermen and the Amish hands seated themselves on the sofas and chairs downstairs, along with Jose and Rob Lozano, the foreman. Mr. Gunderson stood beside the sheriff, Oliver Tanner, and the Colorado Wildlife warden, a tall, middle-aged African-American man whom he introduced as Dane Peters.

The warden wasted no time in coming to the point. "You men probably know that poaching is a year-round business, but around these parts we don't usually have so many incidents together in a cluster. This makes me wonder if there isn't something else going on. But for now, how about you tell me what you heard and saw on your pack trip." He checked his notebook. "Mr. Riehl, how about we start with you, from the moment you woke up in camp last Wednesday morning."

Samuel went through it—even though the beginning felt like a betrayal, when he had to say he couldn't find his friends, and the warden made a note. He and Jose tracking the deer, then his friends coming back into camp, them going on up to the lake while he tracked the poacher ... all of it. For the most part, Peters didn't interrupt, except to examine the sandwich bag containing the bullet casing, the hairs from the deer, and the cigarette butt when Jose handed it to him.

"And you found nothing else at the blind? No wrappers, or cigarettes, or anything to indicate a second person?"

"No, sir." It took a little to get the word out. Using the

honorific was hard to get used to, but he'd heard others using it and figured he'd better, too. "I walked a perimeter around the blind, and didn't find anything else. And I tried not to touch the casing with my fingers."

"I'm glad to hear it. That you found this so close to the blind tells me one thing, anyway—our poacher was using a bolt-action rifle. If he'd been using a semiautomatic, the casings would have been thrown out several feet. But you say you walked a circle and found nothing more?"

"Yes, sir."

He reached two fingers into a leather pouch on his belt and pulled out a small metal instrument with a circle of glass in it. "Thanks for being so thorough. It helps." He put on a pair of latex gloves and pulled the casing out of the bag. He held up the instrument. "Know what this is?"

Samuel shook his head.

"This is a loupe, like they use in jewelry shops to tell the quality of a diamond. It's a real strong magnifier, and gives me an idea of the marks on this casing. Every rifle's rimfire is different, so it'll make different marks. Understand me?"

"Yes, sir." Simon and Ben nodded, watching the man examine the casing.

"Looks like this particular firearm makes a pretty deep score on either side when the bullet leaves the barrel. Someone's not cleaning their guns as well as they should." He glanced at Mr. Gunderson. "I'd like to use my field kit to test all your rifles, if that would be all right."

"You won't find anything, but sure," the ranch owner said with gruff confidence. "Do what you need to do."

"I'd be happy not to find anything. That would mean your hands haven't been out poaching deer for their antlers." He said to Samuel, "Thank you, young man. I like a good, thorough account."

"Jose showed me what to do, sir." Relief that his part was over, at least, flooded through him the way adrenaline did when he was scared.

The warden's keen brown eyes turned to Simon and Ben, though Samuel noticed that Mr. Gunderson's gaze rested on Simon alone. "Now, if you'll tell me what happened when you left camp? What made you get up?"

"I've got kind of a sensitive nose," Ben said. "Maybe it's allergies, I don't know, but I woke up with a smoke smell and I couldn't go back to sleep. I got up to see what it was, and I kicked Simon by accident, so he woke up, too. We both decided to see if we could find it."

"It wasn't the campfire?"

"No. We'd doused it the night before," Simon said. "No one from Lost Creek leaves a live fire overnight."

The sheriff nodded with approval, and Peters asked, "Where did you go?"

"Up the trail a ways toward the lake."

"Almost a mile," Simon put in.

"But by then it was already starting to fade," Ben went on, "and we couldn't get a fix on it, like whether it was stronger in one direction or another. So we headed back down to camp, to find everyone up and Sam and Jose coming up the slope with a deer between them."

"What'd you tell me the smell was like, Simon?" Jose asked. "Burning rubber?"

But Ben shook his head. "No, not like that. A smoke smell, but maybe like they were burning their trash, too, instead of packing it out."

"And what would cause that kind of smell up in the mountains with no roads and no houses?" Peters mused aloud. "Besides hikers or poachers and a fair-sized campfire, that is."

"That's my bet," Mr. Gunderson said. He hadn't taken his thoughtful gaze off Simon, even when the latter wasn't talking. "But I guess your tests on the rifles will decide one way or the other how important that smoke is."

"I expect so," Peters said. "Mr. Rodriguez, if you'd have the rifles you took up there gathered together, I'll get my kit."

"Not just the ones you took up there," Rob Lozano put in. "Call it overkill, but round up all of them on the place, from the barns and in the house. Test them all so there's no doubt."

"He's right," Mr. Gunderson said. "Rob, you do that while Jose gets the ones we pack."

"I'll be back after I log these." The warden carefully put away the bullet casing, the napkin and hanky, and the cigarette butt in separate small manila envelopes, and stripped off his gloves.

The Amish hands were instructed to clean tack and not go anywhere until the warden was ready. That didn't sound very promising to Samuel, but there was no question of disobeying. The atmosphere had seemed relaxed, but an underlying tension had spread from Mr. Gunderson outward, and Samuel wasn't about to put a finger to that string and pluck it. A spider might come running.

So they cleaned tack like their lives depended on it. Even Simon put some elbow grease into the job, as though it might erase his previous casual attitude to anything except being camp boss. Samuel had to give him credit, though—he knew horses, and cared for them as though each one were his own, no matter what it took in labor and time.

Twenty minutes later, they heard the warden's cell phone ring. His tone, which started out in the low-key bass he'd used to ask his questions, rose as he demanded information from whoever was on the other end. "An *Amish* man? This is nuts. Text me the recording."

Samuel and his friends dropped their work and crowded the door. Mr. Gunderson was already outside, though he'd been supervising the collection of the rifles and laying them out on planks set on a pair of sawhorses in the barn.

But the warden wasn't walking toward him, one hand on the holster of his sidearm and the other gripping his phone. No, he was walking toward the door where the three of them were standing.

Some instinct made Samuel square his shoulders and step out to meet the man. "What is it, Warden?" he asked. "What happened?"

"Some information came in while I've been up here," he said, his gaze fixed on him and the two behind him. "Seems that incident cluster I was talking about earlier just got a little bigger. We got an anonymous tip on the Operation Game Thief hotline that the Amish butcher out on the county road has been packaging up road-kill game and selling it illegally. You boys know anything about that?"

Samuel's jaw hung open as his mind tried to rein in where he'd thought the warden was going, and catch up to where he was going now. "No," he managed.

"Butcher? You mean Joshua King?" Simon asked. A frown made a double furrow between his brows, under curly hair that was going to need a cut before Sunday.

"You know him, do you?" The warden latched on to this as though it was significant.

"We all know him." Jose made his way across the manicured yard, wiping his hands on a rag. "He comes every morning and delivers meat to the ranch."

"What kind of meat?" The words sounded like gravel raining down on a corrugated roof.

Jose gazed at him, crinkles forming at the corners of his eyes as though he were squinting to help him read the warden's face better. "Beef. Pork. Sausage. Chicken once in a while, eggs a lot."

"What's in the sausage?"

"I can take you up to the house to have a look. He labels the contents like the law requires him to do."

"I'll do that." Peters was making notes on his phone. "But for now, let's get these rifles tested and hopefully set our minds at rest about the first things on the list." He eyed Simon, who was just about to step back into the tack room. "Nobody go too far."

Samuel was too interested in the testing to do that. So was everyone else. Even the housekeeping staff abandoned their beds and toilets to come and watch. Hannah sidled up to Ben and took his hand, while Amanda stood to one side, her arms wrapped tightly around her body, as though she were cold.

One at a time, the warden fired a single bullet from every gun on the ranch—even the handgun that one of the fishermen had in his duffel bag. The bullets slapped into a thick series of posts the hands had set up in the paddock. They weren't the important part—the casings that somersaulted out of each rifle or handgun and hit the ground were.

At the end of forty-five minutes, twelve rifles of varying makes and calibers, and a pistol, each casing had been carefully examined, photographed, bagged, and numbered following each shot. When he had packed up his equipment, Warden Peters turned to Mr. Gunderson. The house staff and the hands all watched as though this were one of those crime shows the guys at the RV factory used to follow on their lunch hour.

"I'll send everything to our lab in Denver to be sure," Peters said to Mr. Gunderson, "but from my field examination, it's my opinion that the gun that fired the bullet whose casing Samuel found is not among these ones from the ranch."

A collective breath seemed to be released ... or maybe it was just a breeze crossing the yard and cooling the sweat between Samuel's shoulder blades.

"I'm glad to hear it," Mr. Gunderson said. "So now what?"

"As I said, this is only a field examination. But that still leaves three open questions—whether or not this man Joshua King is involved somehow, and whether or not someone with the rifle that does match was up camping on your land and risking a head start on deer—and fire—season." He gazed at Samuel, Ben, and Simon in turn. "And why this incident cluster of mine seems to involve you Amish folks. That's what puzzles me most of all."

16

Amanda," Teresa Rodriguez said from behind her, "the show's over. Two vanloads of quilters are going to be here at four o'clock, and we have a lot of work to get through by then. Bonita, Jenny, Hannah—I want these new guests all in the main house. They requested to stay together, so that's what they're going to get. Four in the Bighorn suite, and the rest doubled up in Eagle, Hawk, Condor, and Puma."

Amanda rubbed her arms, feeling somehow as though she'd come out of the deep freeze and body parts and brain weren't thawed enough yet to work properly. How could anyone care about rooms when a friend was in such trouble? Because she'd clearly heard what the warden had said when his phone rang.

"How is it possible that— Teresa, how could they think Joshua is involved in poaching in any way, shape, or—"

"Nobody who ever met him thinks that," Teresa said shortly. "It's all nonsense, or a prank, or a vendetta. What it isn't, is any of our business, so get a move on. The quilters are a-comin' and I forgot all about getting those quilts of Mariah's hung. Tyler," she called over to a group of the cowboys, "you and Reese grab a stepladder and meet me up in the great room in five."

But it *was* Amanda's business. If a brother or sister were in need or in trouble, then it was the Amish community's business to help them. But how could she? The most she could do was call down to the butcher shop and offer moral support—but would a man facing such a serious accusation be comforted, or merely annoyed that she had stuck her nose in where it wasn't wanted?

No, of course he wouldn't be annoyed. Except for his puzzling behavior Sunday, he had been so kind to her, she must return that kindness in the best way she knew.

"Teresa, may I use the phone?" she asked as they walked briskly back up the hill to the staff entrance.

"Is it long-distance?"

"No. Local."

"Five minutes, no more. You can use my office while I figure out what I'm going to serve the rest of the week if they don't let Joshua bring us any meat."

This had not occurred to Amanda—that the consequences of even an unfounded accusation could be so swift.

She could hear Jose's voice in the cooler, and the deeper tones of the sheriff and the Wildlife warden as they examined Joshua's neatly wrapped and labeled packages of sausage. She shut herself into Teresa's office down the hall. Would they take the packages at face value? Or would they suspect him of mislabeling them so he could make a bigger profit by using illegal game?

No, she must not think this way. It was not true, and she must stand by her friends.

Teresa's desk was cluttered with papers, the computer, a stack of unread magazines. The pencil holder held one pencil and a couple of pens—as well as a pair of scissors, two screwdrivers, and a small hammer that you'd use to hang pictures. But where would—ah. The number for the butcher shop was written right there on Teresa's blotter, as though she used it often.

"King Cuts and Meats."

"Guder mariye, Wilmer," she said. "This is Amanda Yoder, up at Lost Creek Ranch."

He switched to *Deitsch*, too. *"Wie geht's*, Amanda?"

"I'm well, but can I speak to Joshua? Is he there?"

"Ja, he's here. Just a m—"

"He is? Has he heard from the warden, then, Wilmer? Is he all right?"

A moment of silence hissed along the line. "Should he have? Why wouldn't he be all right?"

If someone had upended a bucket of ice water over her, Amanda could not have been more shocked. Time seemed to stop.

Lieber Gott, hilfen mir. I must be the one to tell him.

Joshua came on the line, but it was clear from his father's muttering in the background that the older man had his ear close to the receiver, too. "Amanda? Is everything all right? Has something happened?"

"Ja," she finally got out, her heart beating up in her throat. "The sheriff and the warden are here. There was a deer shot up at the camp during the fishing trip, and they're investigating."

"Ja?" he said carefully, as though he were trying not to spook her.

"They thought Ben and Simon might have shot it, which is why they're here. But Samuel found a bullet casing that he thinks belonged to the poacher, and the markings on the casings don't match. From the ranch rifles, I mean." Was she even making any sense? She had never had a conversation about bullets in her life.

"That is a relief. Though of course it wasn't them. It was a poacher."

"But that's not why I'm calling. The warden got an anonymous tip that—" Her throat closed up. She must be brave. She must get this out, so that when the big SUV with its powerful engine and its official crest on the doors rolled into the yard, he would be prepared. She must do this for his sake. "That the Amish butcher on the county road was selling road kill and maybe even poached game illegally."

He drew in a breath, and in the background, Wilmer made a sound halfway between a squeak and a shout.

"Joshua—they are examining your packages of sausage in the cooler right this minute."

Another exhalation became a huff of humor—or at least, a brave attempt at one. "Then I hope they like pork sausage with apple and herbs, because that's all they contain, other than a few flakes of Grace Ann's dried chiles."

"I expect they will come to ask you questions about it as soon as they leave here."

"I expect so. It's funny, though."

"Joshua, there nothing funny about this." Her voice cracked.

"Funny strange. I left them phone messages about it, so that's why I'm surprised they didn't come here first. On Saturday two men—father and son—dropped off a deer for processing. Road kill, but they said they had a permit for it. Which I never saw. I haven't seen them, either."

"When were they supposed to come?"

"Today."

"It's only just noon. Maybe they'll come when the warden is there."

"I'll ask if he gave them their permit, because they never called me with the permit number, or the name of the warden who issued it, like they promised."

That didn't sound good. In fact, if she were of a suspicious turn of mind instead of merely terrified, she might think that the whole thing was a lie designed to get Joshua into trouble.

Maybe get all the Amish around Amistad into trouble.

Joshua might be accused of breaking the law. Ben and Simon's integrity had already been called into question. Maybe the *Englisch* folks might start talking among themselves. She and her friends might lose their jobs here at the ranch because they had become a liability instead of a draw. People in Amistad might begin to view their Amish neighbors with suspicion instead of cordiality. And then what might happen?

No, she must stop. Fear produced thoughts like that, not faith. They were in God's hand, and so was this whole situation.

"Amanda? Are you still there?"

"*Ja*, I'm here, but I have to go. Teresa only gave me five minutes. But you'll tell him—the warden—about these two men, won't you? About the permit, and everything?"

"If he'd listened to his messages, he'd already know. Amanda?"

"*Ja?*" Her voice wobbled, she was so close to tears.

"Thank you for telling me. It was a brave thing."

"Will the warden be angry with me?"

"He'll never know. Dat and me are silent on the subject."

"Are you angry with me?"

A pause like a hitch on the line. "How could I be?"

"On Sunday night, at the singing—I hardly saw you. I thought I had offended you."

He released a long breath. "This is what I get for thinking things up in my head and not speaking. No, of course you didn't offend me. I was trying to keep people from talking because we had arrived together. But clearly I should have been talking to you, both then and afterward."

"So you're not offended?"

"Even though I've only known you a short time, I can safely say you're the least likely to offend anyone, Amanda."

"I wouldn't be so sure." *Just ask Bonita, or even Cora and Lydia.* "But I'm glad. God be with you, Joshua."

"He is with us. You're not to worry. Have faith."

She laid the phone in its cradle and gulped back tears of relief and anxiety, all mixed up. She would not cry for an innocent man. She would have faith, and trust in the hand of the One who wrapped them around with His protection and love.

Taking a deep, shuddering breath, Amanda straightened her apron and walked out of the office. The air was clear between her and her friend. That was not as important as his knowing about the warden, but still. Now there was nothing more she could do for him.

However, there was a whole list of things to do to get the evening meal ready for the quilters.

THE LAST THING HANNAH WANTED TO DO WAS PREPARE rooms, especially if it meant being in Bonita's company. Her nerves had been scraped raw this morning, listening to the game warden fire shot after shot with such maddening, slow regularity. Her skin seemed to creep with the waiting while he carefully examined the casings, and wrote his notes, and bagged the evidence ... she was ready to run over to him, grab him by the arm and scream, "Just declare Ben innocent, already!"

And he had. Sort of. But they wouldn't know for sure until the results came back from Denver, and who knew how long that would be? A week? A month?

"Hannah!" Bonita stopped in the doorway of the Bighorn suite and snapped her fingers in Hannah's face. "Pay attention."

Hannah pushed the girl's hand out of the way. "Don't do that. What?"

"As I was saying to Jenny, no one has used these rooms since we opened last month. People want the cabins. We can just check that everything is here, dust the surfaces, and go."

"But Mrs. Gunderson said—"

"You really want to clean a toilet that's already spotless?"

"Well, no, but she—"

"Then come on. I'll do Bighorn and you guys do the rest."

"That's four rooms to this one," Jenny objected. "Twice as much work."

"What work? You're just going down the checklist."

"What about the beds?" Hannah said. "We have to split the kings into doubles and remake them."

"Who said?" Bonita demanded.

"Nobody said. It's obvious. Twelve women means twelve singles, not six kings. Unless they're really good friends."

"There are already two singles in the second room in this suite," Jenny agreed. "That makes only one you have to split, Bee. Come on, let's get on with it."

"Teresa didn't say anything about splitting beds."

"Then you go down and ask her," Hannah suggested.

"Come on, Jenny. Checklist first, and then we'll do the beds together. May as well start next door with Puma."

Bonita flounced out, and two hours of turning king rooms into twin doubles and checking that there were two sets of toiletries, towels, and bathrobes in each room —someone had miscounted in Hawk—meant that the afternoon was nearly over before Hannah and Jenny got back to Bighorn.

Which was just the way they'd left it. No one had split the king bed. Or checked the list, either, Hannah would bet.

"Where did she go?" Jenny leaned through the door of the master bath as though Bonita might be in there placing the handmade herbal soaps in their little wooden rack.

"I don't think she came back," Hannah said. "But it doesn't matter—we can't leave this last bed. It's quarter to four and the van will be rolling in any minute."

They made short work of it—one thing about Jenny, if there was a job to be done, she didn't waste any time. And she had a good sense of humor. If she hadn't been so friendly with Bonita, Hannah might have wanted to hang around with her during their off hours, especially when Ben was away on pack trips.

Using the walkie-talkie app on her phone that the ranch had had them install, Hannah hailed Teresa to tell her they had finished. "We split all the kings to make singles," she reported. "Did Bonita come down to double-check? That's what you wanted, right?"

"Yes, didn't I say?"

"No, but that's okay. It just made sense."

"What do you mean, did Bonita come down?"

Hannah exchanged a puzzled glance with Jenny, who leaned over to say, "She left ages ago to ask you about the beds."

"She did, did she?"

Jenny's eyes went wide and she covered her mouth. "I didn't mean to squeal. I just thought you assigned her somewhere else and she never got back to us."

"No and no. Well, thanks for the heads-up, ladies. I can hear the van outside. Gird your loins."

Teresa signed off and Hannah slipped her phone into one of the deep pockets of her Amish dress. "Don't feel so bad, Jen. You didn't mean to say anything."

"Yes, but Bonita isn't going to see it that way. If Teresa speaks to her, she's going to come down on us like a ton of bricks for ratting her out."

"If she didn't do stupid things like leaving us in the lurch, Teresa wouldn't have to speak to her." If Hannah had learned anything in her months in her Amish parents' home, it was how to put the *I* in responsibility. More than once. "When you do the right thing, you don't have to put your friends in this kind of position."

"Friends?"

"Aren't you?"

Jenny turned the housekeeping cart around and steered it toward the tiny staff elevator at the far end of the broad corridor with its framed oil paintings of the views outside. They'd been painted by a guest who had come for a painting holiday, and who had left them all to be hung. Maybe he thought it would encourage people to go outside and see the actual landscape.

Jenny jerked her chin at the paintings as she steered the cart past them. "She's like these. Nice enough until you see the real thing, and then you see how fake she is. I should have gotten my first clue when she was so mean to Amanda. But I figured it was safer to be on her side than yours."

"I guess ... if you care what she thinks."

"I don't. After this, she's going to hear what I think, with the volume turned up to ten."

"If you need backup, let me know."

"I think I can handle it. Are you going to find Ben?"

"I need to. It's making me crazy, not knowing if he's all right."

"But the Wildlife warden said they were off the hook, didn't he?"

"Not completely. Not until the results come back from Denver. It could be the end of summer before that happens."

Jenny nodded. "It'll be okay, you'll see. Go on. I'll restock the cart and put it away."

Hannah ran downstairs and outside, then down the stone stairs through the landscaping to the barn. The big SUV was gone—probably off to harass poor Joshua King. *Anonymous tip, my foot.* She hadn't known him very long, but he was nice, and funny, and exactly what he appeared to be. No one in their right mind would think he would do anything illegal.

One of the cowboys told her Ben was down in the field with the horses, so she jogged there and found him leaning on the fence, stroking the noses of two of the second string.

"Hey," she said a little breathlessly. "Where are the others?"

He shrugged. "I've had about enough of everybody for now. I came out here to see some intelligent creatures who don't talk back." He scratched between the chestnut's ears, and the mare lifted her head to make his fingers find the itchy spot lower down.

Did *intelligent creatures* include Hannah? Was all this poaching stuff bothering him so much he had to shut her out to get some thinking time? "Do you want me to come back later?"

"I didn't mean you." With his free arm, he gathered her in.

He smelled of hay and grease and sun on hot skin. She kissed the angle of his jaw and settled against his side, both of them leaning on the split rails of the fence.

"Are you okay?" she asked softly.

He shrugged. "I've got nothing to worry about. We didn't do anything wrong. I wish we'd been able to pin down that fire, though. We could have taken the warden up there to prove that we weren't just ..."

"Blowing smoke?"

He smiled at the mare. "That was terrible."

"You almost said it."

"You're right, I almost did. Can I ask you something?"

"You can say anything to me," she assured him softly.

"Do you want to stay here?"

That was the last thing she'd expected. "Stay here? Well, we're not, are we? We're going back to Whinburg Township in three and a half months."

"But you're not counting."

"October first, right? And no, I'm not counting, but I do know how long my job is for. What do you mean, do I want to stay here?"

"It hasn't exactly been peaceful. Poaching nonsense on my side and Bonita on yours—and this is just our first month."

"At least with the poaching, someone might go to jail. With Bonita, we can only dream."

"See, that's what I mean. You're not happy and I'm not happy. What do you say we hop a bus and see how far it takes us?"

She slid out from under his arm and hung onto the fence, warm from the sun sinking over the pines, to gaze at him. Plus, it was something solid to hang on to while she got her bearings. "You're kidding, right? It's just a long week talking."

His eyes were shaded under his straw hat, but his mouth didn't have the easy humor it usually did. "I'm not so sure. I don't think this is the place for me anymore."

Good gravy, he was really serious. "Things with Bonita might be looking up. She skipped out on work this afternoon with twelve guests coming in, and Teresa found out about it. I talked to Jenny, and they're not the friends I thought they were. She sees right through her."

"That's good."

But it wasn't enough, if that bleak expression meant anything. "Ben, are you still thinking about heading farther west?"

He shrugged, and turned back to the horse. "A man could buy a bus ticket all the way to California once he gets his two weeks' pay. And have enough left over for a hamburger."

California! That was as far west as you could get without falling off—a whole other world from what any of them had ever seen. No, no. She'd underestimated how serious he was, and she had to fix that right now. "Hypothetically speaking, maybe he could. But what would he do when he got there?"

Over the horse's shoulder, he squinted into the pines' lengthening shadows. "I don't know. Learn to surf?"

"Right. And after that he'd be homeless and starving."

"Maybe he'd make coffee for people, like you used to do."

"He'd be better off here, where he'd make twice as much, or more, with a bed to sleep in and good food to eat, and people he knows around him."

"*Ja,* maybe." Ben turned to lean on the fence again, his elbows up on the top rail, fingers dangling. The horses investigated the fingers, but finding them empty and lifeless, snorted and moved off into the field.

Hannah pulled her ace out of her sleeve. "The warden said

we all had to stay put until this was resolved, anyway. So unless that happens before we get our first paychecks, it's kind of moot, right?"

"Right."

But from the way he still gazed westward, that didn't sound very convincing.

17

Joshua couldn't ever remember being this thankful for a phone call from a friend when he saw first the sheriff's black-and-white and then the Colorado Wildlife warden's vehicle pull into the butcher shop's yard.

"If Amanda hadn't called, I'm not sure what I'd be thinking right now," Wilmer murmured as the law enforcement officers got out, hiked their belts, and paced across the gravel lot.

"We'd be thinking they finally got my phone messages," Joshua murmured back. "I'm glad they're here, considering what we've seen." He pushed open the door and went outside to greet them. "Afternoon, Sheriff Tanner. Warden Peters."

He'd met Peters before, during the gun safety class he'd had to take before he could get a hunting license, and then once or twice during the course of business. But never under circumstances like these. Never on the business end of that deep, brown-eyed gaze.

The men shook hands, and then Peters took the lead. "I'm afraid we're not here on a social call, Mr. King."

Joshua had known since he was small that there was no bad

time to be truthful. Time to lay the facts on the table. "Come on inside, out of the sun. I hear there's been some trouble up at the Lost Creek Ranch."

"Yes, but that's not why we're here. We got a tip on the hotline saying that you were processing unpermitted road kill, and that you might even be offering wild game for sale in your butcher shop here."

Hearing it like that, in a man's no-nonsense tones, was a whole different experience from hearing it in Amanda's soft, concerned voice. He definitely preferred the latter.

"Well, I hope you don't believe it's true. You've been in here before. You know we run our operation completely above board, with regular health inspections and county permits."

"I do know that. Never had any reason to be concerned," Peters said. "In fact, I want you to prove that tipster wrong."

Joshua nodded toward the cooler. "Step on back here, if you please. I left a few messages in your office over the weekend about a little mystery of my own. Did you get them?"

The warden shook his head. "My niece got married on the weekend, and I was out in the field yesterday."

"Then maybe we can help each other answer our questions."

The sheriff zipped up his jacket and followed Joshua, Wilmer, and the warden into the walk-in cooler. The Phelps deer hung from a hook in the ceiling, directly over a drain. It had stiffened with the cold, and there was frost on its eyelashes. Joshua laid a gentle hand on its side. "This animal was brought to me on Saturday by a man and his son. Phelps was their name, and from what they said, we gathered they lived in Salida."

"Did they show you their permit?" Peters asked.

"That was my mistake," Joshua admitted. "I asked for it,

and they went out and searched their truck, but they couldn't find it. Said they must have left it at home. They said they'd give me the name of the warden who signed off on it, but they didn't do that, and they didn't call back with the permit number, either."

"Probably because it doesn't exist," the sheriff said.

"You're likely right. That doesn't excuse my mistake in accepting the job, though. I should have turned them away when they didn't have their permit."

"Next time I hope you will," the warden said.

"If there is a next time," the sheriff put in. "If we don't suspend your business license and charge you with illegally processing this game." He looked miserable in the cold of the room.

"Let's not get ahead of ourselves," Peters told him. "I'm glad to see you didn't process this animal. When did they say they were coming for their meat?"

"This morning," Joshua said. "Eight o'clock. But when I had a look at it again Saturday, there were a couple of things along with the missing permit that told me to hold off and call you."

The warden had already begun to examine the deer. "I see what you mean." He glanced at the sheriff. "Come look at this. When a deer has been hit by a vehicle, what would you expect to see?"

"Broken bones," the man replied. "Bruising. Paint, maybe."

"Right. And Joshua, what did you find?"

"None of that. Seems a healthy three-year-old buck, except for that wound there by your left hand, which wasn't good for his health at all."

Did that Phelps pair think an experienced butcher would miss something as obvious as a bullet hole? Or that he'd just go along with processing game that had clearly been poached, without asking questions? Joshua shook his head in disbelief.

"Here's another." Peters indicated a second wound. "Not *put* down after being struck, but *brought* down. And look at this." Peters was as tall as Joshua, and taller than the sheriff, who stretched to look up at the animal's hind legs. "Looks like abrasion here around its hooves and on its flanks. Maybe he was dragged out of the bush behind a truck to make it look like road rash."

"Maybe," Joshua acknowledged. "Add all those together, subtract a missing permit, and the sum of the matter is that I didn't process this animal."

"Can we finish this discussion out in the office?" the sheriff asked, his teeth beginning to chatter.

Wilmer closed and locked the cooler while Joshua led the law enforcement officers into the workroom, with its stainless-steel instruments and big block cutting table. "This Phelps man told me he'd be back this morning to collect his deer. He paid cash for the processing. A man might forget to call about a permit, but it's hard to believe he'd forget about meat he'd paid for."

"Do you still have the money?"

"I do."

His father went into the office and got it. "Wasn't about to put this in the bank," he said as he handed over an envelope.

The warden fanned through the money, and handed it to the sheriff. He said to Joshua, "They said they lived in Salida?"

"His exact words after he got done yelling at his boy was that they'd have to drive eighty miles home and eighty miles back with the deer getting warm in the back of the truck, and that was why they wanted the processing done then—on

Saturday. They weren't too happy about waiting until today for it. Or at least, they acted that way."

The sheriff said, "I think we have a bigger problem here than we thought."

"I have a feeling you're right," Peters said. "My incident cluster is growing again, and I don't like it."

"Incident cluster?" Wilmer repeated.

Peters nodded. "Things happening all in the same time frame with Amish folks appearing to be in the middle. Anonymous tips accusing people of crimes greater than simply being accommodating or making a mistake. Poachers roaming the mountains on a ranch where it's known there are Amish folks working. This is what I call an incident cluster, and I'd sure like to know what's behind it."

"So would we," Wilmer said. "What can we do to help?"

"Don't process any animals without permits, for starters," Peters said.

Joshua huffed a rueful laugh. "That I can certainly promise. Are you going to charge me for accepting a poached animal? That is what I deserve."

"Not at all. You did the right thing by not processing it, and calling us as soon as you discovered there was something wrong. And they haven't taken away the meat, so we have evidence and a pair of witnesses. Someone tried to set you up, and you were smart enough not to fall for it. But several days have passed now, which has lowered our chances of catching up to these two."

Joshua wished now he'd called the sheriff as well as the warden. Then maybe they could have gotten started sooner.

Peters seemed to notice his downcast face. "You've been here for three years and never put a foot wrong. This setup was deliberate, Joshua. I will ask you to keep your eyes open. Do you remember what they were driving?"

Joshua could see that truck in his mind's eye as though it were parked right outside. "Black pickup—a newer one, with dually wheels in back. Chevy logo on the grill."

"License plate?"

He shook his head. "I wasn't thinking along those lines at the time. But there was one thing—it had yellow fog lamps up on the push bar."

"That should narrow it down some," the sheriff said. "There must be a million Chevy pickups in this state. Provided their name really is Phelps, I can do some checks in Custer and adjacent counties and see what I come up with."

Warden Peters held out a hand, and Joshua shook it. "We'll get to the bottom of this. You might ask your people to keep an eye out for that truck, too. You never know—sharp-eyed witnesses have turned the tide in many a case."

"I hope something else doesn't happen," Wilmer said, worry beginning to creep into his tone. "A number of our folk have shops in Amistad, some run by wives and mothers. I'd hate for anything bad to happen to them, or to someone in a buggy coming home at night."

"That's just what we're here to prevent," the sheriff said. "Don't borrow trouble, though. We just need a few more pieces to turn this puzzle into a picture."

"I'll have to confiscate that animal in the cooler, Joshua," Peters told him. "If you wouldn't mind giving me a hand getting it out to the truck? And if they do come back for their packages of illegal game, I hope you'll call me immediately." He handed Joshua a card. "That's my cell phone, not the office line. Call if you think of anything else that might help us."

When the two official vehicles finally pulled out onto the county road and headed for the main highway, Wilmer closed the door of the retail shop and collapsed into the office chair. Joshua leaned on the doorframe and wiped his forehead with his hanky.

Wilmer eyed him. "I don't know what I would have done if we'd processed that deer and they'd arrested you."

"If I'd ignored the signs, I would have deserved to be arrested." Joshua scrubbed his face, hard. "What was I thinking, to accept that animal without a permit when I know the law?"

"You were thinking they were honest men, like any of us would," his father said wearily. "It doesn't sit right to treat someone like we expect them to do us a bad turn, but I suppose from now on, we'd better."

Joshua's stomach still felt queasy at what could have happened, as though he'd eaten green apples and couldn't quite throw them up. "Peters is a good man. We should thank the *gut Gott* it was him and not some greenhorn fresh out of the academy wanting to make his mark."

"Now you're the one borrowing trouble," his father told him. "God has all of this in His hand, and we can be grateful He does. Now, I think you'd better call up to the ranch and let that kind-hearted girl know what happened. She's probably on tenterhooks, wondering what is going on down here."

"I'll do one better." Joshua made up his mind in an instant. "If you don't mind watching the store for a little while, I'll take the buggy up there and tell her in person. I have to say a drive will do me good—that ranch road is just the right length for prayer."

"I don't mind at all," his father said. And Joshua could swear he had a twinkle in his eye as he made his way past him and out to the front to greet the *Englisch* customers just pulling in.

❧

THE STAFF DIDN'T NORMALLY JOIN IN THE WELCOME OF NEW guests—the Gundersons did that almost exclusively. But Mrs. Gunderson had come running downstairs to grab Amanda when the quilters arrived. "Come with me. Where's Hannah?"

"I don't know. They were trying to get the rooms done before—"

"Never mind. Come and make these guests feel welcome."

The last thing Amanda wanted to do was wade into a bunch of ladies all talking at once. She wanted to hide here in the kitchen, frying bacon for the roasted Brussels sprouts, while she fretted over what was happening to Joshua, possibly at this very minute.

But she had no choice. She followed Mrs. Gunderson out the door and into the courtyard, where the two ranch vans were disgorging guests.

The quilters came into the house in a chattering flock, exclaiming over the scenery, pulling their suitcases and big plastic bins with wheels that seemed to contain everything from fabric to sewing machines. In the great room, they were stunned into silence by the enormous windows framing the view. Mrs. Gunderson greeted them cordially and welcomed them to the ranch while Amanda stood there wishing she'd had time to wash her hands and hoping she wouldn't need to shake with anyone.

Had Joshua been arrested? Would someone call to let them know? What was happ—

"This is Amanda Yoder, ladies, one of our Amish staff.

She'll be happy to show you the way to your rooms. And then I hope you'll meet me back here in the great room for a welcome beverage and a tour of the property."

"Cowboys and quilts!" one of the women sighed. "I'm *so* in my happy place."

"Cowboys and *Amish* quilts." Another fingered the hem of an Ohio Star that had been folded and draped at an appealing angle over one of the leather sofas. "Look at the work in this one, ladies. This is the real McCoy—ten stitches to the inch, I'll bet."

"Is it for sale?" The first lady joined her, then looked up at Amanda. "Did you make it?"

"Oh, no," Amanda said. "The ladies in Amistad did. And it is for sale. You can visit the quilt shop and see more of them. These are just a few."

"Definitely my happy place." The first lady beamed.

"Are you from here?" someone else asked. "Your covering is Lancaster County, isn't it?"

Goodness, they were well informed. She pushed her worries into a closet in her mind and did her best to answer pleasantly, conscious that Mrs. Gunderson was watching. "Yes. My home is in Whinburg Township, near Strasburg. I'm working here at the ranch for the summer, helping in the kitchen."

"Amish food too?" Another lady clutched the woman next to her. "This was the best idea you've ever had, Maggie. Amish food is to die for. We were in Holmes County last fall and I swear I gained twenty pounds in a single week."

Mrs. Gunderson laughed, a sound like a brook tinkling over rocks. "I'm sorry to disappoint you, ladies, but as you might have seen on our website, the food here is quite unique. Our chef was trained in San Francisco at the CIA, and she apprenticed at the La Fonda Hotel in Santa Fe. So while we might not have mashed potatoes and—and whatever else you might find in Amish country, we do have beef Wellington, steak tartare, and *crepes aux fraises* for breakfast, among many other things."

The woman's face fell. "No whoopie pies?"

"Not here—though there is an Amish bakery near Westcliffe. I'm willing to bet you'd find some there. Maybe we could organize a field trip."

The woman nodded, then said to Amanda, "Do you know how to make whoopie pies?"

"I do," she said, glancing at Mrs. Gunderson to make sure she was supposed to answer the question. The topic of food was a sensitive one, and she didn't want to offend. Her employer lifted her eyebrows in a way she took to be encouraging, so she added, "My favorite is gingerbread with cream cheese filling, though lots of people like chocolate with orange. My nephew likes chocolate with peanut butter spread in the middle."

The woman groaned. "Stop. You're making me hungry."

"Then Amanda will show you where your rooms are, and I'll have something brought up to tide you over until dinner," Mrs. Gunderson said, smiling in a fixed kind of way. "Amanda?"

"Please," she said to the ladies, who followed her down the broad corridor with its stripped log beams and glossy plank floor. And the beautiful paintings, which no one seemed to be interested in. "There are four who want to be together, I understand?" She opened the door to Bighorn and four ladies filed in with their bags and wheeled bins. "The other rooms have two beds apiece. You have this part of the house to yourselves, so feel free to spread out."

"Speaking of spreading out, how about a workroom?" one of them asked. "We'll need a place to sew and lay things out."

"We have a big conference room off the dining area, and you can also work outside on the deck if you like and the wind isn't too bad. I like to do my handwork outside at home in the summer, in the screened porch. They don't have mosquitoes here like they do in Pennsylvania, which is nice."

She stood by the door as two women went into Hawk.

"Seems a bit funny we don't get Amish food," one of them said to Amanda. "That would be the icing on the cake. We booked this place for our retreat because the website said there were Amish folks in this area, as well as some working here. We can't wait to see more—and food is part of it."

Amanda flushed. "You could take it up with Mrs. Gunderson. She creates the menus, and takes the food here very seriously." On impulse, she said, "Maybe one morning we could have a group lesson on making whoopie pies. I could show you—they aren't difficult."

The woman's face creased into a smile, giving her apple cheeks and twinkling eyes. "I'd love that. Mostly we've come to escape cooking, but whoopie pies sound like fun."

When Amanda felt it was safe to leave the chattering group to find its own way back to the great room, she hurried downstairs. She had been in the middle of frying that bacon, so she hoped Teresa hadn't been too inconvenienced by having to finish her job for her.

The bacon was draining on paper towels when she came into the kitchen, and Teresa was up to her elbows in salad greens. "Oh good. Glad you're back. Thank goodness tonight is a barbecue, and Mr. Gunderson looks after it. All we have to do is prepare the meat and clean up afterward. We'll have the same for the staff meal. You can start making carrot curls."

Amanda got busy scrubbing carrots, then used a special peeler to make the curls. "The ladies seem nice. They love the quilts, so it was a good idea you had, to bring some up here."

"Good thing I remembered I had them." Teresa smiled and tossed greens with both gloved hands.

"They might want to learn how to make whoopie pies one morning." Amanda slid the curls into the salad. "I could give a lesson here."

"That would be up to Mrs. Gunderson—and it would mean a trip to town to get ingredients."

"We have everything on hand—they're not complicated." Not even as complicated as that salad, with its chunks of avocado and blueberries.

"I'll think about it later. The Brussels sprouts are in the fridge."

"Oh, Mrs. Gunderson promised some snacks, too."

"She did? Never mind the sprouts, then. The trays are in the pantry—you can take them up. And if you see Tyler, tell him to prep the big grill on the deck."

How did she keep track of everything? Maybe the whoopie pies were a bad idea. Teresa had enough to deal with without a dozen chattering *Englisch* ladies in here making a mess with flour and cocoa. Hopefully they'd be so distracted by everything else there was to enjoy at the ranch that the subject would drop.

After the trays had been set out on the sideboard in the great room, she went in search of Tyler. She found him heading down to the bunkhouse and delivered Teresa's message.

"Thanks, Amanda." He turned toward the house, then glanced back. "By the way, there's a buggy coming up the hill. It might be a delivery."

Her heart jumped. A buggy! Who? Joshua!

The Brussels sprouts—the kitchen—everything went straight out of her head as she picked up her skirts and ran up the hill to the road. And there was Rusty the horse and a familiar face visible through the storm front.

"Joshua!" she gasped as he slowed the horse and she ran alongside. "You're all right—they didn't arrest you!"

He laughed, the best kind of laugh, with his head thrown back. "No, they didn't arrest me—though I'm lucky there isn't a fine for being stupid. Hop in and I'll take you up."

She climbed in and turned toward him on the front seat. "Tell me what happened. I've been so worried."

So he did, briefly because they didn't have far to go, but with enough detail that she could picture exactly what had gone on.

She let out a long breath as he pulled Rusty to a stop in the courtyard. "So the long and the short of it was, I didn't need to worry," she said. "You saw that the animal had been poached and hadn't touched it, and you notified them, even if no one was there to get the message."

"I had a bad moment or two, even so." He paused for a moment. "And it touches my heart that you were worried for my sake."

Her heart was still pounding—from the run up the hill from the bunkhouse, from seeing him, from hearing his story—and she covered it with one hand over the bib front of her apron. "Anyone would be worried. These are serious matters, and now even more serious, if what the Wildlife warden suspects could really be true."

"They are serious matters. But Dane Peters is a good man. A smart man. If anyone can figure out what is going on, it's him. All of us just need to keep an eye out for those Phelps characters and their truck. I hope you'll let the hands know, especially the ones who drive the ranch vans. They'll be out on the highway more, and might see it."

"Of course," she assured him.

"Amanda." He let the reins go loose in their channels in the dashboard.

"Ja? What is it?"

"What you did in calling me was the action of a true friend."

She hardly knew how to reply. So she looked down at her hands, clasped in her lap. "I was very worried. I could hardly concentrate all afternoon. It's a wonder I didn't put the raw bacon in the salad and fry the carrot curls."

He reached out and freed one of her hands from its grip on the other. How warm they were—how rough from leather and knife handles and work. And his eyes—but she didn't dare look up. Instead, her face burned as red as coals in a hot stove.

"Friends worry about one another, don't they?"

"Ja, they do," she managed, her mouth going suddenly dry.

"I hope we are friends."

"I—I do, too."

"A man doesn't often come across a friend who knows a word in season when she sees one. I want to thank you for it."

"Even though it wasn't necessary. You'd already done what was needed."

"You didn't know that. *Denki.*" He had not released her hand, and the Lord would bring the world to an end before she would pull hers away. "Perhaps we might see each other again before Sunday?"

If her heart had been beating fast before, it was nothing to the pace it was setting now—like a galloping horse, running and running to she didn't know where.

But before she could reply, feet crunched in the gravel and

someone banged on the back of the buggy. "Joshua, is that you? Is everything all right?"

Teresa.

Amanda gasped and practically leaped off the bench and out of the door. It wasn't until she was safely in the kitchen that she realized she hadn't answered his question. And that he hadn't repeated it.

But then, maybe he didn't need to. Maybe her hand in his had said everything there was to say.

18

When Amanda walked up to staff cabin number four after the dishes were done that evening, it was lit up like Christmas, with raised voices coming through the thick log walls. She closed her eyes in a brief prayer for strength. It had to be Hannah, getting into it with Bonita. Other than a distant glimpse of Hannah with Ben and the horses, she hadn't seen either of them all afternoon. What could have happened now? And was the whole summer really going to be like this?

The sweet, secret joy of Joshua's holding her hand seemed to recede at the prospect of opening the cabin door, and that loss grieved her.

She went in, only to find that one of the raised voices belonged not to Hannah, but Teresa. Shocked, she hesitated in the doorway one moment too long, and Bonita saw her.

"This is *your* fault!" she snapped.

Teresa turned, her normally generous, good-humored mouth thinned almost to the point of disappearance. "It is not Amanda's fault, or Hannah's. It's the fact that you lied to

Hannah and Jenny and left them to do your work. And not only that, it's your inability to get along that is making it downright unpleasant for the others to work in housekeeping right now."

"Is that what they said?"

"It doesn't matter what they said. It's what I've observed. I'm not blind, Bonita. I'm afraid it's just not going to work out for you here."

"But I do work!" she protested. "I work a lot harder than the other two, especially since you took Amanda off my team."

"It isn't your team, it's mine," Teresa said shortly. "I'll have Mrs. Gunderson cut you a check for the full two weeks' pay, and one of the boys will take you into town to get the bus back to Monte Vista in the morning."

"But I don't want to go."

"I realize you probably don't. But sadly, you've done this to yourself. The guests come first, and no one wants to listen to the housekeeping staff sniping at each other."

Hannah and Jenny stepped up on the rustic little porch just then, at which point Teresa went back to the house and Bonita decided that the cold shoulder was all any of them deserved as she emptied the stuffed closet and packed her things. She was horrid for the rest of the evening.

Maybe that was why Amanda didn't sleep well, tossing with bad dreams in which she had to cook a huge meal all by herself for a crowd of guests, and didn't have any of the ingredients. To add to it, she was looking for something—a Phillips screwdriver—knowing that something awful would happen if she couldn't find it.

In the morning, Bonita had a few more unkind things to share as she got into the van with her bags. When the vehicle disappeared down the long hill, Teresa turned to

Hannah, Jenny, and Amanda with a sigh. "I hate letting people go."

"I can't blame you," Hannah said. "But I have to say, it feels lighter around here already."

"The workload won't," Teresa retorted. She pushed her hair off her forehead. "Amanda, you look tired. And here we've got twelve quilters while we're down two staff. I don't suppose you know anybody who could come and help, do you?"

Amanda's gaze met Hannah's, and the same thought seemed to transmit itself in a split second. "We might," she said. "There are some girls about our age in Amistad who might be able to fill in. Would you like me to find out?"

"Would you?" For the first time since last night, Teresa's face lightened with relief. "That would be great. And now I've got to go and clean up after breakfast. You'd think those ladies would appreciate *crepes aux fraises* a little more than they did." She pronounced it not the way Mrs. Gunderson did, but *crape oh frayzes*. "Oh well. We can eat them cold during our break."

Amanda went into Teresa's office to use the phone, and picked through the collection of things in the pencil holder, looking for a pen to write down the Swarey and Hertzler telephone numbers. As the call rang through, she idly pulled out one of the screwdrivers.

Not a Phillips, like in her dream. Just an ordinary screwdriver, for repairs too small to bother one of the cowboys with.

"King Cuts and Meats."

"Hello, Joshua," she said shyly, dropping the screwdriver back into the jar and pulling out a pen.

"Guder mariye," he said. "This is a treat. You owe me an answer to a question, if I recall."

"I do," she said with a smile. "And it might even be yes, but that's not why I'm calling."

"A maybe yes is good enough for me. What can I do for you?"

"Any sign of that black truck?"

"No, nor the Phelps people, either."

Amanda felt the tingle of shock run through her, as though she'd touched a live wire. "Phelps!" she exclaimed. "Not a Phillips screwdriver, for pity's sake."

"Amanda?" he asked cautiously. "Did I miss something?"

"The name of those poachers. Phelps. I had a dream—never mind." She waggled the screwdriver in the holder and shook her head at the odd workings of the mind. "The point is, Teresa fired a man named Phelps when we first came here—Jackson Phelps. The man I replaced. Don't you think it's odd that the name is the same?"

"How old was he?"

Amanda tried to tamp down her excitement long enough to remember. "Maybe in his mid-twenties. His sister and her children had been staying with him."

"Not the same man in the black truck, then."

She sighed with disappointment.

"The older one was pushing forty, and his boy was only seventeen or eighteen. Nice training he's getting in how to be a good man, I have to say."

Well, it didn't have to be the same man. The same name was coincidence enough. And Amanda didn't believe in those. "Then I wonder if it's a relative. Do you think I ought to tell the Wildlife warden? Or the sheriff?"

"It might be nothing, or it might not. I can do that for you. I've got Dane Peters's card right here. Is that what you called to tell me?"

For a moment Amanda couldn't think past the congruence of Jackson Phelps being fired and the poaching that all seemed to point to Amish folk. But that was not for her to figure out. Her job right now was to figure out how to help Teresa.

"No, I called to see if you knew Cora Swarey and Lydia Hertzler's phone numbers. We have two openings in housekeeping and Teresa is willing to give them jobs if they can come on short notice. As in, this week. Probably tomorrow."

"Is that so? Well, that's good news. If they can come, I could bring them up the mountain when I make my deliveries."

For the first time since she had opened the cabin door last night, Amanda found a smile again. "That would be perfect. Then maybe one of the hands wouldn't mind running them back down at the end of the day when they go to pick up the mail."

"Sounds like you've got it all arranged. How about this—why don't I take Grace Ann for a drive this afternoon, after I talk to the warden. She'll be happy to see her friends, and we can have a visit and ask them at the same time."

"And let Teresa know the answer?"

"I will. And speaking of answers, since you might have said yes some minutes ago, can I take you for a drive on Friday evening? Some of our customers mentioned there's to be a star shower."

A star shower! "I've never heard of such a thing. It sounds beautiful."

"One of *der Herr's* many gifts," Joshua said softly.

"I would like that very much."

"So would I." He cleared his throat. "See you tomorrow morning as usual, then."

Amanda hung up and clasped her hands over her heart to prevent its flying out and winging around the room like a happy bird.

Thank you, Lord, for Your gifts. For a star shower You sent so that Joshua would ask me to come and see it. For peace for Hannah and Jenny and me, and maybe even an opportunity for two girls to find work. Even for a crazy dream that might help the warden figure out what is happening in these mountains. There is so much to thank You for, dear Lord.

Help me, I pray, to be an obedient servant, and to be willing to be led by You. Oh, Father, if it is Your hand that has brought Joshua and me together in this beautiful place, please reveal Your will to us so that everything we do is according to what You want, not what I want or he wants. In the name of Jesus, I pray.

With a deep breath, she opened her eyes and headed for the kitchen to let Teresa know that help might be on the way.

BY LUNCHTIME, AMANDA HADN'T HEARD A WORD FROM anyone, warden or possible new employees, but the workload kept her far too busy to think. It was all she could do to stay on top of the meal. When the plates that had taken all morning to prepare came back with only small spoonsful taken out of them or even none at all, it was really difficult not to take it personally.

Worse, as she and Teresa were glumly looking at the serving dishes on the worktable, Mrs. Gunderson swept into the kitchen and caught them at it.

"This is exactly what I want to talk to you about," she said, pointing at the platters, then picking up a piece of smoked salmon and popping it in her mouth. "Is there something wrong with these dishes that those ladies aren't eating them? Do you know I actually heard one of them suggest going into town to the drive-in for a burger? That is outrageous. Unacceptable. What is going on?"

"Oh, dear," Amanda whispered. A burger? That really was an affront. And she could tell by the droop in Teresa's shoulders that she felt just as bad as Amanda did. Some of the garnishes on that plate alone had taken long minutes of careful work—to say nothing of a cut finger—to create.

"There is nothing wrong with the dishes," Teresa said. "Amanda and I tasted everything."

"Then what's the problem? It can't be the presentation. It's not the freshness, because we source everything locally if we can, and from reputable organic places if we can't. And it can't be our guests, because they seem to love everything else about the ranch. So what is it?"

Could she really not see? The women had told her what they wanted, and she'd brushed it off. Well. Amanda was not going to spend another day on fancy cooking only to see that hurt expression in Teresa's eyes when the dishes came back practically untouched. Not when there was a perfectly obvious solution staring them in the face.

"Mrs. Gunderson, if you don't mind my speaking out of turn—"

"What is it, Amanda?" her employer said wearily. "With all your experience in the kitchen, can you shed some light on this problem?"

Amanda couldn't tell whether she was being sarcastic or not. But it didn't matter. "I believe I can. Those ladies were so excited to see that the Amish community was a part of ranch life. That's a big reason they booked their stay here." There, that was a diplomatic way of saying it. "You hired me to be part of that experience for them, but an equally big part is missing."

"And what would that be?"

Definitely sarcastic—something she wasn't used to. Amanda's sensitive soul quivered, but she plunged on. "The food, Mrs. Gunderson. People who come to a working ranch for a holiday don't want fancy meals that could be on the cover of a magazine. They want healthy, nourishing, homemade things that—well, that make them feel like they're on a ranch, not in a big city at an expensive restaurant."

Mrs. Gunderson stared at her, her gaze as clear and cold as the runoff from the glaciers they could see from the windows. "Is that so?"

"The quilters said it themselves—they wanted some Amish cooking. Good, plain cooking that makes them feel at home."

"Really." That tone would make snow fly in the middle of a room.

But Amanda couldn't stop until she'd said what had to be said. "You saw how much they liked the barbecue on their first night. It was simple and tasty. Let Teresa and me cook their dinner tonight—just one meal—in the way that they want. And then you can see whether they like it or not, and if we ought to change the menu around a little."

Silence fell. Mrs. Gunderson took another piece of smoked salmon, and wiped her fingers on a towel. "Fine. One meal. And don't tell me you have to go to town to get ingredients. This one lunch cost more than I probably paid you today."

Amanda didn't doubt that for a second. "I'm pretty sure we have all we need on hand. The staff supper, too?"

"Of course the staff supper, too. Unless they want to clean this up and give me my money's worth." She waved a hand at the serving dishes and left the room, her boot heels clunking on the floors in a stiff-legged way that told Amanda just how angry she was.

Teresa's eyes were wide as she gazed at the door, then at

Amanda. "I can't believe you said that to her. After all the meals I've made."

"Your cooking is wonderful. But these menus aren't what people want. I had to tell her the truth."

Shaking her head, Teresa said, "You know, for someone so shy, you really know how to put your finger on a problem."

Amanda smiled a little ruefully. "It comes of being an aunt and a sister, with family around all the time. And cooking isn't a problem. It's a solution. Come on—let's take inventory and see what we can come up with."

Amanda had never in the world thought that she'd be teaching a chef of Teresa's caliber how to make simple things like chicken and dumplings, but as the afternoon went by on a swallow's wings, she found herself doing exactly that. Yet one more new experience in an adventure laden with new experiences. Who would ever have imagined the word *adventure* in her vocabulary to begin with? But here she was, laughing along with her student as they mixed and chopped and blended.

Chicken and dumplings, and sausage potato casserole, and jellied salad, and coleslaw (the perfect use for the red cabbage sitting in the bottom of the vegetable crisper). Fresh bread, though Teresa insisted on using the fancy electric breadmaker because it would be faster. The smoked salmon went into the blender along with the ingredients for a salmon puff.

Last but not least were the whoopie pies—chocolate, with mint filling because the vanilla and rum flavorings in the cupboard would absolutely not do.

"I've heard of grasshopper pie, but never like this," Teresa said, sinking into a chair and biting into one when they'd cooled and been assembled. "I feel five pounds coming on as we speak." She put her feet up on the little stepladder they used to reach the things on the top shelves.

"Not the way you work," Amanda said, wiping down the counters and the big wooden worktop. "You never stop moving. It's the same at home. People work hard in the house and in the fields, and they need food that sticks to their ribs when they sit down to a meal."

"Let's hope you're right. I'd cook this way any day—Jose is going to be overjoyed. Maybe after this I can talk Mrs. G. into tortillas and carnitas for those executives coming for Fourth of July."

When she and Amanda carried up the coffee and the small hill of whoopie pies on the oval serving platter, they saw that their work was good. The quilting ladies looked like the cowboys downstairs had, leaning back in their chairs with their hands on their stomachs, the empty dishes whisked away by Carson and Mike.

The lady with the twinkly eyes groaned as Amanda set the oval platter of cream-filled cookies in the middle of the table. "There is no way on earth I could put another bite in my mouth," she said. "At least, not until after a brisk walk. I'm so glad we didn't go to town this afternoon. That was the best meal I've had since my fortieth anniversary—and that was last year."

"I'm glad you enjoyed it," Amanda said shyly. "Chicken and dumplings is Dat's—I mean, my father's favorite."

"See?" said the woman across the table as she reached for a whoopie pie. "Good, old-fashioned Amish food. It's the best, I told you."

"We'll have to arrange some hiking and swimming for you, to wear it off," Teresa suggested with a smile. "Our fishermen are checking out tomorrow, aren't you?" She raised a brow at the oldest of them. "So we can reclaim the river for swimming?"

He glanced at Mr. Gunderson at the head of the big, family style table. "Guess that depends on what the sheriff says. I haven't heard that we can't go, anyway."

"The sheriff?" said the twinkly lady. "Why would he prevent you from going home?"

At which point the fishermen proceeded to tell the quilters about everything that had been going on, a tale that took them all the way through dessert and coffee, and into the evening. Amanda and the waiters cleared away the dishes and left them to it.

The dishes had practically been licked clean. "Between the cowboys downstairs and the guests upstairs, I think we'd better add half again to Mamm's recipe," Amanda said, making notes on a recipe card. "I thought it would feed everyone, and it did, but only just."

"That's a keeper for my recipe file," Teresa said. "I guess you showed Mrs. Gunderson, didn't you?"

Amanda got busy filling the big commercial dishwasher. "I didn't mean to show anybody. I just wanted the guests to enjoy their meal."

"You got your wish. So what's for breakfast?"

Amanda stood with a bowl in her hands. "I don't know. Mrs. Gunderson said we could only make one meal my way. Not any others."

"Mrs. Gunderson says you can make more." They both straightened with a snap as their employer came into the kitchen. "That was good, ladies. Thank you."

"I'm glad you enjoyed it," Amanda said softly. She'd known they'd done well, but knowing it and hearing Mrs. Gunderson say it were two different things.

The week's menu Mrs. Gunderson and Teresa had compiled was tacked to the bulletin board. Their employer flicked it with a manicured nail. "I suppose we'd better toss this and try again—at least while the quilters are here. No one's going to a drive-in for dinner on my watch unless they're suffering from acute fast-food withdrawal and have a doctor's certificate to prove it. Amanda, you'll work with Teresa to come up with meal plans for the rest of the week?"

"Yes, I will." The warmth of happiness flooded her at the thought of making real meals—the food of home and farm. The food she knew would satisfy the people here. "Thank you, Mrs. Gunderson. For letting us try."

Her employer gazed at her, but a warm wind seemed to have softened the wintry color of her eyes. "There is nothing wrong with beautiful presentation and innovative flavor combinations. Don't forget that, even when you're cooking Amish."

"We won't," Amanda said. "But it's like at home—we don't serve pork when Uncle Oskar comes for Christmas because the fat upsets his stomach. We have to choose the food that we want people to enjoy, because it's a part of the memories we're making. And we want them to be good memories."

Serving her family with good food was an act of worship, too, but Amanda wasn't so sure this lady would appreciate that side of it.

Mrs. Gunderson nodded slowly. "I suppose you're right. We certainly want people to go away with good memories—and write good reviews on TripAdvisor." She took down the menu and it fluttered into the recycling bin. "Let me know what you come up with, and we'll see that you have all the supplies you need. Oh—" She stopped in the doorway. "Joshua King called. He says that two Amish girls called Cora and Lydia will be available starting tomorrow, and he'll bring them up the hill." Amanda's delight must have shown on her face, because she went on, "If I'd known you had Amish friends right here in the valley, I'd have hired them, too."

"If you want Amish staff at any time of the year besides summer, it's good to know there are experienced people nearby."

"You're right there. I might just start thinking about a Christmas campaign." She nodded to them both and left, and this time the boot heels on the floor sounded light and quick, as though the thought of business plans made her happy.

19

At six o'clock the following morning, no smile was broader than Joshua's as Cora and Lydia climbed out of the buggy and stood in the courtyard looking up at the house. The two girls, one in a burgundy dress and one in hunter green, black bib aprons knotted behind and *Kapp* strings neatly tied but hanging down their backs out of the way, craned their necks to take in the grandeur of the stone and log house.

"No wonder they need all of us to keep it clean," Cora breathed.

"The wonder is they don't need more," Lydia agreed. "We're going to get lost in there."

"I promise you won't." Hannah Riehl patted Josie the Percheron's nose as she came around the buggy with Teresa and Amanda in her wake. "Hi, Joshua."

"Guder mariye," he said, but his gaze was on Amanda, a fact he noticed that Cora didn't miss, even as Amanda introduced the new staff to Teresa.

As a friend of his sister, he'd taken Cora home from singing twice last year. Gossip might have paired them together because of it, but both of them knew that she was still recovering from her disappointment over Simon Yoder and had no interest in being courted by someone new. She did appreciate finding good friends where she could, though, and he'd been happy to fill that place.

And now Cora had agreed to come and work for the same outfit Simon did, so her heart must have healed enough to be strong when she ran into him occasionally. Maybe the *gut Gott* would see to it there were more than the usual number of pack trips this summer, so that in time the sting would diminish.

But he wouldn't think about love thwarted by selfishness on such a beautiful morning. Not when Amanda was standing there talking with the three girls, her face a little more solemn than usual as a red-faced Lydia said something to her in low, rapid *Deitsch*.

An apology? Perhaps for the way she'd spoken at the singing. If so, that was brave of Lydia. Not only were they to work together, but also they would be sitting on the same bench in church on Sunday, and one couldn't bring a bad spirit into the midst of God's people and expect to receive the gift of hearing His voice. Lydia was making it right beforehand, even ahead of making her living.

And Amanda, instead of merely nodding and going about her business, blushed too—and pulled Lydia in for a hug. Joshua blinked in surprise. It wasn't the Amish way to indulge in public demonstrations. There was clearly something deeper going on that a mere man was not privy to.

He smiled again, and turned to open the back of the buggy, where Tyler and Teresa were waiting for him to unload the day's order. Once it had all been taken in, Teresa handed him an order slip. "This one's new, starting tomorrow."

"On a Friday?" She always gave him the order on Monday morning, which covered the entire week until the following Monday.

"Change of plan. Amanda and I drew up the menus last night, and this is what she needs for the weekend."

"What Amanda needs?" He glanced down the sheet to see some very familiar items. "She's cooking Amish?"

"Mrs. G. took a few gentle suggestions, and the guests practically licked their plates clean. So at least while the quilters are here, we'll be cooking Amish."

Joshua had to laugh. "Good for her. I'll be happy to make these changes. Anything for satisfied guests."

"Have you heard anything from the sheriff? Or Warden Peters?"

"I left a message for the warden last night after Amanda mentioned something to me. I guess all we can do is wait."

"I hate waiting," Teresa grumbled. "I want it cleared up and everything to go back to the way it should be. I hate Jose looking over his shoulder and wondering if everyone he meets could be poaching on Lost Creek land."

Joshua resisted the urge to tell her that it was in God's hands—the safest place for the matter to be. "It will work out. At least you know for sure now that everyone here is on the right side of the law."

"I do." She gripped his shoulder briefly. "Thanks, Joshua. And thanks for bringing the girls up. We'll run them back down the hill at four o'clock."

"Their families will meet them at the mailboxes."

He didn't dare interrupt Amanda's work the way he had done yesterday, but simply caught her eye and smiled in a way that he hoped conveyed his pleasure at the thought of the next evening's star shower. She smiled back, and blushed, and he thought he had never seen anything so delightful in his life.

He backed Josie around and rolled off down the drive, whistling. He was halfway down the long grade when he saw a dust plume rising above the pines—a plume that could only mean a vehicle coming up the hill at a pace well over the speed limit of twenty miles per hour.

"Whoa, Josie, we'd better pull over here." He backed the big horse into the farm road that led to the frontier-era barn in the meadow, and waited for the vehicle to pass.

In just a few moments, the Colorado Wildlife warden's SUV came around the curve and accelerated along the flat toward him. Then it checked—slowed—and rolled to a stop across the mouth of the turnout. The dust cloud kept right on going over their heads as Dane Peters rolled down the passenger window.

"Are you going up or coming down, Joshua?"

"Coming down. Josie and I thought we'd better get out of the way in case there was an emergency. Is everything all right, Warden?"

"I suppose that depends on which side of this mess you're on." He grinned. "I'm glad you and that observant young lady up there are on my side. Come on. I might as well tell you and everyone else the news together."

Joshua regretted not having Rusty this morning, so he could put him into his racing paces once more—the Amish often bought racehorses after their careers were over, but it was dangerous to let them remember their own speed when they were hitched up to a buggy. Josie wasn't a racer, but she'd never come so close to it as now, lengthening her big stride up that hill to the ranch house. He might even have let her break out into a gallop—but not where anyone could see them.

He found the Gundersons and every member of the staff who had seen the SUV—housekeeping, kitchen, barn, and paddock—outside in the courtyard waiting. Though it was barely seven a.m., a few curious faces peered down from the rooms above, too, at the sight of the big official SUV and the Amish wagon pulling up together outside.

Warden Peters waited for him to tie Josie to the old-fashioned wooden hitching rail and join them before he spoke. "First of all, I'd like to thank everyone here for what you've done in helping the sheriff and me to bring some poachers to justice."

Samuel Riehl cheered, clearly surprising himself as much as everyone else.

The warden grinned, his hands resting lightly on his equipment belt. "I couldn't have said it better myself." Then his gaze turned to Teresa Rodriguez. "I understand that a couple of weeks ago, you let a man go by the name of Jackson Phelps."

"I did," Teresa said. This was clearly the last thing she expected him to say. "He was my prep cook, but he came in late and hung over one too many times, so I fired him. Two weeks ago today, in fact."

"An interesting bit of information that came to me last night," Peters said. "Particularly since the two men who left a poached animal with Joshua here to be processed as road kill had the same name. Turns out the sheriff isn't a believer in coincidence, and neither am I. It didn't take us long to track down Jackson Phelps, and when we did, guess what we found parked out behind his residence at the mobile home park?"

"A black pickup with fog lamps?" Joshua guessed.

"Exactly. Belonging to his cousin Neil, who apparently has been helping himself to the local wildlife for some time. When the sheriff brought them in to the office for an interview, it didn't take them long to tell us a sad story about jobs going to Amish folks, and needing to eat, and having to poach animals on the Lost Creek acres. It was just a coincidence that the animals had been brought down in just such a way as to make it look like Amish folks might have done it."

He nodded to Ben who was standing with Hannah, holding her hand tightly. Simon was nowhere in sight.

"Theirs was the campfire you smelled. They'd been shadowing you up the trail, waiting for the right moment to bring down that deer and make it look like you'd done it. Once we'd confiscated their firearms, it was easy enough to prove who really had. The markings were a match for one of their rifles."

Amanda pressed a hand to her heart and exhaled. Joshua felt like doing the same. Instead, concealed in the folds of her skirts, he took her other hand. He felt a shiver go through her, and half expected her to withdraw her hand and step to the other side of Cora, but she didn't. Instead, her fingers twined in his, their palms pressed together.

In the silent joy of it, Joshua nearly missed the Wildlife warden's next words.

"I'd like to thank you folks for your cooperation while we got this figured out." His deep gaze moved to Amanda. "All it takes is one person to put the pieces together, and it all falls into place to show us the right picture. I'll be on my way now. You folks have a good day while I spend mine filling out the highest mountain of paperwork you ever saw."

Joshua squeezed her fingers as the warden swung himself into his vehicle, and released her hand before anyone could see and take it upon themselves to comment. They watched the big SUV make the turn around the corner of the rock garden and move off down the hill.

He drew in a deep breath. Even the air, it seemed, was clean again, and clear of the taint of suspicion and trouble.

"It was good of him to come and tell us in person," Jose said to Mr. Gunderson.

"It was indeed. And I'm glad it's all over."

"Jackson Phelps," Teresa said softly, shaking her head. "Who would have guessed he and his family could have been so angry that they'd take it out on innocent people instead of cleaning up their own mistakes? What kind of person makes a plan that complicated instead of just going and getting another job?"

"We'll probably never know. All I know is, I'm glad he's nowhere near you anymore." Jose wrapped his arm around her waist and gave her a squeeze. "The more important question is —how about I give you a hand with breakfast?"

Laughing, the two of them went in the staff door, and the little crowd took the hint to get busy with the chores that had to be done before everyone sat down to eat.

"I have to go," Amanda said to Joshua as she walked with him over to the buggy. "But I'll see you tomorrow evening—after sunset?"

"I'll be here." He wasn't about to give her a one-armed hug, with Lydia and Cora and the others all standing twenty feet away and talking over the revelations of the morning, but his smile was for her alone.

And from the dawning glow in her face, she knew it.

He untied Josie and backed the wagon around, happiness filling him as though his heart were a pitcher and God was pouring out his blessings into it. It stayed with him all the way down the hill and into his work day, to the point that Dat began to tease him about his good humor. But he couldn't help it. He'd never felt like this about someone before—not even with Jacinda, the woman he thought he knew and hadn't. Thought he'd never get over and had. He'd been excited to see her when they had been courting, sure, but not like this.

He'd never had this feeling of rightness—of making a choice that God approved. Of having prayed and prayed, and finally been given an answer. And wasn't that part of the reason for this happiness?

"The happiest man is the one who has not man's approval, but God's," his *Grossdaadi* used to say.

Well, he had man's approval, if Dane Peters's nod of friendship had been any indication. And he was grateful for it. But God's approval, now ... that was something a man couldn't survive without.

He only hoped that Amanda felt that same warmth of sure knowledge, this same joy in knowing the will of *der Herr* was also within reach.

Tomorrow night, as the stars fell, he would find out for sure.

"AMANDA, FOR GOODNESS SAKE, YOU'RE AS JITTERY AS A rabbit in a lettuce patch, or whatever it is my mother says," Hannah observed over the top of her magazine. She was lying on her bunk in their cabin on Friday night, with Jenny busy on her phone in the opposite bunk. The cabin seemed huge now that Bonita's anger and all her clothes were out of it. Amanda had finally claimed her half of a closet—which had made her laugh because she had so few things to hang in it.

"Jittery as a rabbit in a lettuce patch with a fox walking the fence, you mean. And I know," she moaned, fingers twisting together as she paced the Navajo rug on the floor. "I'm sorry, but I'm so nervous. I've—well, I haven't really been on a proper date before."

Jenny lowered her phone, though Amanda could have sworn she wasn't listening. "Seriously? How old are you?"

"Twenty-four." Two or three years past the point where courting couples would make their intentions known to their parents, and the bishop would make an announcement in church. And miles past the likelihood of any of the young men in Whinburg Township asking her if she'd like a ride home from singing.

"What about Jesse Riehl?" Hannah asked. "You dated him, didn't you?"

"Not really." Two more circuits of the rug. She was going to wear a hole in it at this rate. "We were more like friends sharing our rebellion than two people trying to create ... something more than friendship."

"Like with Joshua the butcher," Jenny said, nodding. "I can see you two together. You're both kind of ... solid."

There had been a time when Amanda would have taken this for a veiled criticism of her weight, but now she seemed to be able to look over the wall of her own shyness and realize that she had been more critical of her own failings than anyone. And wasn't that just a sign of pride, thinking that she could criticize what the hand of God had made? It was sort of the opposite of makeup, in a strange way. The Amish forbade cosmetics because using them to improve your looks was like telling God that He hadn't done a good enough job in the first place. Well, what was she doing? Telling Him that his handiwork could lose some weight, and was embarrassing and awkward, and that no man would want such a person in his home?

Amanda was ashamed of herself. There was humility, and

there was what she had been doing to herself all these years with her low self-confidence: humiliation. And for what? So she wouldn't have to open herself up to the possibility of someone knowing the real woman inside? So she wouldn't have to suffer that woman being rejected?

Hannah rolled off the bed and tossed the magazine down. "Come on. We're going for a walk."

The sun had just slid behind the peaks of the range to the west, turning the sky a glorious golden color that faded slowly into lemon and lavender and deep blue. "This is the day that the Lord hath made; rejoice and be glad in it," Amanda murmured as she and Hannah stood under the trees overlooking the road and took it all in.

"I would be glad," Hannah said. "This whole poaching thing is over and Ben and Simon are cleared. But—"

Amanda suddenly realized there was more to this walk up the path to the trees than burning off nervous energy or even looking at the beautiful view. Something more that she should have noticed, if she hadn't been to wrapped up in her own emotions and fears. She must haul up her runaway anxiety and do her best to be a real friend.

"But?" she prompted.

"But now he's free," Hannah said, as though this were a disaster.

"And you're not glad because ..."

"I am glad. In one way. But he wants to leave, Mandy," Hannah said, her tone tense with worry. "He wants us to cash our paychecks and catch a bus to California."

"California!" Amanda had never known anyone who had gone to California. Usually people from home went to Pinecraft in Florida if they wanted a holiday with sun and sand. California was the home of Hollywood movies and freeways and far too many people. Of worldliness and the rampant love of money—though she had to admit that those two things were found everywhere, like dandelions, even in Amish communities.

She finally found her voice. "What do you want to do?"

"I want to stay here. But what if he goes without me?"

"It wouldn't be forever," Amanda said quietly. "Whatever he's looking for out there is the same thing he's looking for inside himself. He can chase it as far as he wants, but in the end he's going to have to come back to the beginning, and deal with his own heart."

Hannah released a long breath. "Where did you learn to be so wise? Because you and I both know it's more than just coming back to join church."

"I do know that," she admitted. "And I learned anything I know in a hard school. I think we all have to learn that lesson. Home is a house and a town, maybe, but it's also a settled heart. It's where you find love, and peace, and have those things to offer others. Sometimes people have to travel a long way to discover that inside themselves—because you sure can't find it outside."

She gazed at the mountains, and Hannah glanced at her. "Is that what you're doing? You've come a long way, too."

"It's early days yet, but I do feel settled, somehow. Or maybe it's that I've come to that place where two ways meet, and I'm waiting for the Lord to give the bridle a tug and lead me where He wants me to go."

"That's the difference between you and me, then," Hannah said. Her hands fisted in the pockets of the dress she wore only because Mrs. Gunderson wanted her to. "I'm holding my own bridle. Maybe that's why I feel like I'm just going in circles."

"I'm really bad at taking my own reins. I always mess it up.

It's a relief to hand them over to Someone who knows the road ahead much better than I do."

Hannah was silent.

Amanda knew when silence should act like soil. It could cover up a word in season and allow it to grow into a conviction. So she merely pointed over at the glowing horizon. "Look. The evening star."

"That's Venus, you know."

"It's not nearly so pretty a name as *evening star*. And I think we should be getting back so I can get my sweater. I hear the buggy." How could she sound so calm when her heart was leaping like a mountain goat up the side of a hill?

"I think I'll stay out here a while," Hannah said. "Ben said he might come by, and we could watch the star shower from here."

Amanda picked her way down the path in the deepening dusk, collected her sweater, and put off the role of friend to draw on the role of ... what? Special friend? Or even sweetheart? That was really getting ahead of herself.

Lord, please take the reins now.

She met the buggy as Joshua turned into the courtyard. *"Guder owed,"* he said as she climbed in and took her place beside him.

"Guder owed," she said softly. Would this ever be her place? Was she only spinning dreams and telling herself they were the will of *der Herr*?

Please show me, Father. Show me Your will, and prepare my heart to welcome it, whatever it turns out to be.

"Was your day as long as mine, waiting for it to be evening?" Joshua said, his voice rich with humor.

"Nearly, I think. Hannah finally made me go for a walk

with her instead of wearing a hole in the rug. Apparently they're very expensive."

He laughed, and shook the reins over Rusty's back. The lamps on the sides of the buggy were lit, and in their soft glow she saw that the smile didn't fade from his face. Was it because he was content with her riding beside him? Or was he simply happy that the Wildlife warden had declared him innocent once and for all?

"Where are we going?" she asked. "Hannah and Ben are going to watch the star shower from up on the hill. Do you have a hill in mind, too?"

"I think we'll be able to see it from anywhere except the middle of the pine forest. But you're right—I do have a particular place in mind. It's literally off the beaten track—and yet, it's right here, on ranch land."

Before long he guided Rusty off the gravel road and onto a rutted track that hadn't been used in quite a while. Long grass whispered against the bottom of the buggy, and a barbed-wire fence ran along both sides. Before long, though, they came to a gate, which Joshua jumped down to open while she took the reins and guided the horse through it into a long, sloping, south-facing meadow. He held out his hand as she pulled Rusty up.

"I put a blanket and a Thermos flask in the back. If you hand them to me, I'll carry them."

He had a flashlight in his pocket, which he used to light their way across the meadow. He handed it to her, spread the blanket, then invited her down beside him. The moon wasn't up yet, leaving them under a canopy of stars—a river of them—a vast universe of them. Amanda fell back on both hands, feeling a little drunk with the beauty of God's handiwork and the thrill of being alone with Joshua in the midst of it.

When he covered her hand with his, she sat up and moved a little closer, so that he held her hand upon his knee. "This is what I've been waiting for all day," he said.

"The star shower?" But she hoped that wasn't all.

"The star shower will come whether I wait for it or not. But you ... you're a whole different matter."

"I did wait for you," she teased. "All day long."

"But I didn't know that. You could have decided there were other things to do this evening, and gone off with Samuel, or Tyler, or even one of my uncles."

This was so downright crazy that she laughed. A rabbit in the grass startled at the sound and leaped away, the thump of its passing like a tiny heartbeat.

"I wasn't waiting for any of them," she told him, smiling. "I was waiting for the man who promised to take me to see a star shower. None of those others thought to suggest it."

"Good," he said. "Just checking. Because it seems as though I've been waiting a good long time for you, Amanda. Not just today. But for weeks and months and maybe even years before that." He took a breath, and when he went on, his voice was rough, as though each word cost him. "A few years ago, back in Kansas, I was preparing to marry a woman called Jacinda Lapp. I thought I knew her as well as it was possible for a man to know a woman, but it turned out I was wrong, and she married someone else. After that, I doubted my own ability to know anything, much less a woman's heart."

"But God knows our hearts," she said softly. The spurt of fear when he'd said he had almost been married before was something the old Amanda might have experienced, back at home. Fear didn't belong in her heart now. Not with Joshua holding her hand, so warm and steady. So she put the unhealthy emotion away, taking a deep breath to make her heart calm once again.

"He does," Joshua said. "God knew what he was doing when he put the desire for a higher church in her heart. He was keeping me safe ... for you."

If his words had cost him, then surely she was paying the price for her own honesty now. Speaking of what was in her heart—revealing it to the person who could hurt her with it if he chose—

But no. The former things were passed away. This was not Silas Lapp, who wanted a woman who didn't want him. This was not Jesse Riehl, a despondent and angry boy.

This was Joshua. The man whom God had brought straight to her, that first morning when she had heard his voice up on the hillside, and he had seen her as God saw her—worshipping Him in joy at His creation.

"Sometimes, lately ... in my imagination," she said softly, "I see a map of the country, with this valley in the middle, and the mountains on both sides of it. I see two meandering lines tracing a path from Whinburg Township to here, and from Kansas to here."

He squeezed her hand in his strong one. "Two lines that maybe waited years to begin their journey to the same point, but finally made it."

He understood. She hardly dared to let the happiness that was building inside her break free. Could hardly believe that happiness like this could be her portion.

And then—

"Joshua, look!"

Far over their heads, a cluster of lights traced their way across the sky and plummeted earthward, trailing a swath of glitter behind them.

"Three at once!"

And then two more, and five, and— "Oh, it's so beautiful." Her throat closed in sheer joy, and gratitude, and she gave a sob as tears welled into her eyes.

But Joshua was not watching the star shower—not entirely. He was watching her upturned face, and now she tilted her head to gaze into his eyes.

"Are you weeping?" he asked softly. "But why?"

"Because—because I'm so happy," she blurted. "It's so beautiful, and I get to share it with you, and—"

And she couldn't say another word, because words were no longer enough—and far too much. His warm fingers touched her jaw, caressed her as though her skin were priceless and fragile.

And then his lips touched hers.

Overhead, it seemed as though the mighty Creator of the universe was creating celestial fireworks, just for them. But Amanda no longer saw even that rare miracle. In Joshua's kiss she tasted joy, and gratitude, and a promise that neither of them could make in words yet.

Maybe not tonight, or tomorrow, but someday they would.

The meandering lines on the map of their lives would stop and form a knot right here in Amistad. Their lonely journeys would be over, and their hearts would rejoice at seeing the lights of home ... in each other's eyes.

THE END

AFTERWORD

I hope you enjoyed reading *The Highest Mountain* and catching up with friends you might have met in the Whinburg Township Amish series. I hope you'll pick up *The Sweetest Song*, the next book in the series, to find out what happens to Hannah and Ben, and to Cora Swarey and the Youngie of Amistad when Simon Yoder decides to mend his ways ...

You might leave a review on your favorite retailer's site and tell others about my books. And you can find print and digital editions of my series online. I invite you to visit my website at www.adinasenft.com, where you can subscribe to my newsletter and be the first to know of new releases and special promotions.

Denki!

Adina

GLOSSARY

Spelling and definitions from Eugene S. Stine, *Pennsylvania German Dictionary* (Birdboro, PA: Pennsylvania German Society, 1996).

Words used:
Aendi aunt, auntie
Boppli baby
Bruder brother
Dat Dad
Daed Grandpa
Daadi Haus grandfather's house
Demut humility
Denki, denkes thank you, thanks
Deitsch Pennsylvania Dutch
Dochder, Dechter daughter, daughters
Dokterfraa female herbalist or healer
Bruderskind brother's child, nephew or niece
Duchly headscarf
Englisch Someone who is not Amish, the English language

Gelassenheit letting go of the world
Gott God
Gmee congregation
Guder mariye good morning
Guder owed good afternoon
Guder nacht good night
Gut good
Hinkelhaus henhouse
Hochmut lit. highness; being proud
Im e Familye weg in the family way, pregnant
ja yes
Kapp The prayer covering worn by Amish women, which can vary in design from district to district
Kinner children
Kumm mit. Come with me.
Kummst du hier und hilfen mir. Come here and help me.
Lieber Gott, hilfen mir. Dear Lord, help me.
Liewi dear, dearest
Mamm Mom
Maedel young girl
Onkel uncle
Schweschder sister
Onkel uncle
Ordnung rules of the church community
Rumspringe lit. running around, the time of freedom for Amish young folks between age 16 and marriage
Was ischt? What is it?
Wie geht's? How is it going?
wunderbar wonderful
Youngie unmarried young people

READING GROUP GUIDE

1. Did you know there were Amish communities in western states like Montana and Colorado? Have you visited the Amish there?
2. Amanda is conflicted about change—part of her wants a change, part of her fears it. Do you sometimes feel this way? What do you do about it?
3. Do you think it was fair of Sarah Byler to ask Amanda to watch over Simon, her grown son? Why or why not?
4. Do you think Hannah and Ben have more in common than they are different? How?
5. Hannah and Samuel Riehl have a chance at a real brother/sister relationship. Do you think they'll succeed, or has too much time passed?
6. Have you ever been to a dude ranch? What was it like?
7. Was Amanda right in questioning why the ranch owners really wanted her to work there? What would you have done or thought in her place?

8. The Amish enjoy hunting and fishing as much as the *Englisch* do. Have you ever tried it?
9. If you were to go to an Amish singing, what songs would you hope to hear? Do you sing them among your own friends and family?
10. Have you ever seen the Rocky Mountains, of which the Sangre de Cristo Range is a part? How do they make you feel? Can you identify with the Psalmist, as Amanda did?

ALSO BY ADINA SENFT

The Whinburg Township Amish series

The Wounded Heart

The Hidden Life

The Tempted Soul

Herb of Grace

Keys of Heaven

Balm of Gilead

The Longest Road

The Highest Mountain

The Sweetest Song

"The Heart's Return" (novella)

The Montana Millers series

"The Amish Cowboy's Christmas" prequel novella in *More Amish Christmas Miracles*

The Amish Cowboy

The Amish Cowboy's Baby

The Amish Cowboy's Bride

The Amish Cowboy's Letter

The Amish Cowboy's Makeover

The Amish Cowboy's Home

The Glory Prep series (young adult)

Glory Prep

The Fruit of My Lipstick

Be Strong and Curvaceous

Who Made You a Princess?

Tidings of Great Boys

The Chic Shall Inherit the Earth

The Smoke River series

Grounds to Believe

Pocketful of Pearls

The Sound of Your Voice

Over Her Head

Writing as Charlotte Henry

The Rogues of St. Just series (Regency romance)

The Rogue to Ruin

The Rogue Not Taken

One for the Rogue

A Rogue by Any Other Name

ABOUT THE AUTHOR

USA Today bestselling author Adina Senft grew up in a plain house church, where she was often asked by outsiders if she was Amish (the answer was no). She holds a PhD in Creative Writing from Lancaster University in the UK. Adina was the winner of RWA's RITA Award for Best Inspirational Novel in 2005, a finalist for that award in 2006, and was a Christy Award finalist in 2009. She appeared in the 2016 documentary film *Love Between the Covers*, is a popular speaker and convention panelist, and has been a guest on many podcasts, including Worldshapers and Realm of Books.

She writes steampunk adventure and mystery as Shelley Adina; and as Charlotte Henry, writes classic Regency romance. When she's not writing, Adina is usually quilting, sewing historical costumes, or enjoying the garden with her flock of rescued chickens.

Adina loves to talk with readers about books, quilting, and chickens!

www.adinasenft.com
adinasenft@comcast.net